Hotwalker

Rick Neumayer

Literary Wanderlust | Denver, Colorado

Published in the United States by Literary Wanderlust LLC, Denver, Colorado.

https//www.LiteraryWanderlust.com

ISBN Print: 978-1-942856-87-0
ISBN Digital: 978-1-924856-92-4

Printed in the United States of America

For Corie, always

SUNDAY

1

I was having a drink on my dock on the Ohio River when the radio announcer's voice was suddenly drowned out by an earsplitting noise.

I was thrilled that the Kentucky Derby was once again alive and well post-pandemic, but still hoped to avoid the hoopla surrounding it. While every TV and radio station in town blared about Derby Week events, from the hot air balloons to the Pegasus parade and the Great Steamboat Race, everything else got put on hold. It was unlikely that I would have any new clients. Every phone call or piece of mail addressed to Jim Guthrie, Private Investigator, was a past-due request.

"The twin spires rise from Churchill Downs like church steeples, fitting since thoroughbred horse racing is a religion here this time of year, with worshippers substituting bourbon for the sacramental wine and betting windows for collection baskets. Some 160,000 spectators are expected to line the fences at the racetrack to witness the most exciting two minutes in sports."

That's when—startled by the whine of high-powered engines—I glanced upriver to find a red speed boat with a white fiberglass hull hurtling my way. It was bouncing high and slapping the waves hard while throwing up a ten-foot rooster tail. Six miles upriver from the city of Louisville where sailboats and fishermen dotted the channel was no place for a muscle craft like this to zoom close to shore at sixty knots, especially not while recklessly shifting directions and jumping its own wake.

Only a grandstander would do that. This one must've been showing off for the woman standing beside him in a two-piece swimsuit. When I waved him off, he veered to the right. But then he veered back while letting go of the wheel, like a kid on a bicycle riding with no hands. He must not have expected the torque that forced the boat to swerve, pitching him out across the waves. Seconds later, he popped up unhurt and swam for shore. But his passenger was not so lucky. As she flipped overboard, she banged her head on the stern and became entangled with the tow rope. Now she was being dragged feet-first underwater.

With no time to think, instinct took over. The driver-less boat was going around in circles, with each pass coming closer. When it seemed within reach, I sprinted the length of the dock and leaped, barely hurdled the watery gap, and landed on the foredeck with enough force to carry me over the other side. Instead, I grabbed a railing and, almost dislocating my shoulder, pulled myself up. Once in the cockpit, I throttled back, bringing the boat to a lurching halt amid a welter of white water.

I went aft and pulled in the rope towing the woman. When I got her into the boat, she wasn't breathing. I laid her out on the deck and tilted her head back, blowing harsh rhythmic breaths into her mouth until she gagged and began spewing up copper-colored water.

"You okay?" I said, realizing at once what a stupid question that was. She had almost drowned. Her skin was cold and pale. She was trembling, her teeth chattering. Strands of auburn hair were pasted over her freckled cheeks and one green eye.

I eased her into a seat. Keying the high-performance engines, I ran the boat up alongside the dock and tied her off. I was helping the young redhead over the transom when the guy responsible for almost killing her showed up. He stood there in a red Speedo and a dab of sunblock with his chest puffed up like an arrogant but incompetent lifeguard.

"Thanks, Pappy. I'll take it from here," he said and grabbed her arm. "Let's go, Libby."

"No, Chip," the woman said. She tore herself from his grasp.

"What the hell?" he asked.

I stepped up onto the dock. "You heard her, Chipper," I said. "She doesn't want to go with you. Who could blame her, after seeing the way you drive?"

"Listen, whoever you are—"

"Guthrie's my name, Jim Guthrie. You can call me *Mister* Guthrie."

"I don't care if you're James Bond," Chip said. "Get the hell out of my way before I kick your ass."

"Do it."

"What?"

"Kick my ass."

He backpedaled after sizing me up, obviously surprised that a forty-year-old codger like me was calling his bluff. Chip hadn't been paying enough attention or he'd have noticed how my years as a soldier and cop had hardened me. Now awareness slowly dawned at last in his button eyes. Still, he couldn't quite let it go.

"You must not know who I am," he blustered.

"Sure, I do. You're Chip, The Clown, who almost drowned your girlfriend and wrecked a $75,000 boat."

"I'm not his girlfriend," Libby said.

"Listen, my father's Herb Alexander."

"That supposed to mean something?" I asked.

Chip forced a laugh. "You'll find out when I tell him about this."

"Tell him about what?"

The question seemed to throw him. "My father's not somebody you want to piss off."

"Maybe I do, though."

That was enough for Chip, who turned to Libby, saying, "Come on, I said. Let's go."

She didn't budge.

"Then the hell with you both." Chip wriggled eel-like down into the boat.

I watched him cast off and putt-putt away. Once safely out of reach, he worked up the nerve to give me a one-finger salute.

Ignoring him, I took Libby's arm and helped her up the rough plank steps. She paused at the top to look over the place I called my "camp." Really, it was just a rustic cottage on the bluff overlooking the river. Nothing fancy, a one-story concrete-block with a peaked roof and screened-in back porch. But oddly out of place, located at the end of a row of rambling upscale resort houses.

"Want me to call for an ambulance?"

"No, I'll be okay," she said in a drained voice.

"Is there someone else you'd like for me to call?"

She shook her head.

I told her to go inside and get out of those wet clothes and take a hot shower. There were towels and should be plenty of hot water, though sometimes the water heater went on the fritz. The terry robe hooked on the bathroom door would help her warmup. She took a deep breath and walked past me. When I heard the shower, I put on dry cutoffs and a T-shirt. I retrieved a bottle of brandy and two glasses from the kitchen cupboard and sat down in an old wooden rocker on the back porch and poured myself a stiff one.

It was the blue hour when the sun was low on the horizon. The evenly diffused sunlight was perfect for painting, which was a passion of mine and more than a hobby. Hearing actual bird twitter, I observed two of them swooping and soaring as they fought over the feeder next door. The cardinal was driving off the robin when Libby emerged from the back door wearing the robe and a towel wrapped around her head like a turban. She hung her bathing suit over a chair to dry in the river breeze and sat in the swing with her legs tucked under her.

"Thank you for saving my life, Mister Guthrie."

"Call me Jim."

"My name is Libby Fontaine. What exactly happened to me? I seem to have blanked out after hitting my head."

I poured her a brandy.

"You had a close call, nearly drowned."

She let out a sigh and gulped the brandy.

When she remained quiet, I said, "Your boyfriend has a nice boat, but he is a menace."

"Chip's not my boyfriend."

"Then why were you in the boat with him?"

"Guess I felt sorry for him." Libby gazed across the river at the forested Indiana shore as if trying to figure out the answer for herself.

"Why?"

"Chip's a big mouth, but underneath very insecure. He has a strained relationship with his father, who's always yelling at him. When Chip begged me to take a little spin on the river in their fancy new boat, I gave in—I guess out of pity. Some spin. He almost got me killed, didn't he?"

"That he did."

Libby poured herself more brandy and swigged it.

"I don't know what I would've done if you hadn't been there."

I noticed she'd stopped shaking. Her color had improved. Her voice sounded stronger, too.

"How do you know Chip?"

"From Churchill Downs. I'm a volunteer at the Backside Learning Center—or BLC."

"Don't tell me he's a volunteer."

"Not a chance. Chip wouldn't be caught dead volunteering.

He hangs around the Downs because his father owns racehorses."

Ah, the menacing Herb Alexander, who I annoyed at my peril. "Tell me more about him."

"Mister Alexander is wealthy. He owns his own business, has three or four expensive cars, and lives in a mansion on Mockingbird Valley Road."

The exclusive east end area of multi-million-dollar estates to which she referred wound through forested hillside off River Road. I heard the disdain in her voice, presumably for the undeserving rich, but also a touch of envy.

"His company distributes pharmaceuticals or something like that. Herb likes to dabble in horseracing. He's got one in this year's Derby. You may have heard of him. Speckled Band?"

I shook my head.

"Then you must not follow the races."

"I do, but only about one day a year, like most people around here. Is Speckled Band a good horse?"

"He's not the favorite if that's what you mean."

"Does Chip work with his father's horses?"

"Are you kidding? Chip doesn't work, period. He's twenty-two and supposedly a college student, but he hangs out at the track more than he goes to classes."

"Whereas you..."

"Study hard and am majoring in anthropology."

When I asked what she could do with that degree, she listed becoming a researcher, teacher, or community development worker.

"Noble professions," I said.

The conversation lulled as a tug went by pushing a dozen barges humped with coal. I was curious about her and her volunteer work at the Backside Learning Center. I asked her to tell me more about it.

"It's sort of an all-purpose school, library, and recreation center all rolled into one. Volunteers like me staff it mostly. It's open during training months—March through November."

"Who is it for?"

"Any adult who lives and works on the backside. I teach English as a second language. Without English, the immigrant workers who mostly come here from Guatemala and Mexico can't pass their driver's license test. Or earn a GED. Or become a citizen."

"Pretty altruistic of you, Libby. I don't meet many folks like that in my line of work," I said.

"What line of work is that?"

"I'm a private investigator."

"Really? What kind of cases?"

"Whatever puts food on the table."

The sky had dimmed. I took a match from the Blue Diamond box on a low table, struck it, and lighted a candle. A few lights were showing in my neighbors' windows. Libby glanced at them. "Looks like you're doing all right for yourself."

The truth was that I struggled to meet the payroll—and I was the only one on it. "My Uncle Bud left me this place. When he built it, the surrounding area was nothing but woods and a few other hermit fishing camps. Now that land values around here have skyrocketed, the neighbors would like this eyesore torn down."

"That would be sad," Libby said.

We had run out of talk. After listening to the waves faintly slapping the pilings for a while, Libby checked her bathing suit and found it dry.

"It's getting late. I should go."

I finished my second drink while she went inside to get dressed.

"I hope you don't mind," she said, coming back out wearing one of my shirts over her bathing suit.

"Not at all. Want a ride home?"

When she saw my car parked in the driveway, Libby said, "That looks like a classic."

"It's a Bullitt Mustang GT."

Her blank smile made it clear that she had no idea what that meant.

"It's the same model Steve McQueen drove in the movie. You know, the one with the great car chase on the hills of San Francisco?"

She didn't. Well, at least she didn't ask me who Steve McQueen was.

"Have you ever been in a car chase, Jim?"

"A few." But I kept the Bullitt at the speed limit all the way to her place, located fifteen minutes away in the quirky yet desirable Highlands area.

At the curb, she thanked me once more for saving her life and asked for one of my business cards. I took one out of my wallet and gave it to her without asking why, figuring she probably just wanted a souvenir. She was only a kid and I doubted I'd ever see her again.

MONDAY

2

Wrong.

Early next morning, I made the twenty-minute drive downtown to my office, located on the east side in trendy Nu Lu, miles from the festivities dawning at the Downs. I parked behind our old commercial building facing similar structures across a wide thoroughfare. A century ago, cattle and pigs passed by here on their way to slaughter. Now all the old shops were gone, with gentrification well-advanced. My rent would go up soon and I'd be on my way, too.

I grabbed the mail from the stairwell box and creaked up to the second floor, where I unlocked the pebbled glass door stenciled with "James Guthrie Investigations" and let myself in. I turned on the lights. Hung my coat on the corner rack. Dropping into my old wood desk chair, I went through the ads and promotions. Surprise, surprise, one of them was a check for a long-overdue bill. I folded it into my shirt pocket for safekeeping as the landline on my gnarled desk rang.

"Guthrie Investigations," I said.

"Mister Guthrie, I'm so glad you're there. I need your help."

The caller, I was surprised to learn, was Libby Fontaine.

"What's up, Libby? Chip bothering you again?"

"No, this is about a friend who has a problem."

As I mentioned, business was slow on Derby Week, so potentially this was good news.

"What friend? What kind of problem?"

"Carlos Rojas. He's a hotwalker from Guatemala."

I knew what a hotwalker was—someone who after a workout or race cooled a thoroughbred down with a walk around the backside.

"I met Carlos when he came to the backside center to improve his English a year and a half ago. His father, Felipe, had just brought Carlos out of Guatemala because it was unsafe there. Turned out it wasn't safe here, either. Felipe was murdered on the backside a few hours after last year's Derby. At least, that's where his body was found, in a horse barn."

"Hold on," I said, as something clicked in my mind. "I remember reading about that. He was a groom, right? Took care of horses. Lived with horses."

"That's right."

"Tell me more about the murder. Start with how you know it was a murder."

"That's what the police said."

"Cause of death?" I asked.

"Someone hit him over the head."

"And you say they're still investigating?"

"If you can call it that. A year later, and they still have nothing. It's tearing Carlos up. I worry about what he might do if this isn't solved soon. We need you to investigate."

"Stop right there. If this is an ongoing investigation, I can't get involved."

"Why not?"

"Because police frown on that. I could lose my license."

"Carlos lost his father." There was a pleading note in her

voice.

"I'm sorry, Libby. I really am. But what makes this my problem?"

"You saved my life, didn't you? Tell me what made *that* your problem."

"That was different."

"No, it wasn't. I'll bet you've heard that ancient Chinese proverb—the one where, if you save someone's life, you become responsible for them?"

"Even if I believed it, which I don't, how would that obligate me to help Carlos?" I rushed on lest she came up with another argument to tug on my heartstrings. "Besides, a year ago is ancient history in a homicide investigation. If there was anything left to find, the cops would have found it by now. What makes you think I can do any better?"

"How could you do any worse? Look, Carlos believes that nothing will happen because nobody cares what happened to his father."

"What makes him think that?"

"Because he's an immigrant. You understand?"

"I keep up with the news."

Meaning I'd seen pictures of children in cages after their parents were apprehended by the border patrol while trying to cross into the U.S. from Mexico. Meaning that I was no Rip Van Winkle who'd dozed off for decades while our nation's failure to reform immigration laws helped elect Donald Trump President. Meaning I was fully aware that raids by Immigration and Customs Enforcement (ICE) had left immigrants terrified, documented or not.

"Carlos is on the bottom rung," Libby said. "He thinks the police are going through the motions. To them, it's only a job. You're not like them, though."

"You're wrong. I used to be a cop myself."

"But you're not anymore, which means you're free to do what you want."

"That's a misconception." I saw my reflection in a grimy windowpane. My face—which I've been told is impassive often enough for it to be irritating—seemed almost sad. I swiveled away to stare instead at the harshly lit all-night diner scene in the print of Hopper's *Nighthawks* hanging on my wall. As always, my eye was drawn irresistibly to the diner's interior yellow wall and the door whose shape was repeated in the windows of the building across the street. Like art, I mused, detective work was often about finding something new in the familiar.

"We'll pay you," Libby said, sounding desperate now.

I glanced at the ceiling and spotted a spider web crack. Everywhere I looked, I found recriminations and judgment.

"How much do you charge for your services?"

"Libby—"

"How much?"

"My standard fee is fifty dollars an hour, with a nonrefundable $2,000 retainer," I said, shaking my head in resignation.

I heard what sounded like a sharp intake of breath on the other end. "All right, where do I send the check."

"Hold onto your money for now. Against my better judgment, I'm going to let your friend Carlos phone me for an appointment if he wants. I'll listen to what he has to say, but I'm not promising to take the case."

"Thanks, Jim," she said in a whole different tenor filled with relief and hope. "But..."

"But what?"

"Getting to your office could be a problem for him. Carlos works seven days a week, you see, and has transportation issues. Could you meet him at the track instead?"

"Okay." One favor, it seemed, begat another.

"Like maybe this morning?"

"Fine."

"He'll be waiting for you at Gate Five, the backside entrance."

"I'll be there in an hour."

As soon as we disconnected, I tossed the junk mail and

opened my laptop. It was Hemingway, I believe, who said the only way to know you could trust someone was to trust them. Or you could conduct a social media investigation of them online, using software to search popular platforms like LinkedIn, Instagram, and YouTube. It wasn't an infallible approach. Assuming Carlos Rojas stayed off social media for fear of being targeted by ICE, I didn't expect to learn much about him—and I didn't, although I found several other people with the same name. The only mention of my Carlos Rojas was in news reports when his father was murdered a year ago. Nothing else about his father, either.

But as a native-born white American citizen, Libby Fontaine could afford for her personal information to appear on several sites. On Facebook, for instance, I found photographs of her smiling with friends, along with the names of her high school and college, plus photos of Guatemala and the Downs, and posts in Spanish such as one thanking her for donating to a BLC fundraiser.

My next step was to determine whether any of the three had a criminal record. For that, I accessed a site that contained police and court records of felonies and misdemeanors. It didn't take long before both came back clean. Then I conducted a computer search for info about crime at the Downs. The results proved less than earthshaking and limited mainly to the one-too-many-mint-juleps category—public intoxication, disorderly conduct, or the occasional assault. Sometimes out of town pickpockets wound up in handcuffs, too, along with those trying funny stuff with betting tickets. But murder was unknown. In fact, the Felipe Rojas murder was the only one that had ever been committed there, as far as I could determine.

I tapped keys and maneuvered the mouse until I'd located newspaper and online stories of the history-making killing. The earliest piece in the *Courier Journal* had made page one of the metro section. It was a straight-forward account and confirmed most of what Libby had told me:

"A Guatemalan immigrant was found dead on Sunday morning just hours after the Derby was run. Police said the victim, Felipe Rojas, forty-six, was employed as a groom for trainer Ned Ericson. Rojas, who had worked and lived in the stables, was identified by his nineteen-year-old son, who also worked there. Racetrack security officers called the police just before 5:00 a.m. after discovering Rojas's body in a currently unoccupied horse barn."

But Rojas had not been working in that barn, which was recently damaged during a storm. It was unclear why he was there, police said. The death was being investigated as a murder. No arrests had been made.

A next-day follow-up included a one-column photograph of the unsmiling victim, with his droopy black mustache and Cincinnati Reds baseball cap. According to the chief investigator—Lieutenant Leo Brownfield of the LMPD—someone had come forward with information, "but not enough to make assumptions on what occurred."

One wire service had called the slaying "a Kentucky Derby whodunit." Investigators were looking into "several altercations" that took place on the backside before the killing and were interviewing "numerous" witnesses.

A month after the murder, police confirmed that Rojas had died of blunt force trauma and that they believed the motive was robbery.

Three months after the murder, detectives said they were still generating leads and felt optimistic they would close the case.

Six months after the murder, investigators said it was only a matter of time until an arrest was made.

Since then nothing.

No wonder Carlos Rojas was torn up.

3

Traffic was light for the four-mile drive from my downtown office to Central Avenue in the city's blue-collar south end, where I'd grown up. In front of the Downs, one lane in four was already fenced off for use by pedestrians and golf carts. The relatively smooth flow of motor vehicles would end as crowds swelled for Derby festivities. Soon, many streets would be jammed or closed.

I recalled as a kid helping friends park racegoers' cars on their front lawns—and anywhere else we could get away with—for twenty dollars a pop. Since then, much of the old residential neighborhood surrounding the track's original eighty acres had been ruthlessly bulldozed into parking lots and other Downs expansion. Even so, finding a parking space during Derby Week was never easy. The going rate to park on someone's lawn was now sixty bucks. But I managed to find on-street parking.

As instructed, I checked in with security around the back. The silver-haired guard manning the kiosk at Gate Five had an American flag patch stitched on his uniform shoulder. He seemed unimpressed by my wrinkled sport coat and black T-shirt, even less so when I flipped open my leather ID case.

"Private eye, huh?" he grunted.

I figured he was a retired cop with their usual disdain for my profession.

"Ned Ericson's expecting me," I told him, then put away the laminated copy of my P.I. license issued by the Kentucky Board of Licensure.

As he went in and picked up the phone, I caught a dry earthy whiff of hay and horse manure on the breeze. The smell reminded me I was about to enter an area only a few members of the public ever saw. Far from Millionaires Row, it was inhabited only by one thousand-odd workers and a few hundred of the fastest horses on the planet. The guard returned and handed me a clipboard with a visitors' log for me to sign. After I exchanged the register for a visitor's pass, he waved me on through.

Libby had given me directions to the track kitchen, an eatery frequented primarily by backside workers, where I was to meet my prospective client. I set out toward it, walking through forty-eight horse barns laid out with military precision like barracks. Interspersed between them was an ongoing tableau of hay bales, tractors, and farm animals. Few cars visible, but dozens of bicycles chained up in front of a large brick building, evidently a dormitory for the short-statured men and women in Kelly green T-shirts who were standing around talking on cell phones in Spanish.

One woman, who was clearly involved in an argument, said loudly, "You don't think I can live without you? Who do you think you are?"

This was not the first time that Latinos who did not expect an Anglo like me to understand what they were saying had spoken indiscreetly within my hearing. While not fluent in Spanish, I did comprehend it with a reasonably high level of proficiency because I'd grown up as an army brat in Texas, Kentucky, and everywhere else my father had been stationed.

Occasionally, this unanticipated ability had led me into awkward or even comical situations, like a goateed young man interrupting his conversation about last night's crazy party to observe, "Man, you ought to see this lost Gringo wandering around like a fool."

In *Espanol,* I responded, "Hello, lovely day to be at the racetrack, isn't it?" and was tickled by the sight of his jaw dropping in embarrassment.

"*Si lo es,*" the man said sheepishly and turned away.

Entertainment value aside, this encounter proved a useful reminder of what I'd heard: that this backside world was a closed circle where outsiders were shunned—and would've been even if everyone spoke English—because racetrackers were notoriously clannish and tended to clam up around outsiders. If I took on the murder case, I'd have to tease out information, take it slow, be patient, not push too hard.

Leaving phone conversations behind, I trod on through a whispery quietness disturbed only by neighing, heavy breathing horses, and their shoes beating on the nearby turf. I'd heard of this venerable track kitchen where the "real" track workers came to eat. Going inside the simple utilitarian building, I smelled the hearty, complex odors of American and Spanish food being served at a cafeteria-style counter. Among the customers was a young man, early twenties, with short black hair and a round clean-shaven Central American face. He rose from his seat at a vinyl table and waved me over. Although he appeared shy at first, he made steady eye contact and stood tall for his height, which was no more than five-six.

"Mister Guthrie?" he said in English. "I'm Carlos Rojas."

We shook hands. I noticed his were hard and calloused—working man's hands.

"Thanks for coming. Have a seat."

I pulled out a chair.

"You want something to eat or drink?"

"Coffee."

While he went to get it, I couldn't help but observe the wall of windows looking out over the backstretch. They were so close to the track that galloping horses had splotched them with mud.

"Wow, that's some view," I said, as Carlos set a mug in front of me.

"Yeah, lots of people come here just for that."

"I'm here because Libby Fontaine says you want me to investigate your father's murder. You understand that I have not agreed to take the case, right? I'm here to listen and observe."

"I understand. Thanks for coming, Mister Guthrie."

I suggested that we call each other by our first names.

"I speak some Spanish," I began, "but I'm an outsider here, a stranger in a strange land. As such, I may not be the best choice to investigate this crime."

"Sounds like you're trying to talk yourself out of a job, Jim. Don't you want the case?"

"Not sure yet." But I liked his directness and his accented but fluent English.

"Are you a good detective?"

"You could ask around."

"I need a good one. You seem old. How old are you?"

"I'm still in my prime, sonny. That's all you need to know."

"Libby says you saved her life," Carlos chuckled. "Her judgment is good enough for me."

"You two seem close. Closer than student-teacher perhaps?"

"We're friends." Something flared in his eyes like a matchstick struck in a dark room.

"That's what she said, too."

"Does it matter?"

"Not necessarily. I just like to know as much as possible about the people I'm dealing with. By the way, I notice you speak good English—better than my Spanish, for sure."

"Libby's got me reading books." He smiled. "Someday, I hope to be a trainer. That's my dream. If you want to move up, you got to speak English, like the bosses. That's why I'm learning English from Libby."

"It's impressive." I paused, gazing over the restaurant, which was starting to fill up. "If I took the case, I'd need you as a guide."

"I'd have to work around my hotwalking duties, but I could manage. What do you want to see first?"

I suggested starting with the crime scene—or rather where the body was found.

We set off through the shed rows—covered walkways beside the stalls that lined each cinder-block horse barn clustered before us. Seems the backside had its own language, in addition to Spanish and English.

"I understand you're unhappy with the police investigation. Do you know who did it? Murdered your father?"

"It had to be someone who lives here. See that?" Carlos pointed out the razor-wire topped fence completely closing off the backside from the surrounding neighborhood.

Appropriate security, considering the multi-million-dollar horseflesh that needed protection.

"Late at night, there's only one way in or out of here," Carlos said.

A locked-room mystery, albeit a large one, I thought with amusement. Would there be a gathering of suspects at the end to unveil the culprits?

"The night of the murder, nobody came or went after ten o'clock, according to security," Carlos said.

"Those horse barns all seem alike," I said.

Each had a green roof and green and white awnings.

"But are they?"

Carlos told me there were differences. Trainers who leased the barns got to set them up however they wished. However, each included some twenty-odd stalls for equine housing, plus offices, bathrooms, living quarters, and veterinary and equipment storage facilities.

"How about their inner workings? Who does what job?"

As we walked on, he explained that the grooms were at the heart of the system, providing all care. Before dawn, they tacked up the horses for exercise out on the track. On days when a horse raced, the exercise rider would put the horse through a light workout to avoid disrupting the morning routine. He said that grooms usually were responsible for three horses at a time. While the stall was empty, the groom cleaned and prepared it before tacking up the next horse in his care. Supervision was provided by a trainer, barn manager, or foreman.

Carlos said that when the horse returned from its workout or a race, it was untacked and given a bath by the groom. Then a hotwalker like him would lead it around the shed row with periodic water stops for a half-hour, or until it was thoroughly cooled out. By noon, the horses were done for the day. Naptime would last until midafternoon. On race days, the groom would take the horse to the paddock, accompanied by the hotwalker. The trainer would saddle it there while chatting with the jockey.

Feeling my knowledge base vastly expanded by Carlos, I accompanied him to a barn with thick bundles of greenish straw hanging at the entrance as if to ward off evil spirits. At the door, a black cat sat in a rocker with its tail curled into a question mark. This one had stood empty at the time when Felipe Rojas' body was found buried under a pile of hay, but now it was back in use.

As we stepped inside, a chestnut colt poked his head out of his stall and snorted at us. At the same time, a uniformed sheriff's employee stepped up to stop us. I showed him my visitor's pass, but he said it wouldn't do. This week until after the Derby, only those with a valid racing commission license were permitted to enter the barns or have any contact with the horses. But when Carlos fudged and told him that I was investigating his father's murder, the deputy agreed to bend the rules—a breach of security, but not one that I'd report.

"This is it," Carlos said.

The stall where his father's body was found was a typical

12x12 space, empty now but big enough for a horse to turn around, lie down, and get up comfortably. There was a window for natural lighting and fresh air. The upper parts of doors and walls were left open so the horse could see out and be seen. Wood chips and shavings were scattered on the floor along with a fresh bed of straw. Buckets full of fresh water and racehorse oats—unbaked and laced with molasses—were fastened to the front wall. Alfalfa hay was stacked in a corner rack for the horse to munch on throughout the day.

Nothing like a fresh crime scene, I thought, especially one that had been cleaned continuously for the past year. The only obvious thing to learn from it concerned its location, which Carlos pointed out was on a direct route between the poker game in the backside workers' recreation room and Felipe's barn apartment.

"They got a nice TV in that rec room," Carlos said, "plus, ping pong and card tables. A bunch of us were in there partying after the races on Derby night. Everybody was drinking and carrying on. Juan Diaz accused Papa of cheating and a fight broke out. Papa punched his lights out. But I didn't see it because I'd already left."

"Was your father cheating?"

"Hell no! My Papa's no cheat."

Having struck a nerve, I probed a little deeper. "Did he get into many fights?"

"This was the first one I know of. Papa came here to get away from fighting. But he was no push-over and this was a matter of honor. The cops think Papa was jumped, robbed, and killed on his way home from playing cards. But they can't prove who did it."

"Who else was in the game?"

Carlos listed three Guatemalan grooms: Juan Diaz, Miguel Molina, and Wensceslao López. There was also a fourth groom, this one an African American named "Buzzy" Jones. I wrote their names in my moleskin reporter's notebook.

"All of them still in town?"

"Juan, Buzzy, and Miguel are, but I heard Wensceslao moved on to Hialeah. I can get you an address."

"Good. If I took the case, I'd want to talk to all of them. Did any of the four harbor any hard feelings toward your father?"

"No, everybody liked Papa."

Not everybody, I reflected.

"Did the five of them play poker often?"

"Occasionally. Papa was a good poker player, but careful."

"Do you think robbery was why someone killed him?"

"It makes sense. I know he didn't have a dime on him when he was found, but Diaz had $600 in his pocket when the cops searched him. That's more than a week's wages for a groom. The others had only a few bills between them."

"You think Juan Diaz might've done it?"

"I don't know. It seems too simple," Carlos said.

"Why too simple?" Occam's razor came to mind: the simplest explanation is usually the right one. Also, this was the second time I'd asked whom he suspected—and for the second time, he'd hedged.

"Juan just never struck me as a murderer. He's weak. But I don't know who did it. That's your job. To find out."

"If I take the case," I reminded him.

As we left the barn, Carlos said, "What else you want to see?"

"How about the rec hall?"

It proved a short walk and was much as Carlos had described it—a bright space for hardworking horse people to have some fun playing games and to drink when their workday was through. The other end of the building was used as backside headquarters for the media, but this seemed irrelevant.

After scoping out the rec hall, we walked back to where the body was found, presumably taking the same path as Felipe Rojas had that night. I didn't expect to see anything helpful and I didn't. You had to start somewhere, though, and like the cops, I thought it reasonable to assume that a disgruntled card player—

or someone else, for unknown reasons of their own—had lain in wait here for Felipe Rojas, whether to rob him or take his life.

"Now what?" Carlos said. "The schedule's light today. But I'm gonna have to get back to work soon."

I told him I'd seen enough for now.

Theories were fine, I thought, as he accompanied me back to the gate, but investigators liked facts. Nevertheless, experience had taught me to trust my intuition when facts were in short supply, as here. I had an inkling that Carlos might be on to something about the motive being too simple.

"Earlier, you said your dream was to become a trainer, Carlos. Was that your father's dream, too?"

He said it was, along with bringing the rest of the Rojas family to live in the U.S.

"Was that because of troubles back home?"

"Thirty-four years ago, my grandfather was murdered by a death squad," he said, in a choked voice.At the time, Carlos' father was only fourteen but supporting his entire extended family. The year he himself was born, Carlos said, the long bloody civil war between the U.S.-backed government and leftist rebels ended and Guatemala finally saw better times. But there was still far too much poverty, crime, and drug trade. Felipe had undertaken the harrowing journey to America hoping to find a better life, only to learn that a hard and lonely existence still awaited him here.

"When was the last time your father saw the rest of his family?"

"Almost nine years ago."

Felipe Rojas must have felt trapped while working his way up from hotwalker to groom. He was cut off. Alone. Yet he still believed that it was worth the sacrifice strongly enough to keep saving his money to bring Carlos and the others here. Carlos had not yet told me how he had made his journey northward, but it was obvious the kid had grit. His strong desire to assume his father's burden showed that.

Quite a sob story. Trouble was it was getting to me.

Carlos chose that moment to inquire how much I would charge for my services. So, Libby had not told him. I had not made up my mind to take the case, and if I did, he could never afford me. But I had grown interested despite myself and now didn't want to let go of it. Libby had offered to pay me, too, but I could not accept her money, either. This was no way to run a business, I told myself.

Despite that, I said, "All right, I'll take the case pro bono. That means for free."

Carlos tipped his head back and closed his eyes. "Thank you, Jim."

"Don't thank me yet. I haven't done anything."

"You will."

His faith was touching, if misplaced. I felt for the check I'd received in the mail from another client that morning and was glad it was still there in my pocket.

4

After leaving the Downs, my next stop was LMPD headquarters. For decades, it had been housed at Seventh and Jefferson downtown. But when an overflow of prisoners from the new jail across the street occupied an ancient cell block on the third floor, the homicide squad had to ago.

Their new digs, located on Old Louisville's western edge, were very un-copshop-like indeed, with an open floor plan, airy ceilings, and modern office style furniture trimmed in avocado. Computer workstations abounded. If I hadn't known better, I'd have thought I was in a Silicon Valley startup.

The five acres of asphalt and barbed wire surrounding the huge building hinted otherwise. The Edison Center was a repurposed warehouse on a formerly contaminated industrial site. It had been re-named after the famous inventor, a one-time Louisville resident whose electric light bulb had been unveiled during an 1880s fair held nearby.

After parking, I entered the lobby, checked in, and followed corridors past meeting rooms to Leo Brownfield's desk, where he sat with his shirt sleeves rolled up and his yellow tie hanging loose. His sharp gray suit coat hung on a hanger on a rack.

"Hello, Leo," I said.

The broad-shouldered homicide lieutenant looked up from the file he was reading when I came in and frowned.

"Well, if it isn't Jim Guthrie, Louisville's grittiest crime fighter since Kinsey Millhone. What was that last case of yours? *B is for bullshit?*"

"You're confusing me with someone else."

"Collared any colorful culprits lately, Guthrie?"

"You know, I think secretly you'd rather be a crime fiction writer than a cop."

"The hours are better, and you meet more blondes. Or so I'm told. What can I do for you, Jimbo?"

Brownfield knew that I hated that nickname. He hadn't changed much over the years. Maybe a few more wrinkles in his round, nut-brown face, some extra gray in his "clean and short" haircut. Corded forearms and a smile still full of white teeth.

"Got time to talk?"

"Always happy to drop everything for you, Jimbo."

He nodded at a chair in front of his desk, where I took a seat.

"I need some information."

"Really? And here I thought you'd come to discuss Picasso. Or Michelangelo."

The sarcastic bastard also enjoyed needling me about my interest in painting. Perhaps because he despised all private eyes, especially former cops like me, whom he labeled as turncoats for supposedly helping defense lawyers keep criminals out of jail. But Brownfield knew he owed me a debt that he could never repay—one that I'd never let him forget.

It had been two years after I left the force before our paths crossed again. At the time, I was chasing a thief down an alley on foot and gaining steadily when I rounded a corner in time to see a perp, who I later learned was high on crystal meth, knock a uniform to the ground. As I broke off my pursuit and rushed toward them, the meth-head straddled the patrolman and began beating him.

I saw him go for the cop's gun and tried to distract him by yelling, "Officer down." One bullet went zinging past my ear, but a second struck my chest, spinning me to the ground. The cop I'd come to help managed to disarm and handcuff the shooter. As I passed out, I heard him say, "Officer down," into his shoulder mic. That was Brownfield.

The bullet had missed any vital organs and, after a week in the hospital, I was released. I had recovered completely, except for the occasional shoulder twinge when the weather changed. But I'd taken one for Brownfield, and that was something for which he'd never forgive me.

"I need to know whatever you know about the Felipe Rojas killing," I said.

"The groom murdered at the track on Derby Day? That's an ongoing case."

"One you've been sitting on for a year."

"What's your interest?"

"My interest? Finding out the truth and putting the bad guys away."

A long-suffering grin appeared on Brownfield's hard cop's face. "You wound me, Guthrie. We don't have the manpower to investigate the hundred murders already committed in this town so far this year, let alone something that happened a year ago. You were police once. You should understand that."

"I do. But I still wonder why there's been no progress."

"Because nobody on the backside will talk to us about it, and until they do, there's not a chance of getting to the bottom of this. Who's your client?"

"Can't tell you that."

"It's the groom's kid, isn't it? He's been nipping at our heels ever since it happened." Brownfield sipped coffee from a foam cup.

"Who's the anonymous witness I read about," I countered,

"the one who came forward with information, but not enough to make assumptions about what happened?"

"Can't tell you that."

"What were the leads that made you optimistic you'd close the case nine months ago?"

"Can't tell you that, either."

"Well, what the hell can you tell me, Leo?"

"Investigating this is a slow process, Guthrie, partly due to the backside workers' transient lifestyle. They roam from track to track, season to season. But whenever there's a meet at the Downs, conversations take place. The killing always gets brought up and we learn some information that helps us."

"There's one going on now, I believe. How does the information generated get back to you? A snitch?"

"If I had a confidential informant that would be classified as ...confidential."

"So, you have nothing, but you're keeping the case open anyway. Come on, Leo. Give me your blessing to look into this."

Brownfield twisted his mouth into a pained frown. For a minute, I thought I'd have to take a sidelong glance at my shoulder to remind him of his debt, but he sat back and clasped his hands behind his head in a gesture of submission.

"Okay, Guthrie. Go ahead, poke around. But keep me informed. And no headlines suggesting that homicide isn't doing its job."

"There won't be any. News reports said abrasions found on the victim indicated that he was dragged. How far?"

"Judging by the amount of tissue damage, not far. A few feet."

"You think that the victim was attacked outside the barn and then dragged inside?"

He nodded. "I do."

"Who could have done it?"

"The backside is locked down at night. But about a thousand workers live there. It could be almost anyone," he said.

"Motive?"

"We think robbery."

"Any proof of that?"

"Not really."

"I understand there was a fight after Diaz accused the victim of cheating at poker."

"That's right."

"But when the players were searched, Diaz was the only one with plenty of money in his pockets. How did he explain the contradiction?"

"Said he'd been saving it up. We had no way to disprove that."

"What about the other poker players? Did you question them?"

"Of course. Nobody knew nothin'."

"Did any of them benefit from Rojas' death?"

"Only Molina, who got the victim's job. Trouble is that Molina was already employed as a groom. The lateral move didn't seem like enough to kill someone over."

"How about grudges or bad blood? Anyone know of any between them?"

Brownfield shook his head. "Not that we've heard."

"Any of the card players have a sheet?"

"Three of them."

Jones, López, and Diaz all had arrest records for being drunk and disorderly. But no other priors.

"Are any of them in the country illegally?"

"Not as far as we know."

"Didn't you check?"

"They were considered as witnesses, not suspects," Brownfield frowned. "We're not the border patrol. Not yet anyway."

But soon that might change. Up to now, he said, Louisville Metro cops had been barred from helping ICE make arrests unless they had a warrant signed by a judge. That policy was meant to show LMPD officers were a separate law enforcement arm from the feds. But that situation likely would be transformed if, and when, the state legislature passed a law mandating enforcement of immigration laws by all public institutions.

If the rumors proved true that some of Churchill's employees were undocumented, then the Downs might be in serious trouble, I thought. Those immigrants from the south were about the only ones willing to work the long hard hours demanded by racetrack life. While the new Biden administration was reversing many Trump immigration policies, undocumented workers were terrified by already occurring ICE raids. Brownfield knew this as well as I did.

"What if robbery wasn't the motive? Are there any jealous wives or husbands in the picture?"

"Don't know of any." Brownfield took a sip of coffee, frowned, and pushed the rest away.

"How about a drug angle?" I was referring to the fact that while Louisville had effectively decriminalized marijuana, the whole state suffered from an opioid epidemic. Methamphetamine and heroin abuse remained rampant, as well.

But Brownfield read it another way. "No drug angle, unless you mean the drugs the horses were taking."

"What do you mean? Are you talking about cheating?"

"It's as old as the sport of kings. But there's a horse fly in this particular ointment."

"And that is?"

"None of the longshots won any races that day. The favorites won. That means no huge payouts, so no cheating."

"I see." Puncturing that trial balloon had left Brownfield too pleased with himself. "Mind if I took a look at the Rojas file?"

"You know better than that," he barked. "It's still an active case."

"But growing colder than frost on a tombstone," I needled.

At this, a cloud of vexation descended upon his face and the veins in his neck stood out.

"Get the horsehair out of your ears, Guthrie. It's against department policy."

I nodded almost imperceptibly at my shoulder.

Brownfield gazed thoughtfully at me and sighed heavily before getting up out of his chair and going over to a row of beige and blue file cabinets. Rooting through the drawers, he pulled out a clump of manila folders, which he divided into two stacks. One stack he kept, the other he laid in front of me.

I thumbed through the reports, quickly skimming individual pages and making notes. I started with the crime scene photographs, which didn't tell me much. Police had interviewed numerous witnesses, whose names and contact information I wrote down. I read the autopsy report submitted by the chief deputy coroner. It was mostly the same as what I'd seen in the papers.

"What about the murder weapon?" I asked.

"Never found."

"The coroner's office initially refused to release some details. What was held back?"

It was standard procedure for police to withhold information known only to a killer, or any witness, for obvious reasons, including to weed out any false confessions.

Brownfield shook his head. "You know I can't tell you that."

"Come on, Leo. Give me something. You've been sitting on your secrets for a year now."

"One condition. You keep your mouth shut about this. Understood?"

I nodded.

"I'll tell you this much. From the angle of the blow, we believe whoever used the murder weapon was right-handed, and at least the same height as his victim. Felipe Rojas was five-nine. From the position of the wound, we think the killer was standing behind the victim. And since it only took one blow to crush the victim's skull, we know the killer was powerful."

"Like Barry Bonds wielding a baseball bat?"

"Bonds hit southpaw."

"Hank Aaron then. How tall are these other poker players?"

"About the same height as the victim."

"Well, that rules nobody out. Are they all right-handed, as well?"

"Except for López. I checked."

"So that's it? That's all you got for me?"

Brownfield nodded. "And this better not come back and bite me in the ass."

"It won't. You can trust me." I stood up to go.

"Get out of here, Guthrie."

I went.

5

By 9:30, I was back at the Downs going through a tunnel under the track that leads to the grandstand. I took an elevator to the sixth-floor office of security chief Ray Hines, which was the standard manager in size and décor. Hines himself was spit-shined and squared-away like someone ex-military.

"Welcome, Mister Guthrie. Let's get you some ID."

We'd spoken on the phone. During our call, he'd mentioned the need for a valid racing commission license to be in contact with the horses. That included trainers and their crews, racing officials, and select visitors such as owners.

"The racing commission determines if someone has a criminal background," Hines said. "Your P.I. license serves the same purpose. Let's take your picture and you'll be set to go in a minute or two."

Hines photographed me with a digital camera. Then he used a computer app and a heavy-duty laminating machine to produce a photo ID of me against a sky-blue background, which he said indicated access to most of the facilities.

"If you need to go anywhere sensitive, we'll escort you," he said.

"What's considered sensitive?"

"Wherever there's money. So, what else can I do for you?"

I asked to see the CCTV tapes from the night of the murder.

"Both the police and my staff have reviewed them. There's nothing there of interest," Hines said.

"I'd like to see for myself."

"Sure. No problem. My people are kinda busy right now, but I can arrange it later today."

I said that was fine. I'd come back.

"Anything else?"

"Yeah, it said in the papers that the body was found by a track security official. I need the name. I want to talk to him."

"That would be the night watchman, George Duffy," Hines said. "You'll have to reach him at home. George retired after last year's spring meet."

I raised my eyebrows. "Did you find that at all suspicious?"

"No. Why should I? There was no connection between finding a body and retirement, after all."

He was probably right. Still..." How long had Duffy worked here?"

"About five years."

"And before that?"

"Private security firm. George is a good man. He was in poor health. It was just time for him to hang it up. Let me get you his number."

Hines consulted his records and printed out Duffy's phone number and address for me.

"Is there anything else you can tell me about the murder?" I asked. "Anything that could have been overlooked? Any suspicions about who was involved?"

"Seemed pretty straight-forward to me," he said. "Too much alcohol, a card game, a fight. Somebody waylaid Rojas, robbed him, and killed him. That's probably all there was to it. You'll never get anything out of these racetrackers. They close ranks."

I thanked him for his help and returned to the grandstand, where I placed a call to the phone number Hines had given me for Duffy. No answer. I didn't leave a message. Thinking that I'd try it again later, I went to find Carlos Rojas on the backside. He was standing at the rail, watching a spotted white colt with black mane and tail gallop around the track.

"Go Speckled Band," someone in the crowd shouted.

When the workout was finished, Carlos and I returned to the Ericson barn, where he worked. Despite his long odds and dodgy pedigree, Speckled Band was the star of the stable. Visitors lingered outside the window, taking pictures on their phones of him just in case he should prove himself a champion. A very fit-looking exercise rider, her calf-length boots dangling out of the stirrups, guided the sweaty Derby colt through the fans and the barn door. Proceeding down the aisle, she ducked as she entered his box stall. The horse tossed his head and gave out a high neigh.

"How did he do?" Carlos said in Spanish.

The rider hopped off. "This little snot is on the muscle from his workout. He's ornery."

The horse didn't look it, with his flaring nostrils and expressive ears. His eyes were wide and set far apart, his bright alert expression appealing.

The thirtyish rider removed her helmet and shook out her dark hair. Metal studs winked in her ears.

"You have to push him, but he can really go when he wants to. Today, he didn't."

Carlos nodded. Then as if suddenly remembering my presence, said in English, "Daniela Torres, meet Jim Guthrie."

"*Hola,*" I said.

"*Entonces hablas Español?*"

I held up my right thumb and forefinger an inch apart and, from here on, stuck to speaking Spanish.

"You're the private eye."

"How do you know that?"

"Everybody knew two minutes after you arrived. Nobody on the backside will talk to you, though."

"Why not?"

"When folks get scared, they quit talking."

"What are they so scared of?"

No reply.

Exactly as Hines—and Brownfield—had predicted. The Downs publicly denied employing anyone without legal status, but they didn't do the hiring. Individual trainers did. And trainers complained that the current system kept them from knowing if they were even going to have a workforce.

Being legal or not was essential to how the immigrants thought and acted. Some might have been picked up randomly in raids by the feds. Others possibly had returned to their home country for legal work authorization, only to be barred from returning to the U.S. for ten years.

"I'm not a cop, Daniela. I wouldn't have to report any illegality I might uncover, like selling weed or immigration status, if it was irrelevant to my investigation. Workers on the backside don't need to worry about me—not unless they killed Carlos's father."

We locked eyes. Hers glittered, unreadable. "I have to go now. Maybe later."

She hurried off. I told Carlos that I thought my Spanish was good enough for interviewing other backside workers. He agreed but seemed a bit disappointed that he wouldn't be serving as my translator. He brightened up, however, when I said it was okay for him to continue practicing his English on me.

"Time for Speckled Band to have his morning bath," Carlos said.

As we left the barn, the circus continued playing out all around us. They called it the Derby Festival for a reason. No nude mud wrestling, streaking, flagpole sitting, or public sex yet. That was reserved for the infield on Saturday. But there was already a jolly atmosphere and an abundance of alcohol. People were enjoying themselves. One young guy drank a morning beer while he studied the Racing Form. The girl with him had two mint juleps and was sipping from both.

At the wash station, Carlos and another Latino, who I assumed was the animal's groom, maneuvered Speckled Band onto a rubber mat covering a stall-sized concrete base. The horse nickered while being tied to a ring attached to the barn and pushed his nose forward to touch the groom's outstretched hand. Carlos continued holding the colt steady as the groom lathered him up and then rinsed off the suds with a soft wash of water from a hose resembling a gardening wand. A rub down came next, followed by brushing Speckled Band's smooth hide with a curry comb. After the final step, which was throwing a head-to-tail cooler blanket over the colt, Carlos introduced me to Miguel Molina, his dead father's replacement, telling him that I had some questions to ask about the night Felipe Rojas was murdered.

Molina, who had a shaved scalp and was mostly neck and shoulders, did not respond immediately. So, Carlos told him I was there at his request to solve his father's murder.

"Okay," Molina said.

With that, Carlos set off to hotwalk the horse.

I began, in Spanish, by thanking Molina for agreeing to speak with me. Then I asked about any cheating that went on during the poker game on the night Rojas was killed. "Do you think Rojas was cheating?"

"Nah," Molina said, adding that Juan Diaz, who made the accusation, had a "snoot-full of tequila when he shot off his mouth." Felipe had knocked him down, and that was it. Then another fight broke out and things "got hairy."

"What was this other fight about?"

"A couple of drunks got out of hand. It happens, you know. The cops came and broke it up. After that, the party petered out."

"Did you notice anything unusual, or suspicious, after the fight?"

Molina shook his head. "I lost track of him in all the confusion. Like I told the cops, everybody went home."

"I understand that when Felipe was killed, you got his job. Some might think Carlos should have gotten it."

"It was not up to me. Mister Ned made the offer and I accepted."

"But you were already a groom for someone else. Why switch?"

"I felt like I needed a change, that's all."

"How's that working out?"

"Fine. Excuse me. I gotta get back to work."

As Molina strode off, I caught up with my client and asked how he'd felt about Molina replacing his father as an Ericson groom. "Didn't you hope to get the job yourself?"

"I was okay with it," he said. "Miguel's a good guy. Mister Ned said I wasn't ready yet."

"What's it take to be ready?"

"A lot. Getting in with the in crowd's not easy. You gotta prove yourself first."

"How do you do that?" I asked.

"By being a good hotwalker, to begin with. Trainers only use people they trust. Don't want their animals rearing, striking, getting loose, and injuring themselves—or you. You gotta be on your toes, read what their bodies are telling you—your life depends on it."

"Sounds dangerous."

"'Cause, it is. Racehorses are different than other nags. They're *not* mild-mannered. They're mouthy. Full of spirit and spunk. It's what trainers want—energy. They get so fit that training doesn't take the unruly off 'em. It's less about control than managing energy. Setting a pace the horse can handle without getting upset. Like walking fast enough to fly a kite."

"If it takes that much to be a hotwalker, what more do you

have to know to be a groom?"

"Everything. How to take care of the horse, know when he's sick, what he needs to get well. It's like raising a baby. Your baby."

"Did Ned say when he thought you would be ready?"

"No."

Carlos had shown considerable patience under the circumstances. But what other choice did he have? I asked if he believed the hulking Molina was telling the truth.

"Yes, I do."

One thing for sure, though: Molina was big and strong enough to have murdered Felipe Rojas with one swipe of a blunt instrument.

6

That made one card-playing person of interest down and two to go. I asked where to find the other card players for an interview.

"Follow me," Carlos said and headed off through the shed rows.

A crowing rooster startled me as he strutted across our path. He wasn't the first barnyard creature I'd encountered today. There were cats, goats, and chickens all over the place, too. When I asked about this, Carlos explained that horses were herd animals who felt more comfortable having small non-threatening creatures around.

"Don't we all?"

Carlos said that goats acted as security blankets for skittish horses. So did cats. They helped control the rodent population, too.

"But no dogs," I said. "Not one. How come?"

"Horses don't like dogs. They get spooked easily by them. Too much like wolves maybe."

At the next barn stop, we encountered a thin older man with white-hair and dark skin who was cleaning up the workspace. In his classic hard brim tweed racing flat cap and scuffed work boots, he appeared as ingrained in the fabric of the place as the horses themselves.

"That's Buzzy Jones," Carlos said.

Only a question or two after we were introduced, I knew that Buzzy—like Miguel Molina and Daniela Torres before him—didn't feel comfortable with talking freely to me about the night of the poker game or anything else. But the situation changed when Carlos began coaxing him to tell me how he got his nickname.

"He don't care about that," Jones muttered.

"Yeah, he does. Tell him about the old days."

"You tryin' to play me, boy?"

"Hell no, Buzzy," Carlos said. "Just talk to the man while I walk this horse."

Jones looked at me skeptically. "You wanna know?"

"I do."

"I got it 'cause I had a buzz haircut."

"I used to have one of those," I said. "When I was a kid. More of a flattop, I guess."

"Flattop. Yeah, I remember those," Jones said.

He began to talk about the barber shop he used to frequent, how it had been a community meeting place where men came for more than just haircuts—to share local gossip and talk politics, as well as play dominoes or chess.

"Ain't like that no more, though," he said. "Old place is gone now, along with the whole damn neighborhood."

"Highland Park?" I asked, referring to a small mixed-race community that had been uprooted for airport expansion some years ago. "I used to date a girl who lived there."

"White girl?" Jones asked, giving me a sharp look.

"Yeah, back when I was in high school."

Suspicions confirmed, he nodded. "Wasn't no paradise, but

folks there got along pretty good."

Now that the ice between us had been broken, I hoped we could have a conversation.

Buzzy—real name Walter, he said—had started his racetrack career at the age of eight, when his father, a groom, had brought him to the Downs and began teaching him everything about working with horses.

"We loved the work. I was in the barn day and night. Takin' care of the horses. Then drinkin' some bourbon and shootin' dice. Can't do that no more. But in those days, you could. Wasn't nobody cared about it, long as it didn't interfere with your work. Now you lucky to play cards on a Friday night."

Or perhaps unlucky, in Felipe Rojas' case.

He went on painting a vivid picture of backside life as it used to be, saying that it mostly remained the same today, except that Latinos like Carlos had largely replaced the African Americans who'd helped pioneer the racing industry. Racetrack life was still a revolving door, with horses and workers coming and going seasonally. I asked him about the night of the poker game and whether Rojas had been cheating. Buzzy didn't think so.

"Any idea who murdered Felipe Rojas?"

He shrugged.

Carlos returned not long afterward.

"Two down and one to go. Let's hunt up Juan Diaz," I said.

One barn was cordoned off from onlookers by a row of white sawhorses. As we arrived, a tall, white-haired man with an aura of celebrity strode inside.

"Who is that guy?" I asked.

"That, amigo, is one real big horse conditioner."

"A what?"

"A top-level trainer, one of the best."

His name was Keene Kessinger.

"He started with nothing, slept on a cot in a tack room. But now he's got all the high-end horse owners on a string, wanting him to train their thoroughbreds. He's training about 150 or so right now, including Cat Chaser, the Derby favorite, in case you don't know. Kessinger-trained horses have won the Derby, Belmont, and Preakness but never all in the same year. That's what he's after now—the Triple Crown."

Moving on, we turned a corner and found ourselves with a wide-angle view of the track as a helmeted rider thundered by, the steady rhythm of hooves pounding on the yellow-brown dirt. Farther on we encountered a lumbering man who was apparently trying to choke a wet sponge to death. Carlos introduced the sponge strangler as Juan Diaz, a Kessinger groom. He was also the final poker-playing person of interest on my list.

I told him, in Spanish, that I was investigating Felipe's murder and needed to ask him some questions.

"Don't wanna," Diaz slurred.

Suddenly realizing this behemoth, who was surrounded by hoses and water buckets, was intoxicated—so drunk, in fact, he could barely stand up—I pressed him hard. "Come on, Juan. On the night Felipe Rojas was murdered, witnesses say you accused him of cheating at poker and got into a fight with him. What do you have to say about that? And what do you know about his death?"

"Nothin.' Go 'way." He dropped the sponge, picked it back up.

"Guthrie," Carlos hissed as a beautiful horse approached, long tail flying, regal head held high.

I glanced at my client.

"That's Cat Chaser," he said.

The Derby favorite was impressive. Impossible not to admire the way his muscles undulated under his glossy black coat. Surely such a highly vaunted beast would be accompanied by his entourage. But no, there was only the horse and his hotwalker, a small but sturdy-looking Latina in her forties. Juan Diaz was too busy throttling the inanimate object in his hammy fists to notice her or the horse. But the woman noticed him, all right.

"Juan!" she shouted, as he kept dropping the sponge over and over. "What the hell are you doing?"

"Juan's wife, Sandy Diaz," Carlos explained, *sotto vocce*.

When Diaz lost his balance and was about to tumble to the ground, Sandy impressed me by steadying him with one hand while keeping Cat Chaser under control with her other. Noticing me, as if for the first time, she said, "Who are you?" When I told her I was a private investigator, she said, "Not the police? Then we don't have to talk to you." She turned. Grabbing a fistful of her husband's faded sweatshirt, she shook him like a terrier wagging a Saint Bernard and said, "Juan, you damn fool. Are you drunk?"

The big guy's eyes widened, and he answered the question with a slap that knocked her to the ground, causing her to drop the lead shank and lose control of Cat Chaser, who whinnied and stamped, reared, and pawed the air. As the spooked animal walked on his hind legs, threatening to trample them both, Carlos alertly scooped up the rope. He spoke softly trying to calm Cat Chaser and it worked as the panic-stricken colt instinctively backed away from what had frightened him and stopped thrashing around.

Freed of her hotwalking responsibilities, Sandy Diaz rose and went after her husband. All of my training and experience told me not to get involved. Domestic disputes are treacherous. But when Diaz swung his fist and hit his wife, I acted instinctively, yanking him by the scruff of his thick neck and sending him spinning. He wound up flat on his back.

This time when Sandy scrambled up, as I feared she might, she turned on me, pounding my chest with her fists and trying to kick me in the groin. I turned sideways to protect myself and spun her around, pinning her arms to her sides and scissoring her legs with mine. She was a handful, a fiercely angry woman made strong by physical labor. I hoped she wouldn't bite.

I saw the white-haired celebrity trainer from earlier come

jogging toward us, apparently bent on saving the day. But no, as it turned out, he was only interested in keeping his multi-million-dollar investment out of harm's way. That became clear well before he slipped on the foamy surface of the bathing station and, in somewhat comical fashion, lost his footing. But he didn't go down. Instead, he snatched the lead rope away from Carlos just as Sandy was beginning to tire from her violent contortions.

"It's all right now, you're okay," Kessinger cooed—not in Sandy's ear but Cat Chaser's.

Once the horse settled down, Kessinger scowled at Juan Diaz, who by then was being pulled to his feet by his wife—not for the first time, I guessed.

"What the hell's going on, Juan?" the trainer demanded.

Diaz pointed at me, implying this was somehow all my fault. But Kessinger wasn't buying it.

"Are you drunk, Juan?"

"Sorry, boss," Diaz muttered.

Shaking his head, the trainer let out a deep breath and said, "You know you could have killed my horse? I've warned you before. Now I'm going to have to let you go. You're through."

Looking stricken, Sandy pleaded, "Please, Mister Kessinger."

"I'm sorry, Sandy. Get him out of here."

Kessinger gave his horse a peppermint and guided him over to the wash area where the trainer had slipped. Carlos tagged along. As the big horse conditioner held up a water bucket for Cat Chaser to take a drink, Sandy was holding up her inebriated man so he could stagger away.

"You okay, Rojas?" Kessinger said.

"Never better, sir."

"Good. That was nice work."

"Thanks, Mister Kessinger."

"No, it's me who should thank you. And your help won't be forgotten."

Kessinger turned the hose on Cat Chaser.

"He's a real horseman," Carlos said to me quietly. "I mean

Mister Kessinger knows and cares about horses. Not all trainers do."

One of the TV people tried to interview Kessinger while he was still up to his elbows in soap suds. "Not now, damn it."

As the journalist backed away, a gravelly voice boomed from the far edge of the crowd.

"What's the matter, Your Lordship? Too good to speak with us ordinary folk of the working press?"

The possessor of this distinctive vocal instrument turned out to be a hard-to-miss-looking character with a foul-smelling cigar clamped in his teeth. He was wearing a bright orange Hawaiian shirt with a kilt, of all things, a gaudy outfit likely to offend anyone's fashion sense, but most certainly Hawaiians and Scotsmen.

I nudged Carlos. "Who the hell is that?"

"That's Whitlow, the tip sheet guy."

"Which tip sheet?" I asked.

"You've never heard of *The Late Mail?*"

Oddly, I hadn't. But I was familiar with tip sheets in general. At some tracks, they were known as tout, pink, or bull sheets and usually sold from kiosks along with racing forms. But the publisher of *The Late Mail* was giving his sheets away. I watched him distribute the photocopied newsletter, wondering how he could make any money doing that. I concluded he must carry advertising.

While onlookers accepted copies of the tip sheet, I sensed an undercurrent of resentment from a band of green T-shirted track workers. And when the tipster approached Keene Kessinger with a copy, the trainer told him to go to hell. Kessinger adjusted the water faucet and began hosing down Cat Chaser. With an exaggerated shrug, the publisher moved on to me.

I accepted a single-page edition and scanned the front. Unlike most other tipsheets I'd seen, this one did not just offer three best picks for every race. No, *The Late Mail* seemed far more ambitious, a hybrid tabloid that appeared to value controversy for its shock value. I came to this conclusion after seeing a cartoon of a jockey and the unlikely headline: "Deceased Jockey Wins Race." A sub-head posed the question, "Who Needs Jockeys?" After reassuring readers that they had read the headline correctly, the sheet reported:

"No, we're not talking about the lethargic performance of a certain rider on yesterday's card at Churchill who only looked dead in the saddle. The reference is to jockey Frank Hayse, who—back in 1923—suffered a fatal heart attack while riding in a race at Belmont Park but stayed in the saddle to win as a 20-1 long shot. Seems like the adage about the more things change, the more they stay the same, is still true."

When I looked up, the publisher was standing in front of me, puffy blue eyes staring out at me from a deeply lined face, adding years to his appearance.

"I'm Wyatt Whitlow," he said, as we exchanged a firm handshake. "The scuttlebutt is that you're the private eye reopening the Rojas murder case."

"That's right. I couldn't help overhearing you having words with Kessinger," I said.

"His Lordship can be a right arsehole." With a roguish grin, he indicated the cartoon. "Probably leaped to the conclusion that our art was modeled after his top jockey."

"Was it?"

"Of course not," he winked. "Any resemblance is purely coincidental."

I had to smile.

"You're on the case, yeah? That predisposes me in your favor."

"Why should it?"

"Makes you a better story. Anything you'd like to share with my readers about the investigation?"

"Who are your readers?"

I already had a pretty good idea—besides people who only wanted the three best picks for every race, there were also those who enjoyed unsubstantiated attacks on racing figures and other such tittle-tattle.

"Who are my readers?" Whitlow asked. "Why, anyone who's interested in racing, or who wants a hot tip and the latest gossip. Or who appreciates brilliant, witty commentary, that's who."

"What do you know about the Rojas murder?" I asked. "Maybe we can trade information."

"I doubt you got much to trade yet. These Mexicans are the most close-mouth bunch you'll ever meet. You'll get squat out of them."

"Felipe Rojas was Guatemalan."

"What's the difference?"

Now I understood the resentment toward him I'd sensed from Latino onlookers. "What's your beef with Kessinger?"

"How perceptive of you. My tip sheet offends His Lordship's sensibilities. What I call 'irreverent satirical commentary' he calls 'low blows.' I think he just can't take a joke. I am a funny guy. Sarcasm and caustic humor are the tools of my trade. But some people are too dumb to get the humor."

"Maybe they get it, but think your ridicule is in bad taste."

"Naw, that can't be it." He rolled his cigar from one side of his mouth to the other. "Like the great American playwright Edward Albee said: 'What I mean by an educated taste is someone who has the same tastes that I have.'"

I was more interested in Whitlow's knowledge of the backside. I suspected he knew more gossip than anyone else because it was his business to do so. I wanted to pick his teeming brain in the worst way, but I got the feeling that he never gave anything away except the tip sheet. It would not behoove me to come across as too eager at first blush. On the other hand, there was plenty I'd like to share with Whitlow's readers.

Unlike a normal investigation where discretion and a low profile are paramount, those strategies offered no advantages here, where the more people who knew what I was doing, the better. I wanted to get everyone talking about the murder and worrying the murderer.

"Exactly how low would you stoop for a scoop, Whitlow?"

"Why? You got one for me?"

"Maybe."

"Well, like Albee says, 'Takes a swine to show you where the truffles are.'"

I wasn't sure why he was calling me a swine, but I didn't let that stop me from going after the truffles, whatever they were.

"It might help if you'd publish a story to the effect that a certain private investigator is following a new line of inquiry and may be close to cracking the Rojas murder case."

"On your first day?" Whitlow cleared his throat. "What new line of inquiry? How close?"

I shook my head. "That's what I want the murderer to wonder."

"You want me to rattle their cage for you?"

"Isn't that what you do best?"

"I like you, shamus, and I'm willing to plant your item—for a small fee, of course." He waggled his eyebrows. "Call it advertising."

"How much?"

"Fifty simoleons."

I winced, recollecting my current bank imbalance, but told him it was a deal. As we shook hands on it, I slipped him the money. He gave me a business card, which I slid into my wallet.

"Are you sure you don't know anything about the murder that would help me?" I asked.

"Buy me a drink sometime at the Rail Runner Saloon on Taylor Boulevard. Alcohol has been known to oil my brain and loosen my tongue."

I felt certain that it would take far more than one drink to get anything out of Wyatt Whitlow. I decided to put that line of inquiry on a back burner. Instead, I carried my folded copy of *The Late Mail* over to the Ericson stable, where a strong but not unpleasant horsey musk lingered. Sweat and leather. Oats and grass and manure.

With nobody around the entrance, I leaned against the barn door and read the tip sheet.

I knew that "late mail" was a racing term meaning timely tips whispered by informed sources about such topics as last-minute scratches, jockeys, and track conditions. While I did not recognize the names of today's top three picks at the Downs, I assumed Whitlow must be a decent handicapper to stay in business, as I assumed the wily tattler knew precisely what he could get away with and how far to go. The cartoon jockey was captioned "Old Sleepy-eye." As I suspected, there were ads, primarily for local businesses.

And then suddenly the world was filled with song.

7

The voice was as smooth as Wyatt Whitlow's was raspy. I recognize the song, "El Paso," as a Marty Robbins classic from before I was born.

A security guard checked my ID and let me in. I crept toward a brightly illuminated stall at the far end of the row where a gray-haired man who had to be trainer Ned Ericson sang about a doomed love affair between two wild young cowboys and a bar maid in West Texas. As he sang the part about stealing a good horse and off he did ride, he was holding Speckled Band's tail with a surgically gloved hand.

In his other was a rectal thermometer. Ericson looked too old and frail for that kind of chore. His jeans were stuffed into the tops of his boots like he meant business, but his worn flannel shirt hung on him as if he'd experienced a sudden weight loss, consistent with illness. He finished the song at the same moment he finished taking the horse's temperature. The stall door I was leaning on suddenly let out a loud squeak and man and horse swiveled their heads toward me at the same time, all ears perked as if ready to make a threat assessment. The horse shifted restlessly, haunches quivering, in the deep bedding straw.

"How'd you know he'd be a Marty Robbins fan?" I asked.

Ericson's eyes gleamed. "Who the hell isn't? You're the one investigating Felipe Rojas' murder."

I admitted it.

"Well, I won't offer to shake hands."

"Probably best," I agreed. "Why do you sing to him?"

The colt nibbled at Ericson's shirt. The trainer pulled a carrot out of his pocket and fed it to him.

"Horses are lightning rods. They pick up the attitudes of other horses, and humans, too. If you come in upset, it's likely your horse will be upset. Speckled Band is the only horse I've found that singing works on. It calms us both down."

Ericson picked up a cotton ball from a shelf and began soaking it in what smelled like alcohol. Then he wiped off the thermometer with it.

"I'd like to ask you some questions concerning the murder," I said.

"Go ahead. Ask them."

"Rojas worked for you a long time."

"Almost nine years."

"In that time, what was your view of his character? Could he have been involved in something shady?"

"Such as?"

"Drug trafficking? Race fixing?"

"Are you joking? Felipe never used drugs, as far as I know. He did not work for a drug cartel, either. And race fixing! You mean *my* races? Now, that's downright offensive. Besides, if you wanted to fix a race, you'd need a jockey or a trainer, not a groom. As for anything else illegal, the man never gave me any reason to doubt him."

Ericson coughed deep in his chest.

"It's a senseless, dirty shame what happened to Felipe.

Whatever you do, at least don't soil his reputation. A man's good name is all he's got, you know. In this case, it's all his son has left of him."

"Not my intention. I'll follow the facts."

"Where have they led you so far?"

"El Paso?"

But Ned Ericson's jovial mood was gone. "How can you take the kid's money? If the murderer could be caught, wouldn't the police have already done it?"

"That's what I told him. But they have lots of other cases to worry about. I have only this one. Carlos wants his father's killer brought to justice. That's what I mean to do."

"How much is he paying you?"

"How much did you make last year?"

Ericson took my point. Stripping off his gloves, he dropped them in a hanging bucket.

"What about known associates? Who were Felipe's friends?"

"I don't think he had many. Miguel Molina occasionally went with him to the Latino bar on Third Street."

"How about women?"

"You mean like the kind you'd meet in a bar? No, he was married and kept to himself. All he cared about was bringing his family here. He wouldn't have done anything to jeopardize that."

"What about this fight he was in on the night he got killed?"

Ericson grabbed a towel and dried his hands.

"Didn't see it. Juan Diaz is who you want to talk to. Better catch him early, while he's still sober."

"Guess you haven't heard. Keene Kessinger fired him a little while ago."

Ericson sighed. "Oh, no. I'm sorry to hear that. Diaz has got a wife and a little girl. I don't know what will happen to them now. These Guatemalans. They're so tough."

"One more thing. Where were you on the night Rojas was killed?"

The trainer gave Speckled Band a final pat and closed the stall door behind him.

"Not sure I remember. Why?"

Before I provided the obvious answer, a wiry-looking young man sauntered in wearing a blue and white University of Kentucky baseball cap over light-brown curls that barely touched his shoulders. He wore cowboy boots and bore a strong resemblance to Ned.

"Who is this, Dad?" he said.

"Jim Guthrie, this is Luke, my assistant trainer, who runs our operation now. Guthrie's a private eye."

"Private eye? What do you want?" Luke asked.

The old man smiled.

"I just have a few questions," I said.

"Questions about what?" Luke said.

"Guthrie's looking into Felipe Rojas' murder," Ned said.

"I thought the police were handling that," Luke said.

"They've run into a wall. I've been asked to investigate."

"Who hired you?" Luke asked.

"I told you that's confidential. What I'd like to do is eliminate both of you as possible suspects."

"Suspects?" Luke turned to Ned. "Sounds like he's interested in your alibi, Dad."

"My alibi? Are you kidding?" Ned guffawed.

"Yours, too, Luke. It's routine in a murder investigation," I said.

"Routine, my ass," Luke said in a huff.

"Take it easy, son. Guthrie here's only trying to do his job." Ned scratched his neck and rolled his shoulders. "I was just trying to recall what we did after last year's Derby. Do you remember?"

"You must be losing it, Dad. We went to a party at Dale Romans' house."

Romans was a big-time local trainer.

"That's right, we did."

"How big a party was it?" I asked.

"Big. We were there until the wee hours," Luke said.

"That shouldn't be hard to verify," I said.

"Yeah, you can verify the hell out of it," Luke said. "Listen, Dad, Cinnamon Skin's acting up again. Could you take a look at him? Give him the old magic touch?"

"All right. You talk to Guthrie while I'm seeing to the colt. And finish recording Speckled Band's vitals for me, too."

"Will do."

"Felipe was a good man. Treat his memory right," the old man said, heading for the door.

"Who are you working for?" Luke said.

"That's confidential. Why would you care?"

He took off his ball cap and ran a hand through his hair.

"Look, all this died down. Now you're raking it up again. For what?"

"To find the killer."

"He's probably in Timbuktu by now. Look, my father's not well. He's been battling cancer for the past ten years. It's starting to wear him down. He doesn't need to be bothered with this crap. How about leaving him alone from now on?"

"I won't bother him unless I have to."

"I'll hold you to that."

Speckled Band pricked up his ears.

"Anything you can tell me, Luke? Was Rojas involved in any disputes? Did anybody have it in for him?"

The younger Ericson reached over and gently massaged the colt's forehead.

"Not that I know of."

"Did he seem bothered by anything?"

Luke shook his head slowly. "His death stunned all of us."

As he spoke, a fit-looking woman wearing a light jacket over a loose-fitting shirt brushed past us silently. She was in her thirties with long dark hair tied back in a ponytail. She opened Speckled Band's stall door and stepped inside.

"Doctor Freya Hall, our veterinarian," Luke said. "This is Jim Guthrie, private eye."

"Luke!" Ned shouted somewhere outside the barn.

"Excuse me. I need to see what Dad needs." Luke stepped away.

The veterinarian began pinching Speckled Band's neck. "I hope you're better at investigating than the police."

"Why are you pinching that horse, Doctor Hall?" I asked, admiring the woman's good-looks and intelligent alert eyes.

She smiled, seeming pleased by my attention.

"It's Freya. I'm checking to see if he's hydrated. If he is, in less than one second after I let go, his skin will flatten back into place."

She demonstrated, releasing Speckled Band's skin. It flattened out, exactly as she'd said.

"I take it that he's been getting enough water."

"Hm, a quick learner. I like that." The colt nosed at Freya, she gave him a carrot. "Learned anything new about the case, Jim?"

I told her I had a few leads I was following up.

"Already? You must be an ace investigator."

"I am."

She smirked. "What's your secret? The police have been stalled for a year."

"I poke and prod, see who gets upset. What did you think of Felipe Rojas?"

"Good man, good groom. We all felt terrible about what happened to him."

"How about his son?"

"Carlos? He's a natural. Horses love him."

"I'm curious. How does someone your size manage to handle a thousand-pound horse?"

"It's all in your head. Just like with a man. You only need enough strength to make him stand still. Like for an x-ray, or an exam."

"You really seem to know horses."

She brushed her hands on her jeans.

"I'm a vet. I grew up around them, loving them, studying them, taking care of them. It's my dream job." Freya stepped out of the stall. "What about you? Did you read about Sam Spade and dream of becoming a private eye?"

"Not quite. I was in the army. They turned me into an investigator. I was an MP and good at it, so when I got out I joined the cops."

"For how long?"

"Four years."

"But then you went private. Why?"

"Long story. Best told over a drink. Let's get back to you. Where did you study to be a vet?"

"I earned my DVM degree at UK."

"Did you know Luke Ericson there?"

"Yeah, though it was quite a while before I became his vet. I started out being more interested in research."

"What kind?"

Freya stroked Speckled Band's mane. "You sure you're interested?"

"Absolutely."

"I did a study concerning the effect of aging on thoroughbred racing performance."

"What did you find?"

"That a three-year-old Derby winner would typically finish six horse lengths ahead of a two-year-old Breeders' Cup Juvenile winner."

"How'd you do that?"

"By using statistics and quadratic equations from other models."

"I love it when women talk dirty to me."

She laughed softly. "I warned you. Practical value? My research proved performance improved substantially up to about age five, then gradually declined."

"You said practical value?"

"There were implications for how long to race a horse, and when to put one out to stud."

"Ah, sounds like important work."

"The research or being put out to stud?"

I grinned.

"So, why give up such important work just to use a rectal thermometer?"

"Well, there is a little more to a vet's job than that. To pay off my student loans, I worked for a large mobile animal practice, making house calls for horses. I did research on the side. One day, I ran into Luke again. His father needed a vet. I got the job. Now their stable is my primary practice."

My phone rang. I dug it from my pocket. It was Hines calling to say now would be a good time to watch the CCTV footage. I told him I'd be right there.

"Sorry, Freya, but I have to go now. Maybe we can talk again—if I think of any more questions."

"A handsome man like you doesn't need any questions to see me."

It was always a thrill to hear a woman offer such a compliment, especially one as attractive as her. It was what came after that worried me.

Seeming to sense this, Freya reached out and pinched my neck. "You seem a bit dehydrated. A drink might be nice."

8

I thought about that drink—and Dr. Freya Hall's feminine allure—while taking the tunnel under the track and riding the elevator up to see Ray Hines. She was both fetching and charming. And I liked the way she wasn't afraid to show that she liked me. But her proximity to the murder victim also made her a potential suspect. I'd had both good luck and bad with women, including a femme fatale or two. Finding a keeper had been harder, as evidenced by my divorce. I needed to be cautious with Dr. Hall.

On my way to Hines' office, I phoned Riley Simmonds, an old army buddy based in south Florida, and after explaining what I needed to know, offered to pay his usual rate to interview Wensceslao López. I'd caught Riley at a down time, he said, and agreed to start right away. I didn't expect much to come of this, but as the Oracle of Delphi once advised, when digging for buried treasure, leave no stone unturned.

Hines took me to an unmarked door made of galvanized steel three-inches thick and designed for heavy security. He punched a keypad on the wall to let us in. No mechanical locks. Everything accessed by key card ports. Another sign of the times—even in an antiquated gentleman's club like Churchill Downs where the horse was still king.

"This is it," Hines said, as the door swung open, "the control room."

Inside, a team of four surveillance operators sat at computer workstations facing multiple wall-mounted monitors.

"This equipment is state-of-the-art," Hines said, with a sweeping gesture.

Seemed like you couldn't solve anything these days without surveillance cameras and cell phones. Thirty-six cams had been installed three years ago. Their coverage included the entire track complex. Hines seemed awfully proud of his toys, which were wireless, outdoor, high definition, and infrared.

"No cassette tapes, huh?" I said, deadpan.

"Hardly. The best way of handling surveillance footage now is via virtual technology."

"I'm virtually clueless. You'll have to explain all that to this poor antiquated private eye."

"Stuck in the past, eh? It's not like in the old days with VHS when isolating part of a recording was tedious. Nowadays, the footage can be modified for clearer video and sharper details, too. Some of our cams have night vision, and motion-activated recording."

"How long are you able to record for?"

"Up to forty-eight hours. We've got intelligent search options that can pinpoint the exact date and time stamp of any image captured."

"Including the night of the murder?"

"Yes," Hines said.

They used something called a "camera map" to help select the best way to view any scene. The cams were numbered on the map. I told him I was interested in the footage from 11:30 at night until the body was found.

"The good news is that we had eyes on it all night long. The bad news is that only three cams were dedicated to covering the backside, and those three were set to sweep the area on a one-minute cycle rather than stay static."

"You're saying you don't have continuous coverage?" I groaned inwardly.

The security chief sucked in his cheeks. "Didn't think we needed it. We had all the usual Derby Day enhanced security, from our own spotters to the military, FBI, CIA, ATF, and Secret Service. The TV networks were here, too, of course. When you're talking about security, that's about as good as it gets."

"But not good enough to catch the murderer on tape?"

Hines licked his lips. "Cams were set up to watch over the loading dock, betting locations, general offices, inside the clubhouse, plus other zones. Unfortunately, as I said, there were some gaps in coverage. We'll have all the bugs in the system worked out next year."

"Won't that be lovely. Too bad it won't help me now. You've seen the footage. What does it show?"

"Nothing much, like I said. Nobody there who shouldn't have been. No suspicious movements during the times you're interested in."

"Police have seen this, right?"

"Yeah. We've set up a spot for you to review the footage. Even with AVI computer files to skim and jump rapidly between different points, it will take a while."

Hines detailed a technician to show me how to scan the images.

—

Two hours later, I phoned Carlos and arranged to meet him at his apartment above the Ericson stables. A white plank staircase led me to a second-floor landing with two doors. I knocked on the one on the right. Carlos opened it.

"Come on in."

Only one room inside, not much bigger than the horse stalls downstairs. Might as well have been a monk's cell, dimly lit by a lonely ceiling bulb, with the only window covered by a sheet. I sat on his single bed and updated him on my progress. But I held back the fact that I'd paid Wyatt Whitlow to publish a lie. The fewer people who knew about that, the better. When Carlos heard that the CCTV cameras had been no help, he grunted, a simple exhalation that conveyed not only his lack of surprise but also suspicion and disillusionment.

"I scanned it backward and forward, at normal speed and in super slow-motion, but the only person I saw enter that barn was the night watchman, followed by other security, around dawn. The watchman later retired which I found interesting. Did you ever talk to him?"

"George Duffy? Yeah, I did. He said he was sorry about Papa, but didn't seem to know much. You think he was involved?"

"Who knows? I plan to talk to him. I was surprised to learn so many people—upwards of a hundred probably—knew how those backside cameras are set up. When they were installed, Hines gave a demonstration for all the bigwigs—money people, trainers, horse owners, corporate, and others. If our killer knew about the one-minute sweep cycle, he'd know exactly when to stay hidden and when to haul ass."

"Is that what you think happened?"

"It seems likely."

"That's already more than the cops found out."

"I'm not sure it gets us any closer, though, Carlos."

I told him about the chief deputy coroner's autopsy report, how it had differed little from media accounts. How judging from the angle of the blow, Felipe's murderer was probably right-handed. How the coroner thought he was also about the victim's height.

"Know if any of the poker players are left-handed?"

"Wensceslao."

I told him about the call I'd made to Miami. I hoped I was

not wasting money—my money—by hiring the operative. While we talked, my eyes swept the room. I noticed a small mirror on the wall. Under it was a table with toothpaste and a toothbrush, a bar of soap, and a large wash basin. Plain white towels hung from a rack. When I asked how long Carlos had lived here, he said ever since he'd rejoined his father.

"Shouldn't this apartment have gone to Felipe's replacement? Wasn't that the custom?"

"Yeah, but Mister Ned let me keep it anyway."

"Didn't Miguel Molina mind?"

"I don't think so. Miguel's got a decent space downstairs."

This apartment wasn't much. A mattress, a chest of drawers, and a packing crate with a twelve-inch TV on top. A stack of paperbacks recommended by Libby, according to Carlos. Someone had hammered hooks into the rafters to serve with a broom handle as a makeshift closet. His mantra appeared to be travel light, since only a navy windbreaker, one dress shirt, and two pairs of jeans hung on the bar.

"Did your father leave any important documents or keepsakes behind?"

"No. I gave everything away, except for those." He pointed to a rosary, a crucifix, and a small statue of the Virgin Mary. Also, partly visible among them was a small brass figurine. I picked it up.

"What's this?"

"Papa's good luck charm."

It was a man-in-a-black suit and wide-brimmed hat. He had a bent black mustache—like Felipe Rojas's—and was holding a money bag and a flagstaff.

"What does it mean?"

"It means 'the saint of gamblers and drunkards.'"

I set the charm down. "Gamblers and drunkards? Did your father drink much?"

"No, he didn't like alcohol."

"How about betting? Did he like that? Seems like everybody

else around here does. They all bet on the races, especially when they've got a hot tip, correct? Your father played poker, too. How could he afford to gamble on a groom's wages and still pay your way to America?"

"All I know," Carlos said, seeming to struggle for words, "is that when it came to racing Papa only bet on a sure thing."

"Do those really exist?"

"Oh, yeah. If you work with horses, you know who feels good today and who doesn't. Whether somebody's holding his horse back, trying to darken the form. Like that."

"Such information would be extremely valuable, would it not?"

"Uh-huh. That's why you don't hear much about it unless you're an insider."

"Have you won any bets on sure things?"

"One or two."

I asked him to tell me more. But he said he didn't want to unless I was sure it had to do with the case. I wasn't, though, so that was the end of that. For now, anyway. I couldn't help thinking that in the end, Felipe's good luck charm hadn't brought him much luck.

9

Mrs. George Duffy lived in a neat California bungalow on a side street not far from the Downs. The small white frame house had a dormer window and a covered concrete front porch with flowerpots. It was bordered by an alley on the east and an open lot to the west. The small front yard was shaded by a mature maple.

A pale cheerless woman with steel gray hair worn in a wispy layered bob answered my knock and my question with a confused look. "Yes, I'm Missus Duffy. Who are you?"

"My name is Guthrie."

"What do you want?" She held her stomach as if in pain.

"Is your husband at home?"

"George? Why?"

"I want to talk to him for a few minutes about when he worked at Churchill Downs. Could I see him please?"

"He's not here." The woman's hands were trembling. "Are you a policeman?"

"Private investigator. What's the matter?"

"George is dead."

"Dead? Since when?"

"He had a heart attack three months ago."

"I'm sorry." I put on a sympathetic look. "If I could come in for a minute?"

"What for?" She looked alarmed again.

"Just a brief word. Won't take long."

"All right." She pulled the door open and I stepped inside a carpeted hallway. We went from there to the over-furnished living room, which included a green sofa, an upholstered chair, a table, and a glass-fronted cabinet.

"Won't you sit down?"

I sat on the chair. She took the sofa. The only light came from a small window. We looked at each other in the dimness.

"I know this is painful for you, Mrs. Duffy, but I'd be glad if you could answer just a few questions."

"I've been expecting you."

"Why?"

"I'm just surprised it took so long. Did someone say something to you about George?"

"Like what? What is it you want to tell me, Mrs. Duffy?"

"You've come to take it back, haven't you?" Her eyes filled with tears. She wrung her hands and began rocking in place.

"Take what back?"

"The money," she said miserably. "The $2,000."

I fired a shot in the dark. "The money George stole from the dead man, you mean?"

She nodded. "He was never the same after finding that body."

"Where is the money now?"

"Gone. Spent."

"On what?"

"Medicine. I have COPD. I didn't know it was stolen."

"Where did you think it came from?"

"He wouldn't say, but I figured it out. He'd come home that

morning with a big wad of cash. We argued about it. I didn't want to keep it. He said we had to. He couldn't continue working. The money would pay for my medicines for a while. It worried me to death. He was afraid all the time, too."

"Of what?"

"Being caught. And now we have been. Are you going to arrest me?"

"I told you, I'm not a cop. But that money belonged to the family of my client, and they need it back."

"It's long gone. I'm sorry."

"What about your husband's life insurance? Can you pay them back out of that?"

"Didn't have any. Couldn't afford it so we let it lapse. All I have is George's pension. It's barely enough to live on."

Judging by her surroundings, I believed her.

—

For the next twenty minutes on my way home for the day, I went over the case again.

First, no matter how much Carlos Rojas could have used the stolen money, there was no legal remedy to recover it. Mrs. Duffy said she had not stolen it, had not known it was stolen, and George, the actual thief, was dead. In fact, the only evidence of the money's existence had come from George, and that was hearsay.

But something important had been revealed. The current thinking was that Felipe Rojas had been murdered during a robbery. If $2,000 had still been on the body when the night watchman found it, then robbery was not the motive. I was willing to bet that my Miami colleague would report that Wensceslao López had lost a substantial sum at poker. If he had debts, this might account for his somewhat hasty departure from town.

As for the murderer, I still hadn't an ounce of solid evidence, not a single grainy photo, not so much as a strand of hair to analyze for DNA. About all I really knew was that I wasn't looking for a left-handed midget—unless in the unlikely event he had been standing on a stool when he clubbed Rojas and had used his non-dominant hand just to confuse investigators. Probably not a woman, either, although I'd seen women who worked on the backside routinely throw around standard hundred-pound hay bales.

By the time I pulled into my driveway, it was late afternoon.

I grabbed a beer and made my way down to the dock. At first, the Ohio's rich rotting reek repelled me. But as always as I watched the river go by, I felt inspired by its power and beauty. Of late the artistic spirit hadn't moved me. I'd begun painting in high school, stopped when I joined the army and picked it back up again four or five years ago when I was going through my bleak period. But now with the sun dropping in a fiery glow behind the knobs, for some reason, I felt ready to start on a new painting.

Up in my spare bedroom/art studio, a large wooden easel stood at the far wall. Finished and half-finished paintings leaned against one another, along with fresh canvases still packaged in cellophane. I unwrapped a canvas and positioned it on the easel. People were often surprised to hear that I painted. Didn't seem to go with being a private eye, I guess. But I'd known private investigators who tied fishing lures for fun, and others who collected stamps, rare books, or even orchids. What was wrong with painting?

I didn't paint much if my personal life went on hold during a case, but I didn't want to relentlessly pursue an investigation simply because I had nothing better to do, either. I wanted more out of life than that. Sitting on the stool, I saw what painters and detectives alike dreaded the most: a blank white slate. I squeezed acrylic burnt umber and a touch of cadmium red onto my red palette. Dipping a two-inch wide brush in water and then paint, I began to cover the surface with slashing strokes, mixing the colors.

When it was done, I swished my brushes around in the water, getting most of the paint off, and used an old towel to dry the bristles. I put the brush bristle-side up in the jar with the others. Looking over what I'd accomplished, I was reminded by the expensive red paint of Dr. Freya Hall's red lipstick. Freya, who was tall and could handle large animals. Freya, whose angling for a drink made me wonder if she was trying to keep me from considering her as a suspect. Or if she simply found me irresistible. It could happen.

TUESDAY

10

On my second visit in two days to an online crime database, I discovered that Luke Ericson had a DUI, plus an arrest for assault and battery growing out of a bar fight four years ago. Freya Hall's driver's license had been suspended for two counts of reckless driving around the same time. Wyatt Whitlow had a clean crime sheet but had been involved in numerous lawsuits related to his publication, which had been banned at several racetracks over alleged racist remarks it contained. None of which was very helpful as I made my way back to the Downs, where an early morning event was transpiring.

Normally, most gates didn't open until eleven o'clock. But today when I arrived, herds of fans were already loping through the backside like a mass migration across the Serengeti, some tapping away on their smart phones while others took selfies. They'd come for "Dawn at the Downs," a special event providing a chance to watch workouts by the racehorses, plus breakfast.

Outlandish Derby hats were all the rage. I saw a woman being interviewed about hers, which resembled a pineapple rum drink with a pink flamingo feather on top. Like images of the infield to come, the scene was oddly reminiscent of Bruegel's painting *The Fight between Carnival and Lent,* an allegory of gluttony and greed.

This was also the day for trainers to make the traditional draw for Derby post positions—no small issue, since from some of the starting spots no horse had won the Derby. TV personalities discussed this on-air, while in the background tractors pulled harrows between gallops by exercise riders to break up the soil and smooth out the track's surface. Other commentators offered tips about what to look out for in the paddock, such as horses with shiny coats and a prancing demeanor.

I went looking for Sandy Diaz and, after dodging a golf cart off-loading hay bales, found her leading Cat Chaser toward the Kessinger barn. The fact that the trainer continued to entrust her with his ultra-valuable Derby horse showed his confidence in her. And it seemed justified since she had the solid black colt firmly under control even as he flared his nostrils and bobbed his head.

I followed the hotwalker and horse into the barn. Seeing it was me, she swung around and hissed, "What do you want now?"

"I need to apologize. I also need to talk to you."

"Haven't you done enough?"

She was wearing dark sunglasses, no doubt to conceal the black eye her husband had given her yesterday. Despite her bruises—or maybe because of them—I saw something I'd previously missed: the character etched in her long-suffering face. She was the kind of woman who looked better the longer you looked.

As she laid her hands on her hips and drew back, her posture exposed a necklace tucked in her V-neck sweater. Hanging from it was an amulet of a man-in-a-black suit, like the one I'd seen in Carlos's room. I wanted to ask her about it, but she pushed past me and went on, leaving me to sputter, "I'm sorry. I—"

Clearly the wrong time for our chat.

I went outside and phoned Miami. Simmons, my contact there, said he'd interviewed Wensceslao López last night. As I'd anticipated, the wayfaring groom had indeed lost a substantial sum at poker on the night of the murder.

"He claimed that Felipe Rojas had cheated him out of it by using marked cards and dealing off the bottom of the deck," Simmons said.

So, who was telling the truth about Felipe Rojas—his son or López? Or could it be that Carlos just did not know that his father cheated?

"López had won the two-grand on the Derby. For him, it was a case of easy come, easy go. But he felt his luck had run out in Kentucky, so it was time for him to get out," Simmons said.

That was it. I thanked Riley and we talked about doing some sail fishing next time I was down his way. Then I told him to send me his bill and hung up.

—

I found Carlos holding the lead rope for a horse I didn't recognize who was being lathered up by a groom I also didn't recognize. When the job was done, I took Carlos aside and asked about the unfamiliar colt's workout today.

"Bud wasn't happy with him," he said.

"I presume that would be Bud Devlin, the jockey who is riding Speckled Band in the Derby?"

"Yeah. This horse doesn't react well sometimes."

"I noticed something earlier. That man-in-a-black suit good luck charm of your father's you showed me? Well, Sandy Diaz is wearing one that looks exactly like it."

Carlos lowered his gaze. "A Maximon charm? You don't say. I didn't know that."

"It popped out of her sweater when she struck a pose to show me how irritated she was to see me again."

"Sandy Diaz is irritated all the time, man. You'd be irritated, too, if Juan was your husband."

"Yeah, drunks are hard to live with. Has he always been a drunk?"

"As long as I been here anyway."

"How common are those charms, Carlos?"

"Fairly common in Guatemala, but not so much here."

"Guatemala is a Catholic country, right? Is there some conflict between Catholic teachings and Native Mayan religion?"

"Oh, yeah. I was taught by the priests. But we also believe in Maximon. He's kind of a folk-saint and a fertility symbol. It's complicated."

"I see. How close was your father to the Diaz family?"

"Not especially, although we're Mayan and speak Quiché." He explained that there were over twenty separate Mayan groups, each with its own language. The Quiché was the largest. "But Papa kept mostly to himself."

"Are you close to them?"

"Not really. We're friendly, that's all."

"I'm glad Sandy's still hotwalking. Too bad about Juan losing his job. They can't live on what a hotwalker makes. What will they do now?"

"Family's gonna be hurtin.' Libby works with Ana Lucia, their seven-year-old, at the Backside Learning Center. People will try to help them, but they could all wind up back in Guatemala."

I told him that was not what I'd hoped to hear.

"Hey, it was Juan's own fault for being drunk on the job. You know, people and horses can get hurt when the one who's supposed to take care of them doesn't do his job."

Carlos's unsympathetic attitude toward the Diaz family surprised me, even though I'd had the same thoughts. I was considering whether to tell him of my deal with the tip sheet publisher when Miguel Molina emerged from the barn.

"*Hola,*" Carlos said to the big man in the green T-shirt.

"I'd like to ask you about the night of the murder if that's okay," I said.

Molina glanced at Carlos, who nodded.

"One of the poker players, Wasceslao López, accused Felipe Rojas of cheating. You were in that game, too, along with López and Juan Diaz. Was Rojas cheating?"

"Nah," Molina said.

So, was he, or wasn't he? Hard to tell with such conflicting testimony. I asked Molina if he'd noticed anything unusual or suspicious, after Felipe's fight. Molina claimed he had not. He said he'd told the cops that he lost track of Felipe in all the confusion when everybody went home.

"When Felipe was killed, you took over his job."

The groom answered with a "so what?" shrug.

"It means you had something to gain from Felipe's death."

"Are you're saying I had something to do with the killing?" Molina said as the chords in his neck swelled.

"Did you?"

With a snort of contempt, Molina strode away. I wanted to keep digging, but someone else—a mustachioed Latino with the hard, lean look of a jockey—caught my eye.

"Do you know him?" I asked Carlos about the man, who was reading *The Late Mail*.

"Yeah. That's Francisco Segura, a jock. You want to meet him?

When Carlos told Segura I had been hired to investigate his father's murder, the jockey said, "I hope you can solve it."

"Me, too. Know anything that might help me?"

Segura shook his head. "I don't know what that would be."

A clutch of boisterous racing fans distracted me while snapping photos of a nearby colt. When I looked again for Segura, he was gone.

"Damn," I said. "Where did he go?"

Carlo shrugged. "I was looking at the woman with the camera."

"Does Segura have a mount in the Derby?"

"No, he's been on a long losing streak. No win, no ride."

I felt like I was running in place, getting nowhere.

We walked on until we encountered a man with biceps like Popeye who was shoeing a chestnut colt. It was like visiting an earlier century when blacksmithing was a central part of every community. We watched as he pulled the horse's foot out and held it between his own legs while tapping nails into the hoof. Then he smoothed out uneven spots with a rasp. Another vivid reminder that we were in an antique world where everyday life was distinctly different for the inhabitants. Carlos told me the farrier, a man named J.T. Young, worked for Keene Kessinger.

"Well, well," said a familiar gravelly voice, "if it isn't Sherlock Holmes and Doctor Watson."

I turned around to find Wyatt Whitlow handing out copies of *The Late Mail*. "Caught the culprit yet?" said Whitlow, looking resplendent in another Hawaiian shirt—aqua this time, no kilt.

"Not yet."

"Take a look at this." Whitlow handed each of us a copy of today's tip sheet, which read:

VILLAINS BEWARE

A local private eye, without so much as a trench coat or fedora to his name, nevertheless claims to be hot on the trail in the long-stalled Felipe Rojas murder investigation. P.I. Jim Guthrie says he's following a new line of inquiry and may be close to cracking the case. Anyone with information about the murder should contact him. Inquiring minds wonder where it all will lead.

"What do you think?" Whitlow asked.

"I think it's great. Worth every penny I paid you."

"Shh, let's keep that on the down-low."

I scanned the sheet and found another intriguing headline:

CHEATING AT CHURCHILL

As if one investigation at Churchill Downs wasn't enough, an undercover whistleblower reports that another inquiry by an animal rights group has been ongoing for months. Results are due any day now. One snowy-headed trainer and his favorite machine jock reportedly were overheard bragging about how many buzzers they've smuggled onto the racetrack. For the virgins in the crowd, buzzers are electric devices used illegally to make racehorses run faster by shocking them. Watch this space for upcoming details.

"Is this true? Is there really another investigation by PETA?" Carlos asked.

"This is the first I've heard of it." I needed to talk to Whitlow, but he'd already disappeared into the crowd. Because of my own arrangement with the tip sheet publisher, I couldn't help but wonder at the timing of this claim, not to mention the name of the alleged whistleblower. Whitlow was not above making stuff up. Still, I couldn't see what benefit, other than a temporary boost to circulation, he hoped to get out of the claim. Maybe that was enough.

"Did you look at this other piece?"

"Uh-huh. Are you truly close to solving the case? If so, why haven't you told me?" Carlos said.

"It's a ruse, Carlos. I'm trying to rattle your father's killer, hoping he'll make a mistake and give himself away."

"Do you think that has any chance of working?"

I shrugged. "It might. Who knows? Anyway, I'm a year behind the police on this. I have to try something."

"This could get dangerous." Carlos ground the toe of his boot into the soil.

"Only to me. Look, if you want to catch your father's killer, we'll have to take some risks."

"Okay, you're the detective. But geez, Mister Guthrie, I sure wouldn't want your job."

"Oh, I don't know about that. Being a hotwalker's a bit like being a detective, isn't it? Once the big event—the crime rather than the race—is over, a detective looks for clues about his suspects while a hotwalker is picking up clues about his horse."

"Never thought of it like that."

Neither had I. But detecting was what I did and who I'd become. I left Carlos to his sleuthing and walked toward the track.

11

Half a dozen covered decks had been constructed alongside the backside rail as observation posts. Each bare wood structure rose three steps high, creating a clear view of the sandy racing surface that wound around the infield like a silk cord. On the far side of the track, some of the city's tallest buildings served as a backdrop for the green and white grandstands.

A knot of onlookers stood on one of the viewing stands watching Speckled Band go through his afternoon workout.

As Carlos and I approached, I noticed Luke Ericson and Freya Hall among viewers. The rider was Daniela Torres. She dug her boot heels into the colt and hit him with the whip as he neared the red and white striped pole marking the workout finish line. Instead of speeding up, though, Speckled Band broke stride and slowed down.

"Can't you give him something to make him go faster?" groused the well-dressed, red-faced man standing beside Ned Ericson.

"We don't do that, Mister Alexander," Ned said.

"Well, maybe you goddamn well better start before it's too late."

"I expect it was only an off day," Ned said wearily. "Try to be patient, Herb. Speckled Band just needs a little more time."

"More time? Hell's bells, Ned, the Derby's only five days away. You realize that no horse has ever won the Derby from the post position we drew?"

"Seventeen's not ideal, but we'll work with what we have. I think this is our year. We've put in a lot of hard work. We can pull it off if things go our way."

"They'd better. I got a pot of money invested in this nag and it's your job to get it back for me. If you can't do that, then maybe it's time to find somebody who can."

"Hey now," Luke Ericson said, stepping between them, "let's all take a breath, dial this down a little, huh? Best you come over to the stables where we can talk privately, Mr. Alexander."

"I want less talk and more action," Alexander said and stomped off.

That's when I saw Chip Alexander. The little wiseass fell into line behind his father and I knew we were destined to meet again. Indeed, Chip's eyes widened at the sight of me. The wheels were clearly turning. I assumed he'd already told his father his version of the boat story. Since he knew mine would differ significantly, and not to his credit, he predictably started blabbing and pointing his finger at me.

"Dad," I heard him say, "that's him. That's the jerk who messed up our boat and pushed me around."

My, that really was a different version.

"You sure about all that?" Herb Alexander asked his son.

"'Course I'm sure. He was in our horse's stall, too."

Exuding menace, the father stomped toward me. Perhaps he intended to stomp me, too. He looked about six feet tall, well built with slabs of muscle on his shoulders and chest. Mid-forties, square-jawed, with angry blue eyes. He halted about an arm's length away.

"Who the hell are you, and what are you doing here?"

I gave him the answers, though I don't know if they were the ones he wanted or not.

"Well," he said, arms folded, "I don't give a rat's ass about some year-old murder case that has nothing to do with me. What I do want to know is whether what Chip told me is true. Namely, that you're the son of a bitch who scratched up my boat, cut the tow rope, and put your hands on my son."

"That's not how it was. Chip is playing you, Mister Alexander. Did he mention Libby Fontaine?"

"What's she got to do with this, Chip?" Father glared at son.

Gaze darting, fingers twitching, Chip said, "She fell overboard, Dad. I'd have had things under control if this jerk hadn't butted in."

"She almost drowned because of the stunt your son pulled," I said.

Alexander turned back to me. "You admit being there?"

"Sure. But he's lying about what happened. Ask Libby if you don't believe me."

Knowing his son, Alexander might have realized that Chip was in the wrong here. I saw doubt in his eyes and thought I had convinced him. But as matters turned out, I was wrong.

"We all make mistakes, Chip," I said. "I wasn't going to rat you out, but you left me no choice."

Legs planted wide, fists clenched, Herb Alexander said, "I'm going to kick your ass."

"You're making a mistake," I said.

"You're the one who made the mistake," he said and began grappling with me, trying to force me backward and off my feet.

He was right about me making a mistake. I should have decked him the instant he laid hands on me. Instead, in trying to avoid a senseless fight, I let him jerk me toward him and use the momentum created to flip me over onto my back. I landed hard with the wind knocked out of me. As I scrambled to my feet, Alexander let out a piercing yell and threw himself at me in a half-crouch. He wheeled sideways and lashed out with one foot. I rotated my hips to protect my crotch, but he aimed higher and kicked me in the ribs. It hurt. A lot.

While I was doubled over in pain, he jammed his foot into my hip, grabbed my ankle, and shoved. Then with his other foot, he let fly a nifty sweeping kick that cut my legs out from under me. He followed that with a vicious kick that crashed into my jaw, shattering reality into shiny stained-glass fragments. I hadn't laid a glove on him and now as I lay helpless and spread-eagled on the ground, he snarled, "The lesson here is don't ever fuck with me again."

He seemed eager to continue the beating, but a pair of burly security guards arrived in time to stop him. The next I knew Ned Ericson was telling someone to call EMS, followed by someone else croaking, "No."

Me.

Looking down at me, the trainer said, "Are you sure about that?"

"Yeah, I'm okay."

"Listen, you could have internal injuries. You ought to get checked out."

As an amateur boxer I'd taken plenty of punches—and many more since then—and had always been able to shake it off. This time, though, I wasn't so sure. I was in agony and my whole world was spinning.

"What about him? He started it," I said as the same burly African American guards who'd saved me now gripped my arms on either side to usher me off the premises.

"Mister Alexander will be leaving by a different exit," one said.

"You're throwing him out, too?"

"That's right."

But nobody had laid a hand on Alexander yet. While all animals were equal, some were more equal than others.

"Now let's go," the talkative guard said.

I wrenched free and wobbled toward the exit while focusing on keeping my balance and my dignity intact.

"Here's some advice. Don't come back here," the guard told me.

"Oh, I'll be back, all right. Count on it."

"Not today, you're won't."

"Let's see what your boss has to say about that."

"No problem. Meanwhile, you're barred. Have a nice day."

The Mustang was parked five blocks away. I'd never make it without first finding somewhere to sit down. On the other side of Fourth Street stood a rambling old white building made of brick and wood. It had a green awning and a sign on the front that read, "Wagner's...Since 1922." I knew the place. Everybody did.

Seeking refuge, I stumbled over there and peeked through the front window. Noontime sunlight was streaming in, brightening the dining room. A wave of thick greasy cooking smells washed over me as I opened the door and stepped inside. All the tables and booths were taken, so I claimed the only unoccupied seat in the joint—a stool at the far end of the old-fashioned soda fountain.

As I slid onto it with my head pulsating and my stomach roiling, I caught a truly ghastly sight—my own reflection in the wide mirror. My jaw was numb and swollen, and I was gashed here and knotted there. A wonder that no one had called an ambulance. Three aproned women busy at the sizzling griddle didn't notice me at first. Then the one whose name tag read Tallulah asked if I wanted coffee.

As she lifted the metal pot to pour, she said, "Honey, what in the world happened to you?"

"Got my brains scrambled by a horse-owning karat expert," I rasped.

"Don't run into many of them, I bet. How bad does it hurt?"

"Like somebody's jack-hammering up the pavement in my

head."

"You need some medicine. Lots of painkillers in the back of the store."

Wagner's had been a pharmacy, as well as a café and grocery, for ninety-five years, according to the laminated menu.

"Let me help you," Tallulah offered.

"Washroom?" I gasped and forked over an Andrew Jackson.

"That way," she nodded.

Dismounting from my trusty stool, I tottered through a tangle of tables to a door marked with a capital "M." I lingered in the empty restroom until the spasms racking my digestive system eased, then returned to my place at the counter. A container of pain pills awaited me there. I took three, thinking that probably wouldn't be enough. As I sipped my coffee, I studied the racing memorabilia hanging on the walls. It included framed photographs of numerous Derby winners like Secretariat and Spectacular Bid.

"How are you doing, hon?" Tallulah asked as she refilled my cup.

"Is that a trick question?"

"You want some food?"

I shook my head and winced.

"Who done this to you?" she said.

"Guy named Herb Alexander."

"I don't like to talk about my customers, but I know that one. He struts in here like he owns the place. Arrogant fool thinks he knows more about horses than the trainers. A big mouth, always trying to show everybody how important he is. I didn't know he was violent, though. Why did he hurt you like that?"

"He disliked what I said about his parenting skills."

Tallulah made a face as if fearing she'd crossed a line and went off with the coffee pot. Later, she returned with a damp sponge and wiped off the counter, lingering in front of me as if eager to talk.

"Bet you've heard your share of tales in here," I croaked.

"I've heard a few," she said.

"Ever hear the one about a murder on the backside?"

"Felipe Rojas? Like yesterday. I knew that poor soul. A real gentleman. Always pleasant when he come in and left a decent tip, though I know he didn't have much. Not like some of them we get. I reminded him of his mother. Called me 'Mama.' He'd come in maybe twice a week. Order salmon croquettes or pimento cheese. I couldn't believe it when I saw his face on TV and in the paper. He'd been in here the day before he was killed. I remembered because he always came in by himself, but on that last day he was with a woman."

"Anyone you knew?" I asked, my quickening pulse giving me a headache.

"Never saw her before."

"Can you describe her?"

"Mid-thirties. Hispanic. Slender. Had a crooked little smile. Wore jeans and a T-shirt."

A description that fit half of the women I'd seen on the backside.

"How did she and Rojas act around each other? Could anything have been going on there between them?"

"Now, how would I know that, Sugar?"

I wanted more, but she had already told me everything she knew or was willing to share. Since I couldn't get anything else out of her, I finished my coffee and departed, leaving her a hefty tip.

12

Slowly, I made my way back to the Mustang. Stinging heat rolled out at me like a desert wind when I opened the door. While waiting for the interior to cool down, I pondered the mystery woman's identity. Who was she? Why had Rojas met her there? And was their rendezvous somehow linked to his murder? No law against lunching with a member of the opposite sex, of course, and no known reason to read anything sinister into it. Nonetheless, unusual behavior for Felipe Rojas.

He had seemed like a decent man. His son certainly thought so, as did others. But even a good man can have a dark side. As I drove home, I had the nagging suspicion that, far from being a simple man, Felipe Rojas had been an enigma. He was a survivor, to be sure, having not only escaped from the horrors of his homeland but had also rescued his son. Maybe this had toughened him up enough that nothing could stand in his way when trying to complete the mission of saving the rest of his family. Maybe he had become willing to do whatever it takes, even engaging in a little racetrack skullduggery.

But this was only conjecture—like my hunch that Herb Alexander's attack on me was something other than an ingrained habit of visiting violence on anyone who annoyed him.

Either way, by the time I got to my place, I was barely able to drag myself up the steps without swooning. My jaw ached. Pain seared my rib cage with each cough. After swallowing four more painkillers, I stripped off my bloody clothing and turned on the shower. I let steam gather before stepping in, hoping it would loosen up my rigid muscles. It did, but only after camping there practically overnight. I got out when fatigue outweighed suffering. Another look at myself in the mirror convinced me I was not the fairest of them all anymore if I ever had been—not with all these welts, a split lip.

By tomorrow morning, I'd have a better idea of whether I'd broken any bones or had other permanent damage. Hearing someone knocking on the door, I wrapped a bath towel around my waist and went to peer through the curtains. A familiar face appeared, that of my friend and neighbor, Clive Thistledawn, whose waxed mustache and goatee reminded me of Shakespeare's familiar portrait on the First Folio.

"Good God, Guthrie, what happened to you?" he asked when I let him in.

"Bumped into a piece of scenery."

"Even with your lack of coordination, I find that rather hard to believe," he said.

"Must've tripped over a prop then."

"Are you sure it wasn't a red herring?"

Thistledawn was a semi-retired actor who'd worked mostly in regional theatre. We had a running joke about whether acting or detecting was the more dangerous profession. Clive, who could only afford to live here because of his many TV commercials, held up a bottle of champagne. "Looks like you could use some of this bubbly."

"It's a bit early for me." Not a good idea to mix painkillers with alcohol. "What the hell. Let me get dressed."

"That's the spirit. I'll fetch goblets and wait for you out here."

Wearing a T-shirt and cutoffs, I eased out to the porch with the grace of an arthritic octogenarian. Clive was ensconced in a cane-backed rocker, so I sank into the creaking swing.

"Here's to crime," he said and poured me a glass.

"And punishment." I sipped as a barge chugged by on the river below us. "What are you doing here, Clive? I thought you had a show to direct."

Nowadays when he wasn't drinking champagne or otherwise salubriously engaged, Clive free-lanced as an actor/director with local production companies.

"I do have a show to direct, a revival of *High School Musical,* with a cast of blessed community theatre locals and randy high school students. But rehearsals won't start until next week, so I'm having a party tomorrow night. You should come."

"I don't know," I grimaced. "I'm in the middle of a murder investigation."

"Come on. It'll do you good. Speaking of which, you look terrible."

"How bad?"

"What's the line in *Jaws?* 'He disagreed with something that ate him?' That's how bad."

"What the hell happened?"

Normally, I wouldn't discuss an ongoing investigation, but something told me that in this case fresh eyes were needed to produce fresh insights. I described the beating I had absorbed courtesy of Herb Alexander and being banned from Churchill Downs in consequence.

"What? That doesn't sound right."

"I agree."

"Hey, your assailant was in the news. Something about his business having money problems," Clive said, sipping.

"What else did you hear?" For a city of nearly a million, Louisville remained in many ways a small town where everybody knows everybody else's business.

"Nothing more. Going to clock this clown?"

"An eye for an eye and the whole world would be blind, right?"

"Oh, please, Guthrie. You're a thug, not Kahlil Gibran."

"True, but I can barely lift this glass."

"You'll bounce back. You always do."

"Thanks for the sympathy."

"Don't mention it. So, tell me—whodunit?"

Clive's one starring TV series role had been as a St. Louis private eye who can't stand the sight of blood. The experience had left him with delusions of adequacy as an investigator.

"I wish I knew."

"Who are the main suspects?"

"There is a multitude. I haven't narrowed it down yet."

"Oh, come now, someone must stand out."

I ran it down for him—from the poker game and the dispute over whether the victim had been cheating, to the CCTV coverage at the Downs, to the night watchman who had robbed the dead body and left his widow guilt-stricken and penniless when he died months later, and all the rest.

"Marvelous. A veritable stew of clues. What's the matter? You look ill."

"I am ill. I feel like Sonny Liston after Ali whupped him for the heavyweight title."

"You're identifying with the wrong boxer. Are you going to turn the widow in?"

"What would be the point? She didn't do anything illegal, at least not knowingly. It won't bring the money back. Why bother?" I drank. The champagne tickled the roof of my mouth. "What matters is that the police still believe that robbery was the motive for the murder. But if that much money was still in the groom's pockets when the watchman found him, it wasn't robbery."

"Well, what was it then?"

"Not sure. But I ought to tell them."

"I don't see why? It gives you an edge. Just let it ride."

"Lieutenant Brownfield might not see it that way."

"So what? You've already found out more in two days than he did in a year."

We drank. The Ohio churned on, endlessly retracing its southwesterly course. Every bone in my body stiffened.

"What about Herb Alexander? He sounds capable of killing with one blow and nuts enough to do it."

"What's his motive, Clive?"

"If Alexander's company is in financial trouble, it could be that he needs to win a lot of money on his horse."

"Maybe, but it doesn't explain why he'd kill the groom who was taking care of his horse. Besides, Alexander was not on the backside that night."

"Who was?"

"About twelve hundred other workers."

"It could have been any of them then. All right, that leaves the client. In murder mysteries, it's often the client who's guilty."

"Not the butler?" I gave him a wan smile. "Accusing Carlos makes no sense to me. Why would he kill his own father, who brought him to the U.S. from Guatemala? And why would Carlos hire me if he was the killer?"

"To cover his tracks?"

"What tracks? There are no tracks." I was fading.

"What about the dispute over cheating at cards? What about this mystery woman at Wagner's? What about Felipe Rojas' Man in Black good luck charm—and the Diaz woman having one just like it?"

"Could be a coincidence or just isolated facts. I need evidence for proof."

"Get some."

Clive rose, smug as the cat who licked up all the cream. "Let me know when you need my help again."

I said I would as the Ohio rolled on by, reeking faintly.

WEDNESDAY

13

I tossed and turned all night, the discomfort increasing with every movement. In the morning, I felt much worse than before. I was nauseated and had a sharp ache in my head. My jaw throbbed. So did my ribs, shoulder, back, neck. Easier to say what didn't. Other parts of my anatomy, hitherto hidden, were now alive and screaming.

I made toast and coffee and flipped on the TV.

On the news, racing fans were warned to brace for scattered showers, along with stalled traffic, long lines, and big crowds. This was the time of year when locals and guests alike went a little berserk, with much of it only semi-connected to horse racing. Derby Week festivities had begun two weeks ago with "Thunder Over Louisville," a huge airshow and fireworks display over the river that attracted more than six hundred thousand annually. Two other big events, the hot air balloon race, and the mini-marathon had already taken place, too, obstructing traffic in parts of the city.

Today, historic paddle-wheelers would compete in the

Great Steamboat Race, where the only anticipated danger was if somebody got too drunk and fell overboard. Tomorrow, however, a beefed-up police presence was planned to discourage rowdyism at the Pegasus Parade on Broadway. And then there were the parties. Ah, Louisville in early May.

Despite my depleted condition, I arose determined to get re-admitted to the backside. This would necessitate having a conversation with Ned Ericson, who I discovered wasn't taking my calls. But I managed to reach Libby Fontaine.

"Carlos told me about what happened. I hope you're all right after being mauled," she said.

"Stiff as a slab, but that's still better than going *to* the mall."

"Not funny."

"Come on, it's just part of the punishment."

"Ouch.. I feel terrible about what happened."

"Not your fault. I do this for a living, remember? Part of the job. You're not even my client."

"But Carlos is, and I'm the one who asked you to get involved. Have you heard that he was let go?"

My stomach lurched. "No, I didn't. What happened?"

"Chip's father forced Ned to fire Carlos. He claimed it was because Carlos hired you. But I think the real reason is that Chip is jealous of Carlos. I tried to talk to his father. I wanted to explain that you hadn't done anything wrong. But Herb wouldn't listen. He kept saying you'd rue the day you embarrassed his son, and so would I. This is serious. If Carlos doesn't have a job, he could be deported."

"Where is Carlos staying? I assume he's been evicted from his apartment."

"He slept in the church attic last night."

"Which church?"

"Victory Memorial, on Southern Parkway. It's where the Backside Learning Center for children is held."

"I thought that was, you know, on the backside."

"It is," Libby said. "But due to liability issues, Churchill

Downs doesn't allow children on the backside property. They come to the church instead."

"Are you with Carlos at the church now? Let me speak to him."

"If Herb follows through on his threats, immigration enforcement agents could be on their way here right now. What are we going to do?"

"Put Carlos on the line."

"Hello?" he said.

"Hey, I hear we're both unemployed now."

"Not you. I still want you to find my father's killer."

"Listen, even if Alexander has some juice with ICE, which I doubt, nothing involving the government ever happens quickly. And he doesn't even know where to look for you, does he?"

"I don't think so. But what if he finds out?"

"He probably won't if you stay put and out of sight. One thing I've learned about people on the backside—they don't snitch, especially not to rich jackasses like Alexander. Give me directions to the church."

It was only a few blocks from Churchill Downs.

"Sit tight."

Wind filled the trees along the river. A flock of Canadian geese floated by on updrafts. I smelled rain and heartache and blood. To avoid Derby congestion, I went the long way around and still got to Iroquois Park in twenty minutes. From there, it was a short haul through light traffic on an Olmsted-designed four-lane thoroughfare through the shady deep-lawn neighborhood.

Rain was clicking on my roof like handfuls of bird shot as I crossed the bridle path and frontage road between the parkway and the church. I struggled out of the Mustang and, hunching my shoulders against the wind, splashed to the Georgian building with pediment and thick white columns. I entered the vestibule and made my way to an adjoining red brick wing and the classroom where Libby and other young women were supervising noisy kids.

"Oh, my God!" Libby said when she saw my face. "Did Herb Alexander do that to you?"

"Yeah, I get the feeling he doesn't like me much. What are the kids making?"

"Balloon-powered paper plate racers," she said, gazing around the room.

"Looks like fun."

"It is. Their parents are tied to the track, and a lot of them don't have transportation. So instead of spending all their time at home watching TV, they can come here for fun and educational activities."

"Where's Carlos?" I whispered.

She looked up at the ceiling. "Do you want to see him?"

"No. How well do you get along with Ned Ericson, Libby?"

Before she could answer, a kid who looked about seven or eight came rushing up to her and thrust out her paper plate racer. "Look, Libby."

"Very nice," Libby said. "What color are you going to paint it?"

"Red," the child said, without hesitation.

"Great choice, Ana Lucia. Go do it, girl."

Libby turned to me. "That's Sandy Diaz's daughter."

"Cute kid. I wonder...does she ever talk about her home life?"

Doubt shadowed Libby's eyes.

"I know you feel protective. But it's important to the investigation. Has she said anything you think could help?"

"She told me her father seemed sad these days. He's in and out of their home apparently."

"How about her mother?"

"Worried a lot. I've seen that in Sandy myself."

"And Ned Ericson—does he like you?"

"Well enough, I suppose, because of the work I do here. Why?"

"Think you could convince him to let me onto the backside again to continue the investigation?"

"I can try." She made the call, the trainer took it. I listened in while she made the case. When she began shaking her head as if Ericson wasn't buying it, I motioned for her to give me the phone.

"Mister Ericson? Guthrie here. Look, it's vitally important that we speak."

"I have nothing to say to you," he said, his voice gruff.

"Well, I have a lot to say to you, and people's lives may depend on it. I know Herb Alexander is important to your business. He wants Carlos fired because of me, but also because he's jealous of him for having Libby. He might be trying to get Carlos kicked out of the country. That's not what Felipe Rojas would want, as I'm sure you'll agree. I can't believe you'd let him ruin these young people's lives and quash a murder investigation."

Several seconds of silence later, he said, "How soon can you meet me at Gate Five?"

"Five minutes."

"All right, we'll talk. But don't think I'm going to let you back in after all the trouble you've caused."

I returned the phone to Libby, who hugged me and gave me a high-five.

It was still raining lightly when I left the church on foot, leaving my car behind. Despite the poncho I'd worn, I was soaked by the time I met Ned Ericson. He recoiled from me as if I were a wriggling snake, but he'd agreed to see me and kept his promise. After hearing what really happened in my two encounters with the Alexanders, Ericson frowned and shook his head.

"That rotten son of a bitch and his no-good kid. Enough of this damned foolishness. Guthrie, you may not know it, but this is probably my last go-round."

Of course, I knew. I was counting on it to make a difference.

With twisted lips, Ned said grimly, "Alexander won't want

to replace his trainer this close to the Derby. But if he does, then I say the hell with it. I don't want to win the race so bad that I'd stoop to destroying people. I'll get you reinstated. You tell Carlos to bring his butt back over here."

"I was confident you'd do the right thing," I said.

"Don't be too sure. Hard to tell what a man might do if you put him in a tough enough spot—or wave enough cash under his nose."

"Not a man who sings to his horse."

—

They let me back in and I went looking for Sandy Diaz. I couldn't find her anywhere. Despite the iffy weather, the backside was overrun. I stopped outside the Ericson stables to wait for her to turn up. After a few minutes, I heard a commotion and rushed inside to find Luke trapped in a stall with Speckled Band, who was alternately trying to trample the assistant trainer and kick down the door while a security guard stood by watching helplessly. The rutted wooden planks were holding despite being slammed repeatedly by the horse's hooves, but that didn't help Luke.

Something had spooked the thousand-pound animal. Hard to say what—almost any inanimate object would do—and now Speckled Band was thrashing around and jumping sideways, placing Luke in imminent peril. If it had been me stuck in there, I would have tried to back away toward safety. Luke, however, moved closer to the horse, and I could see he was trying to get the jumpy critter to focus on him instead of whatever had frightened it. If Luke was scared, his calm soothing voice did not betray it as he kept reassuring the colt that everything was okay.

Then Luke began issuing a series of cues—back up, turn left, lower your head, walk forward, stop—and the frazzled creature obeyed! It was a bravura performance.

"Nice work," I said, deeply impressed.

"Guthrie?" he said, producing a carrot that he then fed to the horse. "What are you doing here? I thought you were barred."

"I was. Your old man let me back in."

"Why would he do that?"

"It was the right thing to do." I nodded at the becalmed Speckled Band. "That was quite a show. How'd you do it?"

"By keeping both his feet and his mind busy. That way, he didn't have enough time to think about whatever had spooked him in the first place."

"Misdirection. A slick trick."

"Something like that. Guess we'll have to tolerate you until you screw up again." He gave the horse more carrot. "What was the problem you had with Herb Alexander? Something about his son and a boat, I think I heard."

"A better question might be what was your beef with him?"

"That's none of your business."

"I heard him ask your father to give Speckled Band something to make him run faster. Will he?"

"That was foolish talk, nothing more. Herb knows better. We don't dope our horses. If we did, we wouldn't be dumb enough as to discuss it in front of witnesses."

"I noticed you ushered him out of earshot."

When Speckled Band poked his head out the stall door and whinnied, Luke used the opportunity to change the subject while massaging the colt's ears.

"Hey, I saw that story about you in *The Late Mail,*" he said. "What are these new leads you're supposedly following up?"

"Not ready to say. Do you think Herb Alexander had something to do with Felipe Rojas's murder?"

"Wow, that's out of left field. Why? Because he beat you up? Herb Alexander's a bully, but that doesn't make him a murderer. Look, I have work to do. Time for you to go."

"One more thing," I said. "Do you know if Felipe Rojas had any women in his life from around here?"

"You're one nosy bastard, aren't you? Go around poking your nose into someone else's affairs—even a dead man's."

"Think of it as investigative curiosity. I'm trying to solve his murder. So, why don't you answer the question?"

"This will be the last one. He was married, you know. I never heard of him having any other women. Guy seemed completely celibate."

"Just a thought. By the way, I heard your father singing to Speckled Band. Do you sing to him, too?"

"That's two more questions, but no, I'm not much of a singer. Another way I've managed to disappoint Dad."

As soon as the words left Luke's mouth, I sensed that he wished he could recall them.

Leaving the barn, I tramped through the crowd until I found Freya Hall, who was sitting at a picnic table near the first turn, watching a horse come back from his workout. She flipped her shiny black hair with her fingers as I drew closer.

"Morning," I said.

"Are you okay?"

"I'm fine."

"You don't look fine. Have you been to see a doctor? No, of course, you haven't."

"No time for that."

"Hmm. Come over here a minute." She had me sit down beside her and began kneading my left shoulder with her wise fingers. "Lots of muscle tension and swelling. Long, firm gentle strokes along the large muscle group usually will calm a horse. Often works on humans, too. Better now?"

"Mm."

"So, Mister Private Eye, how many criminals have you put away today?"

"I've lost count."

"Oh, must have been a lot of them then." Her fingertips cleverly worked their way up the base of my skull with slow, circular motions. "Something else I've been wondering. Do you carry a gun?"

"Sometimes."

"When?"

"Whenever I expect my quarry to be armed."

"Your quarry?" She tugged on my hair. Instant bliss. "What kind of gun?"

"A Smith & Wesson .45 semi-automatic."

"Sounds like a big one. Where do you keep it?"

"Handy." At this moment tucked away in the Mustang's glove box.

"Ever shoot anybody?" She stared at me from the corners of her large hazel eyes.

"Nobody who didn't deserve it." The knots in my shoulders were melting under her touch. "I'd rather not talk about it."

"Okay," she said, making a face. After a moment, she smiled and the dark clouds lifted. "How's the investigation going?"

Before I could reply, a voice that sounded like crushed ice said, "Don't let me interrupt anything juicy. But you certainly look ravishing today, Doctor Hall."

"Thanks, Wyatt. That's certainly a colorful outfit."

This time, Whitlow, who'd crept up from behind, was sporting a red Hawaiian shirt with the tail out, a green eye shade, and camouflage cargo shorts. He grinned at Freya around the ever-present cigar clamped in his jaw and said, "Glad you like it."

"Sort of the surfer-bookie look?" she said, wryly.

"I prefer to think of it as West Coast Casual." He handed us each today's tip sheet, adding, "I heard you were barred from the track, Guthrie."

"They let me back in."

"Get any feedback from...you know?"

"Not so far."

"Don't sweat it. Some of these people are slow readers."

I glanced at the top story:

SHOCKING REVELATIONS!

The Late Mail has been doing some snooping of

its own into that secret undercover investigation of cheating we've been telling you about. You won't believe what we've uncovered. Check out tomorrow's edition for shocking revelations!

Before I could ask what revelations, Whitlow said, "Hey, have you heard this one? A woman goes into Wagner's with a duck. She puts the duck on the stool and sits next to it. The waiter comes over and says, 'Hey, that's the ugliest pig I have ever seen.' The woman says, 'It's a duck, not a pig.' The waiter says, 'I was talking to the duck.'"

Freya and I rolled our eyes in disgust, but nothing fazed Whitlow—except perhaps the sight of Keene Kessinger bearing down upon him, tip sheet in hand.

14

"Why do you keep spreading lies about me?" the trainer demanded of the smirking publisher.

"Which ones?" Whitlow asked.

"You've implied that I cheat with buzzers. That's a lie."

"So, how do you cheat?"

"There is no investigation, Whitlow, as you well know. You made it up trying to smear me. Where's your proof? What are these so-called 'shocking revelations' you've supposedly uncovered?"

"Like it says in the sheet, check out tomorrow's edition."

"You little weasel."

"Says the big horse turd."

At this insult, Kessinger rushed forward to slug it out.

For his initial aggression, he received a punch in the nose that bloodied him and left Whitlow free to dance around in jubilation temporarily. Kessinger groaned and shook it off, then landed a heavy blow to the side of Whitlow's head. Swinging back purely out of instinct, Whitlow nailed Kessinger again, this time just below his left eye. It staggered him, but already both men were heaving with exertion.

Seeing Whitlow's colorful plumage in conflict with Kessinger's white shirt and crest was a bit like watching a cockatoo assault a parrot. I wondered who would win the fight—the trainer or the publisher. Whitlow was about the same age but a head shorter and twenty pounds lighter than Kessinger. Still, sometimes the battle does not go to the strong, nor the race to the swift.

The pair bought time by circling each other while trying to suck more oxygen out of the air. Then Whitlow jabbed and missed. Kessinger responded with two hard body shots, doubling the tipster over. Kessinger tried but was too winded to follow up his advantage. As both men grew more deeply exhausted, the match deteriorated into mostly flailing and grunting.

A bloodthirsty throng had gathered to jeer them on, urging the old, out-of-shape brawlers to keep on trying to injure each other. Stopping it now would have been a gesture of mercy, but I wasn't tempted, and neither was Freya, who'd been following the action with rapt attention as the fight continued. I found this faintly troubling.

After another brief flurry of blows that did little damage to either man, a bear-hug resulted in both tumbling to the ground. They landed in a heap and continued to thrash around in the mud like gasping fish. Someone finally took pity and doused them both with a bucket of water. Unfortunately, Whitlow reflexively threw a glancing right that clipped the ear of the would-be peacemaker—Sandy Diaz, as it turned out—who reacted with a solid left hook to Whitlow's chin and then thumped him in the face several times before track security arrived and broke it up.

All three squabbling combatants stoically refused medical treatment. As they were escorted off through the crowd, presumably to be ejected, Freya took my hand and we slipped aside to a quieter out-of-the-way spot, where she drew my face forward with one hand and kissed me.

"Umm, not bad," she murmured.

When I told her that I might be out of practice, she assured me we could take care of that together.

"How about going to a party with me tonight? My friend Clive claims he makes the perfect mint julep." I watched Freya's hazel eyes turn brown, then green.

"I'd love to. Do you have my number?"

"I'm a detective, remember."

"Seems like a smart detective would just ask me for it."

"What's your number?"

She rattled it off, and I wrote it down on my pad, already looking forward to tonight, as my phone began to vibrate. When I fumbled it out of my pocket, Freya said something about needing to get back to work and, following a peck on the cheek, abandoned me.

I was confounded to learn that the call was a text message from Whitlow, urging me to come meet him at the Rail Runner Saloon right away if I wanted to know what was going on.

While I suspected he was promising more than he could deliver, I headed for the bar anyway, located six blocks away on Taylor Boulevard. The place reeked of smoke, sweat, and stale beer. There were framed photos of Derby legends like Citation and Count Fleet on the walls. As I came in the door, a Frank Sinatra hit from his middle-aged heyday in the 1960s was playing on the jukebox.

When I saw Wyatt Whitlow, he was applying ice to his left eye and singing along with Frank about riding high one month and being shot down the next. Whitlow's battered face resembled nothing so much as a study in mud by Jackson Pollock. Unlike the restless half-dozen other customers who were priming themselves with cheap hooch before heading to the track, Whitlow seemed to have settled in for the duration.

"Did you see the fight, Guthrie?" he said, after waving me over. "Did you see us mixing it up?"

"You don't look so good, Wyatt," I said, with a nod.

"I always look better with a fresh drink in my hand."

I nodded to the wizened bartender, who poured him another shot. Whitlow gulped it down.

"I'm going to be sore tomorrow from rolling around on the ground," he said, "but so will butthead. If anyone goes to the doctor it'll be him. I was handling His Lordship all right until somebody else jumped in. Doofus was lucky they did."

"What do you have for me, Whitlow?"

"Buy me another shot of this paint-thinner and I'll tell you."

"Why should I?"

"Because it's cheap at the price. I know everything about thoroughbred horse racing and I'm smarter than you."

"If you're that smart, Whitlow," I said, nodding at the bartender to pour another one, "why don't you tell me who killed Felipe Rojas?"

"I wondered when you'd get around to asking the only person who might know," *The Late Mail* publisher said, with a cagey look.

Before he could toss it back, I put my hand over his topped-up glass. "I'm asking now."

He stared at the offending hand. When I did not move it, he sighed.

"I've always wanted to write a book, but not just any old book. An exposé. Something that would shake up the horse racing world like *All The President's Men*. So, your follow-the-money strategy suited me. After getting into it, I decided to go whole hog and play detective myself."

"So, you followed the money where?"

"You might be surprised."

"Cut the banter, Whitlow. Who are you accusing, and with what proof?"

He raised an eyebrow and chuckled. "The proof's in the pudding, and the pudding's in the oven."

"I've never much liked pudding," I snorted.

"You'll love this pudding. It's ninety proof."

When I removed my hand, he instantly drained the shot glass.

"What have you got?"

"You married, Guthrie?" Whitlow slurred.

Anything to keep him talking. "I was once."

"So was I."

"What happened?"

"She died, a long time ago. What happened to your wife?"

"Divorced."

"You cheat on her?"

"No."

"Then what happened? Did she cheat on you?"

"This is not crying in your beer night at karaoke, Whitlow. If you have something relevant to tell me, now's the time or I'm gone."

He eyed his empty glass again with a morose expression. I decided if one more drink didn't loosen his tongue, this would be his last on me.

"Tell me what you have against Keene Kessinger."

The question helped him focus.

"Oh, His Lordship thinks he's the cock of the walk. Such a stuck-up snob, with all his fancy airs. He has friends in high places, though. They'll ban me from the track but let him and Sandy off Scot-free. Watch and see if they don't."

"Why go out of your way to antagonize the man then?"

"Because it's fun."

"Does he really cheat with buzzers? Where's the proof?"

Whitlow grinned. "The proof is in—"

"Stop it! No more of that. Give me something for all the drinks I bought you."

"Read tomorrow's edition," he said.

"Come on," I said.

"You want a clue? How about this: 'There is no such uncertainty as a sure thing.' Robert Burns."

"What the hell's that supposed to mean?"

"I got to go to the can."

"Wait a minute."

But he was already stumbling down the hall.

Despite Whitlow's insistence, I doubted that Kessinger had cheated by shocking his horses. Still, anything tied up with gambling was easily corrupted. And racing had been a shady business ever since the first horse was domesticated six thousand years ago.

"I'd look out for that one," the ghostly-looking bartender said to me. "He's got a hollow leg."

"Well, this does seem to be his favorite bar."

"Not when I cut off his tab." He lowered his voice. "I'd say Wyatt's about flat broke."

My phone was vibrating again. This time, the caller was Churchill Downs P.R. director Bob Bendix, wanting to see me about the Rojas investigation. It occurred to me there were probably better ways to spend my time than listening to Whitlow gibber about pudding proof. I dropped some bills on the bar and left.

15

I made my way through crowds, police barriers, and stalled traffic back to the track. I continued my journey through the sprawling labyrinth of the grandstands with their many levels reached by oddly tucked away stairs, elevators, and long escalators. Television screens were everywhere. The place was mobbed, humming in anticipation of the day's first race. Guards posted at each stairwell checked tickets and passes, including mine.

Ten minutes till race time.

The professional photographers were bunched up at the rail with their tripods, training telephoto lenses in pursuit of the perfect shot. Everything was in waiting for the first race to begin. Red geraniums encircled the presentation stand of the Winners Circle, which was only used for the Derby, the Oaks, and the Breeder's Cup. I picked up a racing program and saw that Keene Kessinger had a horse in the race after this one.

As a red-coated bugler stepped out to sound the call to the post, I followed winding hallways to a sardined elevator that would take me up to the P.R. director's lair. Riding up to the sixth floor, I wondered if Kessinger had been banned for fighting or would be let into the paddock to saddle his horses.

I realized that Churchill Downs was probably terrified to have an ongoing murder investigation conducted while the eyes of the world were upon it. I felt anxious about this meeting because if they threw me out, my job would get much tougher. But if they decided to shut me out, I could always go public. That would be much worse for them, a real P.R. nightmare, in fact.

The doors slid open. A pink-cheeked man in a green blazer and a lavender shirt ended his conversation to greet me.

I considered it a good sign that I was getting the public relations spokesman instead of the hard-ass security chief again. I had Bendix pegged as a master schmoozer because, in his line of work, he'd almost have to be one. I expected a smooth conversation and coffee from a carafe, not thumbscrews.

"What's this about?" I said after he greeted me.

"Come right this way and I'll explain."

Bendix showed me down the hall to a generous space that was not an office, but a conference room dominated by a large table. Derby posters and other art hung on the walls. And sure enough, there was a carafe on the table.

"Nice view," I said, as sunlight streamed through high windows overlooking the finish line.

"Yes, isn't it?" he smiled.

As if to underscore the observation, the public address announcer said, "The horses are at the starting gate. And they're off!"

There's nothing like a race to focus your attention, and we watched intently as the horses took off with a low-throated roar. Right out of the gate, it was a mad scramble with five mounts no more than two lengths apart. High-stepping hooves kicked up a dust of sand, silt, and clay. All other sounds were quickly muffled by crowd noise. Manes and tails streamed behind like battle flags as the horses charged into the backstretch.

When they reached the turn, with their ears pricked and nostrils flaring, four horses were still knotted along the rail. Into the home stretch, it was down to three, with jockeys whipping frantically and horses foaming with sweat. It seemed as if nobody could outpace the pack, but in the end, one did—winning by a nose.

"What a race," I said.

"I never get tired of watching them," Bendix agreed.

He offered me a seat and took one across from me. After I declined coffee, he said,

"I wanted to check in with you about your murder investigation."

"What would you like to know?"

"About any, and all progress you're making."

"Due respect, Mister Bendix, you're not my client. Why should I report to you?"

"Well, I think we've pretty much bent over backward to be cooperative. We granted your request to see our CCTV footage and have allowed you continuing access to Churchill Downs.

"You have, and I appreciate it."

He smiled. "And you'll continue to receive our full cooperation. You have my word on it."

I thanked him for this quaint assurance, which reminded me once again that Louisville was still half-Southern, and that regardless of horse racing's tawdry reputation, rules of etiquette applied.

"We want the murder solved as much as you do."

"That's good to hear." Authority was not usually in my corner. "But what if I find out something damaging to Churchill Downs?"

My host's pink cheeks turned a shade darker. "We don't believe you will."

I wondered if that was because there wasn't anything to find, or I just wouldn't be able to find it.

"In any event," he said, "we're willing to go wherever the

facts lead."

"Fair enough, Mister Bendix. About the only thing I know right now is that Felipe Rojas wasn't killed because of a robbery."

"How do you know that?"

"That's confidential for the moment. But I'm confident it's true."

"So, why was he killed?"

I threw up my hands. "That I don't know yet."

"There's another matter that we're concerned about," he said. "Aside from the rowdiness in the infield during the Derby, we dislike that sort of behavior around here. We expect the people we do business with to act like gentlemen."

Uh-oh. Maybe he was about to rebuke me for the run-ins I'd had with Herb Alexander and Juan Diaz. But he surprised me.

"Herb Alexander was out of line when he attacked you. I'm sorry that happened. I'm also sorry you were asked to leave."

"Not exactly asked."

"Removed then, especially since we've determined the unfortunate incident was not your fault. We've spoken to Mister Alexander about the matter. Ned Ericson seems to have taken a liking to you."

"Only because he doesn't know me well."

Bendix stared at me for a moment.

"Perhaps it's your sense of humor he likes. In any case, our security people checked you out. Despite what's happened around you the past few days, we know your reputation for honesty and discretion."

Aha. Racetracks didn't like being involved in lawsuits. Not that I had any intention to sue the Downs, but they couldn't count on that. Bendix was wise for apologizing and for appealing to my vanity.

"If you're concerned about that, you must be freaking out over the Whitlow-Kessinger heavyweight bout, since it happened right there in front of God and ABC."

"A tremendous black eye for Churchill Downs," Bendix

winced, perhaps recalling this morning. "What did you see?"

I described the fight briefly.

Bendix said my account matched what he'd heard.

"Whitlow thinks you'll punish him and let the other two go. That right?" I asked.

"That's premature."

Bendix said they were waiting for a copy of the official report from track security. The Kentucky Horse Racing Commission would review it before discussing possible action, such as scheduling a hearing.

"We don't want to overreact."

I stood up. "Got any hot tips on the next race?"

"I'm afraid not."

I stepped into the elevator, then struck out for the paddock. That was the courtyard and stable area where the Downs required that every horse be saddled twenty minutes before post time. The names of all past Derby winners ringed the outer wall along the main building's eaves. I stopped under Seattle Slew, surrounded by elbow-to-elbow fans milling around, talking, and snapping pictures of thoroughbreds in their bright racing silks. The horses bobbed their heads and neighed.

Once they had been identified by their lip tattoos, the entrants for the next race were led from the tunnel to a small asphalt ring encircled by hedges and flowers and a jam-packed brick path. Once there they were saddled and paraded around for everyone to see. I edged forward as the jockeys waited in a grassy area with flowers in the middle to get last-minute instructions from trainers.

Then once again it was, "Riders up" and "They're off."

After the race, I picked up Sandy Diaz and followed her horse, a big bay in red silks with gray polka dots on the sleeves, back to the shed row for the cooling-off process. This one had finished out of the money. Losing tickets layered the cobblestone floors underfoot, deepening with each race. Sandy helped the groom who'd replaced her husband wash the bay down. When he took the horse inside the barn for curry combing, I showed the guard my pass.

"Mrs. Diaz?" I asked.

She clicked her eyes at mine and stepped around me.

"We need to talk," I said, following her.

"You need to leave."

"I will—as soon as you explain why you have a Maximon Man in Black charm identical to the one Felipe Rojas had."

She stopped and, with one arm holding the other at the elbow, said, "Same reason he did, I imagine—for good luck."

"Nothing more?"

"Is there some kind of law against it?"

"No, but I'd like to know why you carry it."

"What makes that your business?" she said, her eyes darting away. You're the one who got Juan fired. We can't even pay our bills because of you."

"I can't tell you how sorry I am about that. But I'm investigating Felipe Rojas' murder, and that means I need to know everything about your relationship with him."

"What relationship? I'm a married woman. Where did you get that?"

"Word gets around," I lied.

She picked up a long-handled pitchfork leaning against the wall. "Get out of here. Right now."

"Okay, Sandy. I'll go. But then I'll just have to ask your husband instead of you. Is that what you want?" She bit her lips. "Put the tool down."

She dropped the pitchfork.

"It's true about you and him, isn't it?"

"No," she said emphatically, "there was nothing between us. But even if it were, what would that have to do with him getting killed?"

"Maybe your husband found out and murdered him in a fit of rage."

"That's crazy. Juan went home with me that night and didn't

leave until the next morning."

"Can anyone else verify that?"

She shook her head. "Please don't tell Juan about your suspicions. He's already accused me of cheating."

"Have you been cheating?"

"I already told you it wasn't true." Her eyes bored into mine. "I've done nothing but wear a good luck charm around my neck. And you're about to break up our marriage over it."

"Do you have any idea who killed Felipe?"

"Not the slightest. Don't tell Juan. What good would it do? Please, I'm begging you."

"Don't know if I can promise that. Juan's a suspect."

"I swear he didn't do it."

"Then who did?"

She brought a shaky hand to her forehead. "I don't know."

We stood there looking at each other and for a long moment, neither of us spoke. Finally, I broke the silence, saying, "Give me your phone number so I can call you if I need to."

She told me and I wrote it down in my notebook.

If she was innocent, as I wanted to believe, she would have nothing to fear from me. But Juan Diaz was another story—a jealous violent drunk. No telling what he might do.

—

Famished and not knowing when I might eat again, I stood in line to buy a foot-long hotdog, then heaped on onions and relish and mustard. As I chewed away, I decided my next job would be to find the Diaz residence. I accomplished that goal by phoning Libby Fontaine, who gave me directions. She wanted to know how much progress I'd made, naturally, but I put her off, for now, saying I was busy, but promising to let her know later.

The Diaz' place proved a small one-story frame from the post-WWII era. Like many of the houses in this dreary little neighborhood, it had been converted into a duplex. It was in bad shape, with a cracked foundation, crumbling sidewalk, and neglected lawn. The residents I saw suggested a mixed population of mostly African Americans and Latinos. Many of the latter group undoubtedly were immigrants who worked at the track like Sandy. If I hadn't initially realized how starkly I stood out here, their vacant stares and vague air of hostility soon made that plain.

I hadn't decided whether to bring up the infidelity issue yet when I walked up the steps to the tiny concrete front porch. But it was probably going to come out anyway, sooner or later. I knocked on the door. When nobody answered, I peered through a curtained front window and detected no sign of life. I rattled the doorknob to make sure it was locked, then gave up and walked away.

16

It was eight o'clock when Freya Hall's MG whipped into my driveway spewing gravel and crunching to a stop beside my Mustang. The first thought I had was that we should breed them and create a new species of automotive elegance. As a scientist and a veterinarian, I thought she'd take a liking to that idea.

But when she stepped from the car, all long legs and smiles, my first two words were, "Wow" and "Wow."

"Am I overdressed?" she said, taking in my black jeans, charcoal blazer, and cream-colored T-shirt.

"Not at all," I said. "That dress looks amazing on you, Freya." She'd done something poufy to her hair and added a blue peacock feather. Her black strapless dress showed just enough cleavage to make my heart palpitate.

"Well, thanks. You look great, too. Your skin tone is like a painting. So many colors..."

She laughed, and I laughed with her. After registering my bruises, she glanced at the camp, perhaps finding it shabby in comparison with the neighboring row of upscale custom residences that belonged in Malibu or Miami Beach.

"I like your place," she said.

"Yeah, fits in like a mule running in the Kentucky Derby, doesn't it?"

I felt a spark when she touched the back of my hand. "Oh, Jim, it's not the stall that makes the stallion. I didn't come here to see your house."

"What did you come to see?"

"Your etchings?"

"Will you settle for some paintings?"

"You're a painter?"

"Does that surprise you?"

"It does. I'd love to see them."

"Maybe later. It's been a long time since I showed them."

Or had a date.

I nodded toward Clive's place. "Party's that way. Our host can't wait to meet you."

"You told him about me?"

I nodded.

"Told him what?"

"Not to get whiplash when he sees you."

She leaned forward and kissed me lightly on the lips. I gripped her shoulders and drew her closer. After a moment, she pulled away and smiled.

We strolled past three doors and veered downhill, for a wide-angle view of the Ohio. Some of my more staid neighbors—women in simple colorful dresses and men in chinos and blazers, who were invited mainly to forestall noise complaints—were clustered on the patio around the bar, while a gaggle of Clive's scruffy theatre friends was already doing drunk renditions of Broadway tunes and making merry on the lawn. These two groups would never mingle on their own. But the four-piece Bluegrass band now playing "The Tennessee Stud" would bring everyone together under the big tent.

As Clive materialized out of the crowd, I noted Freya taking in his loose-fitting ruffled white shirt, black breeches, and knee-length soft boots. She turned to me, alarmed. "Is this a costume party?"

"No, fair lady," Clive called to her. "Why do you ask?"

She looked doubtful.

"Freya," I said, "this is our host, Clive Thistledawn the noted actor."

Clive bowed. "And this must be the enchanting Doctor Freya Hall, who I've heard so much about."

"Oh? And just what have you heard?"

"Nothing inconsistent with your presence. Welcome to our little soiree here on Pipsisewah Beach," he said and kissed her hand.

A tuxedoed server came by with a tray of mint juleps.

"Try one. They're my specialty," Clive said.

We did.

Freya licked her crimson lips. "Mm. Delicious."

"Guthrie prefers his bourbon neat," Clive said.

Freya looked at me. "That right?"

"I don't drink much bourbon anymore, but when I do..." I nodded.

"Well, I like mine anyway it comes," Freya said. "What's your secret, Clive?"

"Uh-uh. That's why it's a secret."

"'Nothing is so heavy a burden as a secret.' French proverb." Freya took another sip.

"Beautiful *and* sophisticated," Clive grinned. "I like her, Guthrie."

"You're an actor?" Freya said. "What have I seen you in?"

"Maybe the TV series where I played a private eye like Jim?"

Freya shook her head. "No, I don't believe so."

"Detective with a nervous stomach? Got good ratings until they started moving the time slot around. Are you sure you never saw it?"

"Afraid not," Freya said while casting a sly look my way,

"though I've always had a soft spot for private eyes. Is it on Netflix?"

"No," Clive frowned.

I braced for more about Clive from Clive, but he became distracted by other arrivals. There were maybe forty guests spread around. We moved slowly from one group to another, working our way toward the big tent. Freya mingled easily, saying the right thing to everyone she met. I assumed she was accustomed to hobnobbing with anyone from destitute immigrants to fat cat horse owners.

When the band struck up a ballad, she took my arm. "Let's dance."

I hadn't slow-danced for a long time. I was half afraid I might've forgotten how. But when I put my arms around her, she pressed tightly against me and I felt exactly where I belonged. Slowly we swayed across the dance floor, completely focused on each other. When the last chord was played, we kissed, and I felt a flutter in my chest that might've been a heart attack.

"Getting hungry?" I asked.

Freya scrutinized the buffet awaiting us, everything from Benedictine spread to Hot Browns, beaten biscuits, grits, Kentucky burgoo, and of course chocolate bourbon nut pie. Bluegrass health food.

"Ravenous," Freya said.

We joined the long line. Clive soon turned up with a much younger woman on his arm. He introduced the glowing beauty with shoulder-length blonde hair as Hailey. She was playing a lead role in his current production. I found it hard to look away from her—until a dagger thrust of Freya's elbow between my extremely tender ribs made me groan.

"Love your outfit," Freya said, eyeing the ingénue's black V-neck camisole and silver harem pants. "So theatrical."

"Why thanks." Hailey's blue eyes seemed amused. "Yours is nice, too."

As we filled our china plates, Freya whispered, "Does your

friend always date teenagers?"

Feeling uncomfortable, I carried our food to a table suitable for conversation—that is, far from the band. A moment later Clive asked if he and Hailey could join us. He pulled back her chair and everyone tucked into their food, which was excellent.

Hailey nibbled on a finger sandwich until asked by Freya to tell us about the role she was playing.

"I'm Gabriella, a shy transfer student who tries out for the school musical, along with the captain of the basketball team." I'd seen the show a couple of years ago when I was dating a member of the tech crew.

"Hailey's doing a great job with the part," Clive said.

"I'll bet," Freya said.

Hailey said she understood that Freya worked with racehorses. When Freya identified herself as an equine veterinarian, Hailey responded that she loved horses.

"All girls do." Freya took a bite of her salad.

"Who do you like in the Derby?" Clive asked.

"Cat Chaser. He is the odds-on favorite. Post position number seven."

"That's a very favorable position," Clive said.

"You follow racing?" Freya asked.

"I do. Enough to place a bet now and then anyway. The trainer you work with must have a horse in the Derby, too, right? What about his chances?"

"Speckled Band," Freya said. "He's rated a longshot."

"How long?" Clive said.

"Long."

"So, you wouldn't bet on him?"

"If you like risk-taking, a wager on Speckled Band could pay off big-time. Not that I'm saying it will, you understand."

A server came by with a tray of drinks. While Clive was distracted momentarily, I said, "Tell me the truth, Freya. Can your colt win?"

"Against the next super horse?" she smiled. "Of course, if

you're in the race, you always have a chance. Probably slim and none in this case, unless Mister Ned's singing produces stronger magic."

We shared a private smile.

Fresh drink in hand, Clive rejoined the conversation.

"I've heard of Speckled Band," he said. "I believe he showed some early promise, enough to qualify for the Derby, at least. But from what I've read lately, he hasn't done very well. Correct?"

"You could say that," Freya said.

"What's wrong with him?"

"Who knows why a horse doesn't perform well? Could be anything. Equipment needing adjustment. Improper diet or medication. Maybe he's injured or feeling sore. Not being handled right. Wrong trainer, wrong jockey, wrong vet."

"Surely you're not going to admit to that," Clive said.

"I'm just being honest. Finding the key to what makes a horse win is an art as much as a science. If it was easy, everybody would do it. But it's not. Could be some weirdness unique to that horse. They're skittish animals who can be spooked by almost anything from a plastic bag blowing in the wind to an object they've never seen before."

"Huh. Thanks for explaining that. So, should I bet on him or not?" Clive asked.

"Up to you. Look, the Derby is like any sporting event. They don't hand you the trophy simply because they think you're better. You have to go out and run the race. Once the horses are out of the starting gate anything can happen. Sometimes the best horse doesn't win," Freya said.

"Isn't Speckled Band owned by Herb Alexander, who also owns a drug company or something?" Clive asked.

"Pharmaceutical distribution company," Freya said.

"Jim was telling me about him. What do you think of the guy?"

"I think he's the owner," Freya said.

"I heard he's a swine," Clive said. "He's been on my shit list ever since I found out he'd clocked Jim."

"Clocked him?" Hailey said, with interest, for perhaps the first time this evening.

"Let's don't go into that," I said.

"Oh, let's do," Hailey said. "Sounds exciting."

"It's not," I said.

Hailey pouted. "All this Derby talk makes me want some Derby Pie," she said.

We obliged her and carried our slices of pie down to Clive's dock, where we could be alone for a while.

"Your friend is certainly flamboyant," Freya observed. "How did you get to know him?" "We met at a party the first day he moved in. At the time, I was a little awed that he'd been in show biz. Clive, on the other hand, was impressed to meet a real-life private eye, having played one on TV. Once he found that out about me, all he wanted to do was hear about my cases. We went on to become friends, mostly because neither of us fit in here."

"Where do you fit in?" Freya asked.

"Nowhere really. Guess I've always been a loner."

We ate some pie.

"So why, and how, did you become a private investigator? You said it was a long story best told over a drink. Well, here's the drink." She held up her mint julep.

I didn't want to rip off that scab yet.

"How about telling me this, then," Freya said. "Are you married?"

"No." The question had taken me by surprise. "Are you?"

She shook her head. "Ever been married?"

"Yeah, I'm divorced. You?"

"No. Guess I haven't found the right man. You have kids?"

"One. My daughter, Sarah. She's a teenager now." I paused. "Let's talk about Doctor Freya Hall. What about your family? Where did you grow up?"

Freya said she didn't like to talk about herself.

"Why not? I find Doctor Hall wonderful."

She smiled and set her plate down on the dock. "I will, but only if you promise to tell me why you became a private eye."

"Okay."

"I grew up on a small farm in Lewis County, which in case you don't know is the poorest county in Kentucky."

"Eastern Kentucky. Up around Maysville."

"Correct."

Freya told me that her parents were farmers, but had jobs, too. Her father, George, ran a hardware store. Her mother, Irma, taught school. As an only child, Freya had had what she considered a normal childhood up to age twelve when her parents splurged on a three-day summer holiday at Lake Cumberland state park and everything changed.

"We went, even though it cost a fortune to us, and nobody could swim a lick."

They rented a tiny cottage with a view of the water. The weather was perfect the first two days, sunny and warm. They fished off the boat dock, happily casting their lines all day long.

"Had ourselves a fine time."

Freya made the statement with a hitherto concealed twang.

On the last day of their holiday, George and Irma wanted to do something special—so even though it was overcast and looked like rain, they rented a boat and baited up at a good spot they found on the lake.

"The sky darkened," Freya said, as if vividly reliving the moment, "and there was lightning."

When it started to rain, George tried to head back to shore. But the storm blew up too fast. Their motor stalled. They were stuck and would have to ride it out. Sheets of rain came down so hard they couldn't see a boat length in front of them. The swells kept getting bigger and rougher. Walls of water battered their little boat, pitching them around as if caught in a squall out at sea. Suddenly, a rental houseboat appeared out of the tempest riding a gigantic wave.

"The fool at the wheel lost control," Freya said. "He ran us down."

Their little boat capsized and they were all swept overboard. Freya, who was wearing the only life vest because Irma had insisted, popped back up. But her parents did not.

"I screamed and screamed for them," she said.

But the roar of the storm had drowned everything else out. Freya was terrified. She struggled hard keeping her head above water, certain she was going to die. The storm went on and on. When it finally let up, another fisherman in a small boat appeared and pulled her aboard. Her parents' bodies later washed up on shore.

"I'm sorry, Freya," I said, thinking that the weight of such grief must have been enormous, a wound that would never entirely heal. "What a tough break."

After that, she stayed with her mother's widowed sister, Emily. She worked part-time all through high school helping a farmer take care of his horses, which had become her obsession.

"That was when I decided to become a vet," she said.

Freya told me she was able to go to college only because Aunt Emily, who died in a car wreck when Freya was twenty-one, had sold the family farm to pay her tuition and living expenses. Her death left Freya with no living relatives.

"That's the story of my life," Freya said. "Your turn. Tell me why you wanted to become a private eye."

By this time, lights were winking across the water, the Bluegrass band was packing up its gear, and most of Clive's guests had gone home.

"I was never much on following orders," I confessed. "In fact, I was a screw up in high school. I got in some trouble with the law but had an otherwise clean record, so the judge gave me a break. He offered me a choice of jail or the army, so I joined the army."

Thinking back on it as I told her the story, I felt astonished all over again that they'd made me an MP. Even more incredible, I'd been so good at it they'd promoted me to an investigator.

"When I got my discharge, having learned no other trade than law enforcement, I joined the cops."

"So," Freya said, with glee, "the juvenile delinquent had morphed into the fuzz."

"Too true," I said. "I was well on my way to becoming a pillar of the community. I accomplished this despite a few minor in-house skirmishes with authority and was promoted. Then I met my wife, Leslie, bought a house, and when my daughter Sarah was born, became a doting father.

I picked up a stone and pitched it into the river.

"Life was just one big ham and cheese sandwich for me at the time. But then one day out of the blue, the bank notified me it was foreclosing on our home loan. I couldn't understand how that was possible until Leslie finally admitted she'd gambled away every cent we had. Up to then, I'd suspected nothing. Some detective, eh? I wanted a divorce. Leslie found a better lawyer, so she got the divorce, along with child custody. When she wanted to move with Sarah out to Las Vegas, the judge allowed it. After that, I went a little crazy. More than a little. Batshit loony, actually."

I took a breath.

"When your child is ripped out of your life and you can't see her anymore on a regular basis, both of you slowly start to lose your memories of each other. No matter how hard you cling to them, they fade like an old photograph exposed too long to sunlight. As time passed, I panicked, worrying about what I was missing as my kid grew up, but also dreading that someday we wouldn't recognize each other anymore."

I paused a moment, listening to the wind playing faintly on the water. I hadn't opened up like this to anyone for a long time. Ever, in fact. Now, having started, I couldn't stop.

"My old friends were oblivious to the pain I felt. New friendships were always missing something, too, like they'd skipped the opening chapter of the story. I'd never had that much faith in humanity, to begin with, but now what I had was totally destroyed. I stopped caring, got sloppy at work. When my boss called me on it, I was insubordinate. Talked myself right out of a job. I didn't care. It was all the same to me whether I lived or died."

"How did you survive?" Freya asked when I finally shut up.

"Luckily, a couple of my friends did care. One of them was an old army buddy, Alan Mason, who'd become a zookeeper. Alan believed in the healing effects of the company of animals. I didn't, but when he got me a job offer as an apprentice keeper at the Louisville Zoo, I took it and started working with chimps. They're scary smart animals and unbelievably strong. I struggled mightily. But after a year at the zoo, I realized how right my friend was about that healing effect because somewhere along the line the dead part of me slowly came back to life.

"I got another lucky break when I ran into Harriet Anderson, who I'd known as a kid. Harriet had become a lawyer, and she needed an investigator. I loved the zoo but still had an itch for detective work. Despite my troubles, Harriet believed in me enough to give me a job. While working for her during a sensational murder trial, I was able to locate a key witness that helped her win the case. Subsequently, she kept me on at the firm until—compelled by my loner instincts, probably—I went solo. And that is how became a humble, but world-class, private investigator."

"Not quite what I expected." Freya took my hand and stared at me, blinking rapidly. After a long silent moment, she said, "Time to show me your paintings."

It was a command, not a request. I obeyed. We walked up the incline to my place.

17

Thanks to pain pills and alcohol, I'd managed so far to smooth out much of the suffering resulting from the beating I took. Now I wondered if my joints were up to an even bigger, more pleasant challenge. When Freya excused herself to use the bathroom, I took advantage of the opportunity to turn off my phone. No interruptions, please.

A few minutes later when she returned, I waved at the stacks of finished and unfinished paintings in my spare room/studio. "Here we are."

She pointed at the painting sitting on the easel. "Tell me about that one."

I went over slowly and stood close behind her. "I've barely started it. At this stage, you might not be able to tell what it will look like. It's the under painting, blocking in where things are going to be."

"Right, but I like the colors you've used."

"Good. But only bits of them will show through when it's finished."

"Kind of like your personal evolution?" She went on quickly. "Got any completed ones handy?"

"Here."

Reaching around her shoulders, I positioned her so she could see the river from a good angle.

"I'm a bit obsessed with painting the Ohio." I pulled up a river scene from the floor rack for purposes of comparison.

"That one is so vivid I can almost imagine jumping right into the water," she said.

"See these little dots and dashes in the back?"

As she studied it more closely, I moved my hand to touch the small of her back.

"Those are the buildings on the other side," I said.

"And these at the front are weeds you've drawn using the tip of your brush?"

I nodded.

Freya flipped through the canvases. "That's a lot of paintings. What makes you do it?"

"It's hard to explain."

"Try."

"Degas said, 'Art is not what you see, but what you make others see.' I like that idea."

She reached for my self-portrait, but it was too full of anguish, so I pulled her away.

"I can't bear for anyone to see that one."

"Why not?"

"I'd rather not say."

She nodded as if understanding. "Jim, you should be in a gallery. Are you?"

I shook my head.

"Why not? You're good."

"Thanks. Maybe someday. For now, painting helps relieve my job stress. It's almost like having a beautiful woman massage my knotted muscles."

"Yes, I know all about your knotted muscles," Freya said,

pinching and stroking and kneading my shoulders with those strong fingers of hers. "Which method of relieving stress do you prefer?

"I think you know."

We reached for each other. As her arms encircled my waist, she locked her mouth over mine, her tongue darting. I slipped my fingers underneath the fabric of her dress, where she was naked, and cupped her breasts, feeling her nipples spring to life. As I buried my face in her soft flesh, she shrugged off the dress. Then her hand snaked to unzip my jeans and we sank to the floor.

—

"I've been meaning to ask how your current investigation is coming along," Freya said, sometime later, nuzzling my neck. "Is what I read about you in *The Late Mail* true? Are you really following a new line of inquiry and close to solving the case?"

"Absolutely," I yawned, "though in general, I wouldn't believe everything you read in that rag."

"You shouldn't feel too bad if you're not close to solving it. After all, the police have been trying to for a year. You've only been on it for what—a few days now?"

"Thanks, but they have lots of other cases. I have only this one right now."

She moved to cock her head at me. "What makes it so hard to unravel?"

"When I began, the trail had gone cold. Most backside workers wouldn't tell me anything. I had to get creative."

"Creative how?"

My pulse quickened as she shifted gently, brushing her fingers across my chest. When she was close like this, it was hard to think about anything else.

"Trade secret," I managed finally.

"You don't trust me, do you?" Her fingers had stopped moving.

"I want to. But my job is persuading people to tell me their secrets, not give mine away. Speaking of which, what have you heard?"

"Not much. I'm considered management, not really part of their private world."

"Well, you've certainly become part of mine."

"Have I?"

"Yes." I kissed her. "Ever hear of any trainers or jockeys who used buzzers to cheat?"

"What have you heard?" She resumed caressing me.

"That a few years ago a famous jockey was caught on tape saying if a horse needs a little help, you gotta plug him in. The jockey was talking about using electrical shocks to prod a horse to run faster. I understand that buzzers have been found hidden in bridles, in the jockey's mouth, even in the jockey's jock. Think there's any truth to it?"

Freya sat up, allowing the sheet to slip in a revealing way. "I don't know. You don't hear about buzzers so much anymore since they started using random magnetic wand scans to detect them."

"How come we, the general public, never hear anything about this?" I asked.

"It's racing's dirty little secret, I guess."

"The only one? Tell me, as a veterinarian, how do you feel about the fact that this goes on?"

"I'm angry," Freya said and pulled the sheet back up. "Also, sad and frustrated. When I became a vet, I swore an oath to protect the animals and prevent them from suffering. And that's what I do."

She sounded like she meant it. I reached out and touched her hair. "What about other ways of cheating?"

"You mean like PEDS—illegal performance-enhancing drugs? That's taken very seriously by the industry since there's just so much at stake. Nobody will bet if they think the race is rigged. But drugs are a way of life in racing, and they're so clever. Many trainers and owners consider the horse only as a commodity. Everything given to horses is to make them run faster and win."

"You sure know a lot about it."

"Don't go getting paranoid on me, Jim. I'm a veterinarian. It's my job to know about it. Anybody who works in the industry could have told you the same thing."

Except nobody had.

"Now I need to get some sleep," she said. "Since I'll be up and out of here by three o'clock, I'll say good night now, handsome."

She leaned over and kissed me.

THURSDAY

18

I was at my desk daydreaming about that kiss when Lt. Leo Brownfield came barging into my office at eight o'clock the next morning. A normally fastidious dresser, he looked rumpled like he'd slept in his suit. He also reeked of dried perspiration and stale coffee. I assumed he'd been out working all night, not that uncommon for a homicide detective.

"Why don't you ever answer your phone when I call, Guthrie?"

"I do," I said, swiveling in my chair to face him. "I just turned it off last night to get some uninterrupted sleep. What's the matter? You look like you haven't slept yourself."

"Never mind that." He sat down in the client chair, giving me a red-eyed glare that served to emphasize his crow's feet. "Where were you at 2:45 this morning?"

An ominous question. "At home in bed. Why?"

"Alone?"

"What makes that your business?"

"Last night, a homeless man found a body in a dumpster

behind the Rail Runner Saloon, a hole-in-the-wall near Central Avenue. I believe you know the place?"

"So what? Where are you going with this, Leo?"

"The 9-1-1 operator said the call came in about 2:45. A patrol car was dispatched. The uniforms confirmed there was a body."

"Who was it?"

"A guy who put out a tip sheet at the Downs named—"

"Not Wyatt Whitlow?" I said, my jaw dropping.

"So, you knew him."

"I saw him yesterday in connection with my investigation of the Rojas murder. Are you sure it's him?"

"He was identified from his driver's license photo. What time did you see Whitlow?"

"Around five o'clock."

"At the Rail Runner Saloon?"

"Yeah. How'd you know?"

"I spoke to the bartender this morning." Brownfield leaned back. "He put someone bearing a strong resemblance to you in the bar yesterday. Want to tell me what you were doing there?"

"Trying to get some information out of Whitlow by buying him cheap hooch."

"What information?"

"About the case."

"You said that already. Okay, we'll come back to it. What time did you leave the bar?"

"Five-thirty or so."

"Did you go back later that night?"

"No."

"You sure about that?"

"Of course, I'm sure."

"Okay, it's just that I was wondering if you might have gone back, say around two a.m., and forgotten about it. If so, that would make you the last person to see Whitlow alive."

"Are you nuts? What the hell, Leo? You think I'm a murderer now?"

"No, of course not, Jimbo. I would never think that, especially if you had an alibi. Do you?"

"This is ridiculous." I didn't want to say it and felt stubborn about it. "I'm hurt that you even asked. I thought you were my friend."

"Whatever gave you that idea?" Brownfield smiled.

"Look, why would I want to kill Wyatt Whitlow?"

"I don't know. He was a racing tout. Maybe he gave you a bad tip."

"Please," I said, meaning don't be absurd.

"Do you have an alibi?"

"Yes."

"Well?"

"I was with a woman until three o'clock in the morning."

"And this woman—she'll confirm that?"

"Yes."

Brownfield scratched his stubbled jaw as if fashioning some devastatingly brilliant pin with which to pop the balloon of my alibi.

"You were together right up to three o'clock, you say?"

Talking to him was like following a long series of switchbacks through the hills, each hazard hidden until the last possible second.

"You got somebody in your life now? Or was this just a one-night stand?"

I tried to smile at him pleasantly. "Why? Are you taking a survey?"

"What's her name?"

"Her name's Doctor Freya Hall."

"A doctor? Sounds a little out of your league, Guthrie."

"Freya's a veterinarian for Ned Ericson, the trainer," I said, ignoring the jibe. "We met during my investigation. She'll tell you."

"Let's hope so. I want to go back to why you were meeting the victim. Did it have anything to do with this?"

Brownfield dropped something on my desk in front of me that turned out to be a news story from this morning's paper. Under the headline, "Prominent trainer involved in a brawl at the Downs," the article read:

A brawl on the backside between a horseman and his persistent critic was the talk of Churchill Downs yesterday morning. The barnyard scuffle was triggered by scathing remarks about well-known trainer Keene Kessinger that appeared in *The Late Mail,* a tip sheet published by Wyatt Whitlow. A third unidentified track worker became involved in the altercation when she tried to stop it by dousing the combatants with a bucket of water. A Churchill spokesman said the matter was turned over to city police.

"I was there when it happened," I said.

"Go on, tell me the rest."

I highlighted how the feud had grown out of Whitlow's caustic witticisms about Kessinger, the latest implying that the trainer and his top jockey were being investigated for cheating.

"Afterward Whitlow texted me to meet him at the bar, claiming he had information to do with my investigation."

"What information?" Brownfield asked.

"That's what I went there to find out, but he never said. Now let me ask you something. What was the cause of death? I'm assuming he didn't crawl into a dumpster to commit suicide. So, how was he killed?"

Brownfield thought that one over. "All right, I'm going to tell you. Then you're going to tell me everything you know. And remember why I agreed to let you investigate the Rojas murder in the first place."

"Fine. I understand."

"Okay," he said, pausing for dramatic effect. "Somebody bashed in his skull from behind."

"Just like Felipe Rojas? Wow, two murders with the same M.O. Both involving the Downs. What are the odds? They must be connected."

"That's how it looks. So, let's try again. A few hours after talking to you, our tip sheet publisher winds up dead. Take it from there, starting with why you got no information from Whitlow when that's why you say he'd summoned you to the bar."

"I don't know. That's the truth. Look, the man was notoriously unreliable. You never could tell if he was giving it to you straight or bullshitting. He certainly wasn't above faking a story in order to get attention. I'd paid him $50 to publish a lie myself—"

"You paid him to do *what?*"

"To publish a claim that I was getting close to solving the Rojas murder."

"Were you?"

"No."

"Then why would you want him to do that?"

"I was trying to stir things up. Poking a stick in a hornet's nest to see what would fly out."

"That was reckless of you, Guthrie. Did it ever occur to you that a hornet might fly out and sting someone?"

"Yeah, but I figured I was the only one who'd get stung. Whitlow claimed to have an exposé of his own about to come out. At the time, I thought he was lying."

"Then why go to the bar?"

"Because maybe he wasn't lying. Whitlow was clever. When I asked who killed Felipe Rojas, he said he wondered when I'd ever get around to asking the right person, meaning him."

"So, when you asked him, what did he say?"

"Whitlow never answered the question. But he liked that idea of following the money."

"Why? What money?"

"I wanted to find out who benefitted financially from Rojas' death."

"Who did?"

"Nobody, as far as I can tell."

"That can't be all that Whitlow said to you."

I went back over the interview in my mind. At first, nothing came to me. Then I remembered.

"Right at the end, Whitlow said he had a clue for me. It was a quote from the Scottish poet Robert Burns."

"I know who Robert Burns is, Guthrie. I'm practically half-Scottish myself."

"Gee, you don't look half-Scottish," I said. "Sometimes it's hard to tell when you're putting me on—"

"Get to the point," Brownfield yelled.

"Okay. As I recall, Whitlow said something like, 'There's nothing as uncertain as a sure thing.'"

"What did you think he meant by that?"

"I don't know. Only thing I could think of was that 'a sure thing' could apply to horse racing."

"Is that it?"

"That's all I got, Leo."

"Come on then." He stood.

"Where?"

"I need you to formally identify Whitlow's body."

"I thought you already did that," I said.

"No."

"Why me?"

"Because I crave your amazing company."

"See, that's what I meant about not knowing when you're being sarcastic."

"What do you think? He doesn't have anyone else. Bar owner told me Whitlow worked and lived alone. He had few friends and no family."

"What about people at the track?"

"Let's go," Brownfield said, heading out the door.

—

We rode in Brownfield's unmarked gray Ford Taurus mostly in silence to far eastern Jefferson County, a thirty-minute drive from downtown. The morgue recently had moved from the aging Urban Government Center on Barrett Avenue to a site known variously over the decades as "the Central Kentucky Lunatic Asylum," "Lakeland," and "Central State Hospital."

Brownfield parked in an ambulance slot by the entrance to the six-story building and we stepped inside. At the county coroner's offices, Brownfield explained the purpose of our visit to a deputy coroner. Then we put on masks and plastic shoe covers. A balding, overweight worker wearing a black polo shirt accompanied us to a large depressing room in the basement with a disturbing formaldehyde reek. Racks of corpses wrapped in clear heavy plastic rose to the ceiling. The bodies had been autopsied and were awaiting pickup by a mortuary, the worker said.

After visiting the old morgue many times over the years, I was used to the rotting fruit odor of a decomposing corpse. It didn't exactly send me away screaming, but it did produce a queasy, nervous feeling in my stomach that I'd prefer to avoid.

"That's him," I said when the worker opened a refrigerated steel cabinet drawer and pulled back the sheet covering Wyatt Whitlow's lifeless face.

The worker turned Whitlow's head sideways at Brownfield's request. The back of the skull was a mushy disaster. It had been penetrated and the hair stained a dark color, apparently caused by blood from the grotesque wound. I wondered who'd ID me when it was my turn to lie lifeless on a gurney with a toe tag.

"The cranial lesions are geometrical and about the same size as a hammer, though none was found at the crime scene. The abrasions, which resemble friction burns, may have been caused by dragging the victim from where he was killed to the dumpster where the body was found," the worker said.

During the autopsy, the medical examiner had measured and calculated the depth of Whitlow's wounds. A forensic pathologist would analyze the direction from which the attack was delivered, along with an assessment of the attacker's state of mind. From this, he would build a profile of Whitlow's attacker.

I wondered how closely this profile would match that of Felipe Rojas's killer.

Brownfield said he had checked Whitlow's hands, fingers, and arms for defensive wounds, which could show how much of a struggle the victim put up and how frenzied the attacker was. But there were none. It appeared that Whitlow never saw it coming. After Brownfield took a few photos, we got out of there.

At the car, he offered me a peppermint to quell the odor of death.

"So now we have not one, but two murder cases to solve," Brownfield said, as we headed back to town. "And you, Guthrie, are the link between them."

I felt my breath catch briefly. "We're not back to my alibi again, are we? What are you implying?"

"I'm not implying, I'm saying. First, you stick your nose into the Rojas case, then you're in the middle of this one. That seems more like cause and effect than coincidence."

"Does it really? There are some other links."

"Such as

"Well, the cast of characters consists solely of backside workers. Juan Diaz played poker with Felipe Rojas on the night he was killed. Diaz worked for Keene Kessinger, who Wyatt Whitlow detested. Whitlow told me he'd always wanted to write an exposé, which may bring us back to the Rojas murder."

Brownfield listened patiently, but I could see he was not satisfied.

"Now it's time for you to tell me the rest you've uncovered during this investigation," he said.

Well, a deal was a deal, though I wasn't ready to reveal my suspicion that Juan Diaz might have killed Felipe for having an affair with his wife—at least not until I was sure there'd been said affair. I'd already helped Juan lose his job. His marriage could be next. And despite what I'd said, I couldn't be certain I was blameless in Whitlow's death, either.

I couldn't shake the feeling that Felipe Rojas's determination to bring his family to America was the key to solving everything. It would have been an expensive undertaking, probably in the $25,000 range per person, so at least fifty-grand more. Rojas didn't have that kind of money, had no way of making that kind of money. It would have taken a huge windfall to accomplish his goal. Yet his son was here.

"Did you ever get a look at Felipe Rojas's bank statements?" I asked.

"He had no bank account," Brownfield said. "Rojas dealt strictly in cash."

"And no drug angle?"

"Not that we could find."

"Me, either. What about Whitlow?"

"He was broke, according to his employer," Brownfield said, "which seems to rule drug trafficking out again."

"Wait a minute. I was thinking some more about that Burns line. You know, Whitlow was always quoting some literary figure or other—but what if he was referring to the Derby? Kessinger's horse is as close to a sure thing as it gets."

"You think he was implying something about this year's race?"

"Who knows? Whitlow loved to tantalize and frustrate. He was probably just trying to keep the free drinks coming from me."

"Do you like Kessinger for the Whitlow murder?"

"No. True, they hated each other. And Whitlow implied having the goods on Kessinger somehow. Yet Kessinger doesn't strike me as the cheating—or the murdering—kind. He's too upstanding."

"Well, that's great detective work, Jimbo. After failing to solve the first murder, you've now all but eliminated my chief suspect in the second."

It didn't seem fair, but I didn't say a word.

19

wondered whether Whitlow's exposé of cheating would appear in today's *Late Mail*. Or even if the tip sheet itself would come out now that he was dead. Either way, the evidence on which his claims were based still needed to be found. The obvious place to look for it was in Whitlow's home, located on Lillian Avenue near the Downs. But when I got there, it was crawling with cops. Patrol cars and uniforms out front. Gloved technicians toting cardboard boxes out the front door.

Figuring Brownfield and I were probably thinking along the same lines, I decided to let LMPD finish their work before beginning mine.

At a nearby fast-food chain outlet, I ordered coffee at the drive-through window and went to the back of the lot to drink it. My intention while so doing was to contemplate the full extent of Whitlow's possible involvement in the case. What I kept thinking about, though, was Freya Hall and that strapless black dress she had worn when we went dancing. I could still feel the blaze she'd ignited in me—followed by the happy contentment I felt holding her tight.

Also coming back to me, however, was Brownfield's jibe about Freya seeming out of my league. Was she? What did the hell did he know about it? Had he even met Freya?

What he said struck a chord, though. Of course, I did not want to believe it, but his words had re-awakened a nagging voice of doubt in my mind. I was fully aware that a woman as beautiful as Freya could turn any man's head, including mine, but I did not believe she had. Still, it was possible that I was merely a means to find out where the investigation was headed. It hurt to think so, though, so, I stopped thinking about it.

When I felt I had waited long enough for the cops to finish, I drove back to Whitlow's place. They were gone. I went up on the front porch and found the door sturdy, but the lock itself old and loose. Slipping on a pair of disposable nitrile gloves, I inserted a credit card between the door and the frame. The plastic was flexible enough for me to push and bend until the lock popped open. I went in.

Whitlow had used the dining room as his office. There was a swivel chair at his L-shaped computer desk, so I sat down, literally putting myself in his place. Police had removed the computer, along with everything connected. They'd emptied a four-drawer file cabinet, too, so no receipts, bills, or photos remained for me to examine. No copies of today's *Late Mail* in sight, either. I didn't know what they'd found, but I figured Whitlow wouldn't have made finding his secrets easy. Possibly he'd rented storage space elsewhere, but I knew he was cash strapped, and nowhere else would have been as convenient a stash as right here.

I went back to the living room to start looking, feeling along the bottom edges of doors and unscrewing air vents and light fixtures and power outlet covers. The searchers had been unusually considerate, tossing the place without wrecking it. Cabinets and drawers stood open, but nothing had been dumped on the floor. Carpets remained intact. Floorboards had not been ripped up. No X cuts in the upholstery. I examined lamp bases, drapes, books, and bookshelves. Found nothing. No hide-a-safes in secret wall compartments or windowsills. Nothing concealed under chair cushions.

In the bedroom, a double bed mattress had been flipped onto the floor. All the dresser drawers were pulled out. In the closet, I found shirts and pants with their pockets turned inside out. I ran my hand along the closet's high shelf, but no messages had been taped there. It was a similar story in the bathroom, where I came across nothing untoward in the cabinet, linen cupboard, or toilet tank.

My last stop was the kitchen. Unless Whitlow had hidden diamonds in the ice cubes, there was nothing in the freezer but a fifth of vodka. The cabinets held coffee mugs, glasses, dishes, and coffee, but no food. On the kitchen counter stood a half-filled wine rack and a pyramid of empty beer cans, testimonials to the occupant's abstemious ways—not. In one drawer, I found an assortment of cutlery. In another, a collection of wine corks. I swept up a handful of corks, wondering why he'd kept dozens of them when I heard somebody fiddling with the front door lock.

Shoving the corks into my pocket, I crept into the living room and stood listening. When I yanked the door open, I found myself face-to-face with a bulky figure with a hoodie pulled down to hide his features. He instantly charged into me, knocking me flat, and took off running wildly down the sidewalk. By the time I got up and chased him, he'd already driven off in an ancient yellow pickup truck.

I jumped into the Mustang and followed him to Central Avenue, where a cop in an orange and blue reflective vest was directing traffic by using two paddles—SLOW and STOP. Ignoring the traffic cop, my quarry rocketed through the intersection with horns blaring at him, barely missing an oncoming city bus.

I followed, careening onto Seventh Street while trying

to read his license plate but the numbers were crusted with mud. The high-speed pursuit went on for several blocks as we cut back and forth through four lanes of heavy traffic, finally skidding through a gravel-spraying left turn onto a side road and crossing a CSX railroad hump. From there, we roared along lightly used two-lane blacktop at seventy, modest homes zipping by on either side, until a flatbed trailer poked its nose out into the road, forcing me to swerve into a shallow ditch and killing the engine.

By the time I got it started again and back on the pavement, the pickup had disappeared. I floored the Mustang and was going eighty-five when a T-shaped intersection with Dixie Highway loomed into view. I hit the brakes while trying to guess which way to turn, chose south, and for a couple of minutes feared I'd gone the wrong way. But at last, I caught a glimpse of the pickup truck ahead.

It turned west onto Manslick Road, then south again, this time entering the old-growth forested knob of Iroquois Park, the biggest and most rugged of Louisville's extensive city park system. The road curved sharply through steep hillsides covered with oaks and other ancient hard woods. The pickup tried to lose me among the park's winding roads, but I knew every inch of it, having lived nearby as a teenager.

No way any pickup truck was going to outrun this Mustang, I thought, just as another vehicle came out of nowhere driving on the wrong side of the road. I yanked the steering wheel hard right and fishtailed all over the pavement. Instinct told me to slam on the brakes, but I did not. I kept my foot on the gas, turning into the skid, which put the rear end back in line with the front tires. By then, the pickup was out of sight.

Scant minutes later, I found it again, this time stopped at the edge of a deserted playground area. The driver let his door hang open while he reeled through the swing sets and sliding boards. I pulled in behind the pickup, blocking its escape, and chased the driver along a well-worn hiking trail. Leaves slapped my face. Branches scratched my arms. My quarry soon ran out of wind, allowing me to catch up. When I did, I forearmed him in the face and stood over where he lay sprawled on his back, all the fight having gone out of him.

It was Juan Diaz.

"How does your head feel?" I asked.

"Hurts," he moaned.

"Get up."

I marched him back to the playground and sat him down on a sawn-off tree trunk.

"I need some answers, Juan. Why were you skulking around Whitlow's place?"

Diaz shrugged and scratched his cheek.

"Did you follow me there?"

When he didn't answer promptly enough, I encouraged him with a slap on the head.

"Damn!" he said, flinching and cradling the spot with both hands. "That hurt."

"Same question. Did you follow me there?"

"Okay, I did. All right?"

"Why? And why were you skulking around Whitlow's place?"

"I didn't know what else to do. I thought maybe I could find something to sell."

"Like what? Whitlow was broke."

"I didn't know that."

"If you're so broke, how can you afford a pickup truck?"

"We saved up. It's not worth much."

That was at least half true. "Why'd you run when I opened the door?"

"I panicked. Thought you might kill me."

"Why would I want to kill you? Say, you're not the one who shot at me last night, are you?"

"Wasn't me." As his gaze clouded and went distant, I grabbed his shirt front. "You sure about that?"

"I don't even got a gun."

I stared at him hard. "Why'd you stop here in the park?"

"Uh, um, ran out of gas."

"Real criminal mastermind, aren't you? Tell me why you murdered Felipe Rojas."

"Hey, I didn't murder nobody," he said, blinking rapidly and licking his lips.

"Did you catch him with Sandy? Is that why?"

"No, I'm telling you. I didn't kill him. And my wife wasn't having no affair."

"Not what I heard."

"Well, you heard wrong."

Beating the truth out of him was an appealing prospect, but the way he stuck to his story was convincing. He did not seem to believe that Sandy had a lover, and I doubted he was that good a liar. If he did not know, then he had no motive for killing Felipe Rojas. I decided not to waste any more time with Diaz and left him stranded there without any gas.

A few blocks from the racetrack, I pulled off the parkway and sat a moment to let my head clear. I needed to find out why Sandy Diaz had failed to show up last night. I had a hard time believing that she was the one who had shot me, but no one else knew where the meeting I was having was going to be held.

Feeling drained and weary, I reached for my handkerchief to wipe my damp forehead. When I did, I found the corks that I had stuck in my pocket earlier. Something else to get rid of.

I got them out and dropped them on the passenger seat. They appeared ordinary—the kind used to stopper expensive or inexpensive wine. Thanks to Clive, a veritable fount of information about "fruits of the vine," I was aware that synthetic corks and screwcaps had been cutting into the traditional cork market for some time now. Someday, they might become a thing of the past but presently natural corks were still the norm. They were also useless once the wine had been consumed. So, why keep them? Clive claimed that used corks would fetch about a dime each on eBay. Whitlow wasn't that desperate.

I picked up a red-stained cork. A grape design was stamped into it. Another cork had a date stamp, a third a blurred French-looking word. Maybe these were some kind of poor man's trophies like that pyramid of beer cans stacked up on the kitchen counter. Maybe the tip sheet publisher had collected them like baseball cards. Nobody thought those things would ever be worth anything, either, but look at them now, some fetching thousands. These corks were all the same size, except for one slightly longer. When I picked it up and pulled on both ends, it came apart! The cork was hollow. Something was hidden inside—a small electronic device, a mini flash drive.

At last, a lead that might produce actual results. I doubted Whitlow would have gone to such lengths to hide the flash drive unless there was something valuable on it. Like what? His exposé perhaps? I went out to get my laptop from the trunk of the Mustang, brought it in, and booted her up. Then I inserted the drive into a USB port. When an icon appeared, I clicked on it.

Password-protected, it said.

I immediately texted my hacker, Mario, who claimed to be "the Clyde Barrow of data banks."

"hey Mario"

"what you need"

"open password-protected flash drive"

"no problem when need?"

"asap usual rate"

"ok"

"sending now"

20

As I drove to the Downs, I heard on the radio that over a hundred thousand racing fans were expected for tomorrow's Kentucky Oaks. Unlike the Derby, the Oaks was for fillies. It used to be the day for locals to go to the track. But since it was harder now to get tickets, the forty thousand local racing fans who hadn't inherited Derby seats went on Thursday instead of Friday for a smaller crowd and greater ease of movement at the racetrack.

"Gates opened this morning at eight for 'Thurby,' as the day was now being marketed," the reporter said. "A light but steady rain is forecast with temperatures hovering in the high forties to low fifties." But a sketchy forecast would not prevent a big crowd from turning out. Serious drinking would already be underway in the hospitality lounges and lines would have formed at the betting windows.

The backside was relatively calm when I arrived. Workers mucked out stalls and completed all the other unglamorous tasks necessary for racing to go on. A tent had been set up for TV people, whose demeanor off-camera often contrasted sharply with the face they showed viewers. Photojournalists, easily recognizable by their backpacks and multi-pocket camo vests stuffed with lenses, tramped about like big game hunters, stalking for that front-page shot.

At the tack room in the Ericson barn, I found Freya surrounded by bits and saddles. She was filling a bowl with cat food.

"Cats seem to do pretty well around here," I said.

"They should. After all, they're intelligent, affectionate, and beautiful."

"Not unlike you."

"If you say so." She smiled. "They need lots of loving attention—and a good place to scratch."

"I may know such a place."

"You must show it to me some time."

"I will," I said, looking into the shadowed depths of her eyes.

She turned to put away the cat food and changed the subject smoothly. "How's the case going?"

I gave her a quick version of my visit to the morgue.

"Sounds grim. Did you learn anything?"

"That both Rojas and Whitlow were killed by blunt force trauma."

She asked if that meant the same person could have killed them both, and I said it did.

"Catch one killer and solve both crimes then," she said.

I nodded. "Will I see you tonight?"

"Take me dancing."

"I don't know. I'm not much of a—"

"I am." She smiled. "Pick me up around 8:30. Dress up."

"Okay." I held her in my arms and kissed her to make it official.

—

Racing continued with its usual color and cachet. The public address announcer was keeping everyone aware of post time. As the crowd roared during the next race, I passed a man walking a white goat on a leash. Just another mindboggling sight on the backside. Seconds later, I saw Sandy Diaz conversing in a confidential manner with Daniela Torres. Wishing I was a fly on the fly to overhear their conversation, I pulled out my telephone and shot a photo of them, just as my phone vibrated.

"Guthrie, where are you?" Carlos said. "You need to get over to Keene Kessinger's stable right away. The cops are there. Something to do with Whitlow's murder. Maybe Papa's, too. Hurry, it's happening right now."

At Kessinger's barn three minutes later, I encountered two uniformed cops who were using the row of white sawhorses to bar the crowd from the entrance. I didn't see Carlos, but Kessinger, his farrier J.T. Young, and Hines were all there.

"This is preposterous," the trainer snarled. "Absolutely insane. What's wrong with the damned police department?"

"They're only doing their job, Mister Kessinger," Hines was saying as I joined the group.

"Well, it's nonsense."

"Probably nothing to it," Hines agreed.

I asked what was going on. Hines took me aside and explained that LMPD officers were scouring the barn for evidence in connection to the Whitlow case.

"Kessinger sounds less than enthusiastic about it. Do they have a warrant?"

Hines nodded.

We stood watching. Soon the tableau attracted several notebook-toting scribes, plus a TV camera crew.

"Doesn't take long for word to get around, does it? Wonder how management will feel about this?"

Hines reacted to my comment with a scowl suitable for a sufferer in an antacid commercial. He lamented the timing and the fact that the national media were out in force. Obviously, the Downs wanted the public's attention focused on horse racing, not murder. On the other hand, solving a murder was not bad publicity.

"Speaking of bad publicity, what did you think of Whitlow?" I asked.

"I sure won't miss him," Hines said, this time with a moue of disdain. "He's been a major pain in the ass for as long as I can remember. In fact, several years ago, he made it personal by assassinating my character in his sheet. For that, he got himself ejected and barred. But he filed suit, and we took a lot of heat for overreacting. Whitlow was back in a few weeks. I didn't like him, but that doesn't mean he deserved to be murdered. Nobody does."

Hines shifted his gaze from the crowd to the barn door.

"And here they come."

The growing knot of onlookers tightened as Brownfield exited the barn along with another plainclothes man and several tech people in light jackets.

"Recognize this?" Brownfield held up a clear plastic evidence bag containing what appeared to be a shoeing hammer.

"Yeah, it looks like one of mine," Young said. "Why do you have it?"

"It's what we've been looking for. We found it in the tack room hidden under some rags on a bottom cupboard shelf."

"I had one stolen about a year ago. I try to keep them out of sight," the farrier said.

"Those are traces of blood and hair," Brownfield said.

"They can't be," Kessinger said.

"We'd like for both of you to accompany us voluntarily to police headquarters to be fingerprinted," Brownfield said.

Young looked like he might put up some resistance, but Kessinger stopped him with a gesture, saying, "We'd be delighted to cooperate with the police in any way we can."

A plainclothesman led them away.

Kessinger's move seemed shrewd. It would spare them both from the humiliation of handcuffs and Miranda warnings in front of the crowd and a television audience. I wondered how someone capable of such clever improvised strategy could have been dumb enough to park a murder weapon on his own property where it was sure to be found. And what had led police to search the stables?

Brownfield, holding an impromptu Q & A for the media gathered at the barn, said it was an anonymous tip.

"Do you believe Wyatt Whitlow was killed with the hammer you found here?" one reporter asked.

"It's possible. We'll know more after DNA and fingerprint evidence is examined."

Brownfield took a couple more questions before cutting them off, saying, "Okay, that's all we have for now."

The throng dispersed. As TV reporters did stand-ups, I pushed my way through until I caught up with Brownfield.

"Leo," I said, "what the hell are you doing? You don't seriously believe either of them left the hammer in Kessinger's barn, do you? Or that they had anything to do with his murder."

"What I believe is not important," he said. "What matters is what the evidence shows. And in this case, the shape of the wound appears to fit the hammer we found. Oh, and look where we found it."

"I get it. You're going after Kessinger because of the fight he had with Whitlow. But what's Young's motive?"

"Revenge. Whitlow recently printed in his tip sheet that the farrier's work was of poor quality and might've caused an injury to a horse. Young is on record that Whitlow's verbal attack harmed his business."

"Look, even with Kessinger's prints and DNA on the hammer, doesn't it seem likely they were planted by the real killer?"

"Why should I believe that, Guthrie? If Kessinger's prints are on Young's hammer, he's got some explaining to do."

"Okay, but Whitlow was murdered off Taylor Boulevard. Why would anyone in his right mind bring the murder weapon all the way back here to his own barn where it was sure to be found?"

"I think you answered your own question. What murderer is in his right mind? Of course, we can't acknowledge that because if we did, everyone would get off on temporary insanity. If we find Kessinger or Young's fingerprints or DNA on that hammer, it'll be an open-and-shut case, Jimbo. Never look a gift horse in the mouth."

Chuckling at his wit, Brownfield went on his way.

He had to know this was a travesty. On the other hand, an arrest was an arrest, especially at the same racetrack where a high-profile homicide case remained unsolved after a year.

My case.

They had it wrong. Maybe the real murderer was named on the mini flash drive. Maybe that's what Juan Diaz was looking for at the tipster's house. Not a theory I was in a position to share with Brownfield, so I phoned Mario instead.

"Have you broken the password on that drive yet?" I asked.

"No."

"Why not?"

As usual, Mario spouted condescending gibberish until I interrupted to ask, "Does that mean you'll be able to open it?"

"I might. Hard to say when, though. Whoever did this could have done something else equally boneheaded, like leaving the password in clear-text."

I had no idea what he was talking about but urged him in the strongest possible terms to keep at it until he could tell me what was on that drive.

Time for another visit to Wagner's. I went across the street and was caught up in a tidal surge of customers that washed through the front entrance to overwhelm the wait staff. While others fought for seats, I stood patiently waiting to speak with Tallulah whenever she had a moment. It wasn't long before I heard her say, "Your bruises look better today. Are we eating, hon?"

"Not now." I showed her the photo I took of the two women.

She recognized the one on the right, said she was at the café with Felipe Rojas on the day of his death. But she wasn't talking about Sandy Diaz. The one on the right was Daniela Torres. Stunned by this revelation, I thanked Tallulah, gave her a hefty tip, and made a beeline back to the track.

21

I found Daniela standing at the rail wearing a leaf bag to keep out the fine drizzle veiling the city's skyline. Rainwater dripped off her makeshift parka but underneath her jeans and purple blouse appeared dry enough. When I flashed her a smile, she turned to walk away. I stopped her by grasping her elbow.

"I just had the most amazing experience. I think it's one you'll find surprising, as well." I pulled her away from other racing fans and put her in the picture about the picture, meaning the one of her and Sandy Diaz at Wagner's.

"So, what if I was there?" she said, shaking off my hand defiantly. "How is that any business of yours?"

"My business is solving Felipe's murder. To do that, I need information about what was going on at the time of his death. I suspect that meeting was significant. I need your cooperation."

"What do you want to know?"

"Were you having an affair with him?"

"No, we were just having lunch, not a quickie." She glared at me flinty-eyed, with her chin held high.

"Even so, tongues would have wagged if you were seen alone with him. It would have been all over the backside in fifteen minutes. You wouldn't take such a risk without having a good reason."

"You're making something out of nothing. We just ran into each other. I was hungry, that's all."

"Am I? Maybe Sandy Diaz was having the affair with Felipe. So, what were you doing there really?"

Daniela bit her lip. "Who told you that?"

"I'm a detective. I deduced it. If Sandy was involved with Felipe, she could no more afford to be seen with him in public than you could. In fact, it would be far worse for her since she was married. Not to mention that Felipe's wife is trapped back in Guatemala. I doubt Sandy would want people to know about him and her. You and Sandy, on the other hand, don't mind showing that you are close friends. It's obvious from the photograph. It's also obvious that you want to protect her, but you can't, not anymore. Things have gotten out of hand. But I might be able to help if you'll level with me about what you know."

"You're reading a lot into one picture—one that you didn't have my permission to take."

"I don't need your permission. Listen you're also both *mestizos*. You both speak the same Mayan language, Quiché."

"Again, so what?"

"I find it intriguing. Felipe spoke Quiché, too. Then there's his good luck charm, which I saw at his apartment, and the identical one Sandy wears."

"That doesn't prove anything, either."

"No, but it's a lot of coincidences and after a while you know that's not what they are. Here's how I see it. Suppose Sandy had a vital message for Felipe right away. She couldn't wait for the normal way to deliver it, whatever that was. So, who else could she trust, turn to for help? I'm betting on her best friend—you."

I was looking for a tell, and when Daniela blinked, I believed

I had found it.

"Maybe you met Felipe at the diner on that same day he was beaten to death because Sandy Diaz asked you for a favor—to pass along a message to her lover. What was the message, Daniela?"

She hesitated, clearing her throat, and seemed finally ready to answer my question. But just then, the track announcer's voice blared, "The horses have reached the starting gate. And they're off!"

Between the roaring crowd and the pelting rain, we could no longer hear each other until the race was over. But when the last horse and jockey had galloped by, I said, "The message, Daniela?"

"Sandy wanted Felipe to meet her that night during the after-Derby party," she sighed.

"Where was this meeting to take place?"

"At my apartment, where they could be alone."

"Was that their regular love nest?"

Closing her eyes, she nodded.

"You served as their regular go-between?"

She nodded again.

"Felipe was trying to bring his wife and family to the U.S. Did that upset Sandy?" I asked.

"How could it when she knew their lives were in danger in Guatemala?"

"But wasn't she afraid he wouldn't leave his wife behind? That would be a strong woman-scorned reason for killing him, wouldn't it?"

"I understand what you're saying. But Sandy would have never hurt Felipe."

"Why not?"

"She loved him too much. She would have let him go if she had to."

Rick and Ilsa back in *Casablanca,* but I was not sure I was buying it. She started to leave.

"Wait." I held up my hand. "Had you ever delivered messages to Felipe at Wagner's before the night he was killed?"

"No, never."

"What made seeing him that night so urgent?"

"I don't know."

Neither did I, but I was damn sure going to find out.

—

At the Ericson stable, my face had become so familiar by now that I barely rated a glance from the security guard. Moisture dripped from the eaves onto soft green hay, giving the place an intense fermented smell that had nothing to do with bourbon, though I spotted a small, square box of mint growing against the wall. My client was mucking out a stall.

"Hey, Carlos. We need to talk."

He leaned the long-handled shovel against the wall and came out of the stall.

His head drooped and he had dark circles under his eyes as if not sleeping well. He looked a little down, too.

"I've got a bone to pick with you," I began. "You lied to me."

"Don't know what you mean."

"I asked you if your father was close to the Diaz family. 'Not especially,' you said."

"He wasn't."

"Not counting his affair with Sandy Diaz?"

"What? Horseshit!" Carlos said.

"No, it's the truth, and we both know it."

"My Papa was a good man. And I'll kick anybody's ass who says different."

"Nobody is saying that. But you've wasted my time. I can't help you if you hide the truth from me."

A sheen of sweat appeared on his cheeks and forehead. "Okay, I messed up. I just didn't want nobody else to know about it."

"How did you find out?"

Carlos shrugged and with a pained expression said, "Little things Papa said and did. Like he'd disappear, and when I'd ask where he'd been, his answers wouldn't add up."

"Have you ever personally talked to the Diaz woman about this?"

Carlos said Sandy expressed her sorrow on the day after his father was killed. "I asked her, 'How sorry are you?' That's when she knew I knew."

"What happened next?"

"She tried to tell me Papa still loved Mama and me, and the family. I said then he sure had a funny way of showing it and how the hell would she know anyway? She said that if he didn't love my Mama, why was he still trying to bring her here? And I said you tell me. She claimed it wasn't about us, only that they were both lonely. She said she had a shitty marriage and that she loved Papa, and he loved her. I asked her how the hell could he love two women at the same time, and she said life was complicated and asked me to keep her secret. I told her to go to hell."

"But you did keep it, Carlos, because you didn't want your father disgraced publicly or for your mother to find out. Sandy didn't want her husband to know. That's why you agreed to keep it between you."

"I didn't think it mattered."

"Stop lying to me. It's the key to everything. What else are you holding back?"

"Nothing, I swear." He looked down at his feet, dejected, then back up with a plea in his eye. "Will you stay on the case?"

Horses snorted. Rain pattered on the roof.

"Only if you promise to be straight with me from here on out," I said, after making him sweat.

"I swear."

"Okay, you looked glum when I got here. Why?"

"It's nothing."

"Don't bullshit me. You just promised to be straight. Now

you're lying again."

"No, I'm not," he said, rocking slightly and sweating.

"Yeah, you are. Last chance. How are you and Libby doing?"

"We're just friends."

"Really? Cause it doesn't sound like it."

He looked away, twisting his hands. "You believe in love, Mister Guthrie? True love?"

"Who doesn't?"

"What if I'm like Papa? Maybe I don't deserve her."

"Hey," I said, as an image of Freya *au natural* flashed through my mind, "I'm the last guy to ask for relationship advice. But I know this. Just because your old man wasn't perfect doesn't mean he was a bad man. Sandy's right. Life is more complicated than that. And you're not him."

Very glib, Guthrie. And true as far as it goes, but exactly how far was that? The simple truth—or simply a rationalization? We all deny what we cannot face. Hearing that his father had been unfaithful to his mother was a hard punch to the ribs for Carlos. Watching him gulp and struggle to breathe reminded me of just how much we all rely on such defense mechanisms. What was I rationalizing? That I had not done enough to save my own family? And if so, why not? It happens to men, who think they've gotten out of a bad situation and don't want to get back in again. Even so, it was essential to be honest with yourself even when you were being dishonest with others.

"Let's talk about Whitlow's murder," I said, changing the subject. "You know Kessinger and his farrier. Do you believe they did it?"

"No, nobody's stupid enough to leave the hammer in his own barn. Sounds like a frame-up."

"I agree. The real killer needs a fall guy."

"But it won't...stand up?"

"Maybe it only needs to for a while," I said.

"Till when?"

"After the Derby, maybe."

"Are you saying what I think you're saying?" Carlos asked.

"Yeah, they want to fix the race."

He whistled. "What's our next move?"

"*My* next, you mean. Yours is to keep your head down. I believe Sandy Diaz knows more. I'm meeting her after midnight."

"Why so late? Like maybe she don't want to be seen with you?"

"I suspect that she's afraid to. It's been over a year since your father's death. Sometimes on anniversaries, events have a way of repeating themselves. We know there are some dangerous people out there. Keep your eyes open. And don't repeat a single word of this."

22

The rain had stopped falling and the skies were clear when I went to pick up Freya around 8:30 that night. I was wearing dress pants and a shirt with a collar plus leather shoes—and hoping not to be mistaken for a waiter. She had texted me her south-end address. It was easy enough to find, a couple of miles from the Downs on Southern Parkway in a neighborhood full of modest houses dating back to World War II. Hers was a one-story, two-bedroom with a front porch and a small green lawn. The bricks had been painted white for that old antebellum effect.

I knocked.

She came to the door looking ready to tango in her low-cut black midi dress. Twin slits in the front showed off her legs. Black suede ankle strap heels completed the outfit. She was wearing her hair up for the evening and it gleamed and shone.

"Jim," she said with a smile.

"You look beautiful, Freya."

She stepped forward to kiss me and said that I looked handsome, but I knew I'd be invisible beside her.

We went into the living room, where there was a fireplace with a lavender mantel, a striped rug of many colors, plus a pair of cream-colored sofas. Very chic. She sat across from me and poured two glasses of sauvignon blanc. "I hope the wine is okay," she said.

I assured her it was.

Then she sat back and, for maximum effect, demurely crossed her well-toned legs. We made small talk. I complimented the house, asked how long she had been living here. She told me a couple of years give or take. She liked the location, being convenient to her work. Housing prices were lower in this part of town and she felt she'd made a good investment. When she went on the road to other racetracks, her neighbors kept an eye on it for her.

After a few more minutes of this, I said, "Where would you like to go dancing? Did you have a particular club in mind?"

"I have a better idea."

She produced two tickets to an exclusive corporate charity bash on the roof garden of the swanky old Brown Hotel. They threw a party every year, she said, adding last time had been fun. No need for dinner. Drinks and finger food would be provided.

"What are we waiting for?" I asked.

We parked in the garage at Fourth and Broadway, passed through the ornate lobby bar, and rode the elevator with three other couples up to the sixteenth floor. A host in a vest and bowtie checked our tickets before admitting us to the party. We passed through double doors to the landscaped roof garden, which offered a broad view of the downtown lights and was big enough for maybe two hundred revelers in fancy dress. Two bars and a bandstand were set up, and the dance floor already was thrumming with couples performing elegant dances of yesteryear.

"I warned you that I wasn't much of a dancer," I said.

"Oh, you'll do fine."

After managing a couple of slow numbers without stepping

on Freya's toes, I asked if she wanted a drink. She did. She said she would meet me after she visited the "powder room," an archaic moniker well-suited to that kind of joint, which oozed with antique charm. I made my way through the crowd and stood in line at the bar facing the river, where two women in white coats were serving up hard liquor, wine, and beer. I overheard a guy in a suit griping about how hard it was during Derby Week to get around town or find a table at a decent restaurant.

When he walked away after being served, I ordered two glasses of red wine. I scanned the dance floor while it was being poured. The merrymakers were about what you'd expect— mostly well-fed middle-aged couples and a few youngsters thrown in for spice. Nothing too earthshattering.

But thirty seconds later, over the dancers' heads, I spotted none other than my least favorite local karate expert, Herb Alexander, engaged in deep conversation with Freya Hall. Feeling a rush of adrenaline as my fight-or-flight instincts kicked in with a vengeance, I took a couple of deep breaths to get myself under control before returning with our drinks. By the time I did, Alexander had departed into the crowd and some other drunk was bothering Freya.

I got a bead on him, but before I could do anything, she had slapped him silly. She struck him so hard it sounded like a gunshot and left a red palm print on his pink cheek.

"Are you okay?" I asked her while watching him stumble away, humiliated.

"I can take care of myself," Freya said.

"I noticed. Good thing strong women don't scare me."

"Maybe you should be scared," Freya said.

"Maybe *you* should be. Wasn't that Herb Alexander you were talking with before? He is a dangerous man, Freya. What did he want?"

"Look, he is part owner of one of our horses. I have to talk to him."

"About what?" I inquired, still trembling with pent-up

aggression.

"Oh, we exchanged opinions on Derby hats. Salmon seems to be the in color this year."

Just then the band struck up a tango.

"Let's dance," she said.

As she marched me onto the floor, I thought, Oh, God, this is going to be a disaster. I admired the tango's acrobatic moves and melancholic flavor, but I was no Antonio Banderas. Fortunately, Freya was a great dancer with a keen sense of rhythm and feather-light on her feet. I followed her in a close embrace.

"That was fun," Freya said, after all the fancy lifts, kicks, and drops.

"No, fun is climbing Mt. Everest. That was scary."

"Was it really as bad as all that?" she purred and rubbed herself up against me, which made up for it, as far as I was concerned.

As we sipped our drinks, I overheard snatches of conversations all around us ranging from tourists who clogged everything up to the Derby itself. One self-proclaimed savant, who'd worn a path to the bar, laid odds that this year's super horse, Cat Chaser, would lose.

"I'll take that bet. Say $100?" said a silver-haired executive type.

When his wager was declined, he turned to Freya with a superior little smile. "No guts, no glory. Didn't we meet here last year? You're a veterinarian, I believe."

Freya smiled. "I'm impressed you remembered."

"Or maybe you're just that memorable," he said.

Freya glanced at me. "What do you think, Jim?"

"Oh, I agree with him."

The Man With The Good Memory asked, "Do you think Cat Chaser will live up to his billing?"

"I'm rooting for Speckled Band. He hasn't won yet as a three-year-old. He looked better in the Louisiana Derby back in March, but he still finished out of the money. That was a mile and an eighth, though, not a mile and a quarter like the Derby. Speckled Band has yet to prove he can go the Derby distance, but if he should win there'll be a big payout."

"Would you bet on him?" asked The Man With The Good Memory.

"Sure. Why not?"

Before he could come up with another question, I dragged her away. That was the problem with beautiful women. Men were drawn to them. We left the hotel and went to her home, where we immediately went to her bedroom and rumpled a perfectly pressed set of sheets.

—

I rolled over, sweating, savoring the pungency of our coupling, and stared dreamily at the ceiling fan's ticking blades. When I looked over, I discovered Freya's eyes fixed on mine.

"Is there something you'd like to tell me?" she asked.

"Like what?"

"I don't know. You seem to have something on your mind."

"Okay, one. Were you and Herb Alexander really discussing Derby hats? Two. I'm out of here at midnight for a meeting. And three, I was thinking that I'd like to paint you."

"One, yes, we were. Two, what meeting? Does it concern the case? And three, I'd love for you to paint me."

Ignoring points one and two, I said, "I'd like to paint you right here on this bed just the way you look right now, with your eyes half-closed and your bare skin beaded with perspiration. You're so damn beautiful. But I'm afraid I'll never do you justice."

She didn't smile, didn't move for a couple of beats. Then she beckoned me toward her. I felt the firmness of her breasts once more as I kissed her. We started unhurriedly but soon caught fire again.

—

The pinging I heard was not my heart but my phone. I fished it out of my pants pocket and glanced at the time. It was 11:30. I was going to be late for my meeting unless I hustled. The text was from Mario, who said he'd finally opened Whitlow's mini flash drive. I texted him back, telling him to send it, and, elated, stepped into the bathroom.

"Jim!" Freya called. "Where are you going?"

"Nowhere. Be right back." I clicked on a screen icon, and a number of folders appeared. I opened one:

CHEATERS

This book is about cheaters. I've been investigating and researching the subject. I know what's going on. I know who some of the biggest cheaters in horse racing are, and you might be surprised to find some of them are right here at Churchill Downs. I've got the facts. I've got the figures. Numbers don't lie. Some horses win when they should, some don't. Some horses lose when they should, while others win when they shouldn't. And some horses die when they shouldn't.

Three years ago, I started listing long shot winners and odds-on favorites who lost at selected tracks, along with injuries and deaths of horses. The statistics on some trainers, jockeys, and owners fell out of the normal ranges. Some of their names seldom appear on my list. Some names appear sometimes. And some names appear all too often.

The latter are the cheaters. If you want to know who they are, buy the book.

Returning to the bedroom, I started gathering up my clothes.

"What are you doing?" Freya sat up.

"I have a secret midnight meeting, remember?"

"Who was that?"

I didn't want to tell her. But I didn't want to ruin a great night, either. "That was Mario, my hacker." I stepped into my pants.

"It must be really important for him to call you now, in the middle of the night."

"Look, I like you a lot. But this is business. And it's confidential." I buttoned up my shirt.

"I understand. You don't trust me."

"Come on."

"No, it's fine. Don't let me hold you up."

Without answering, I put on my socks and shoes. She turned away. And I could feel our connection slipping away with her.

"All I can tell you is that this text could blow the case wide open. Now I have to go."

"Wait." She uncovered herself and slipped out of bed. "Thanks for telling me that."

"Don't mention it to anyone."

"I won't"

I started to go, but she pulled me back. "I really like you, too."

Leaving her was harder than expected. It required a supreme effort of will. I didn't know if I'd ever be able to do it again.

—

A thin slice of moon broke through the clouds as I circled Sandy Diaz's block, my headlights reflecting off the windshields of parked cars. I saw no pedestrians out on the streets, and any pre-Derby parties remained muffled and well-hidden. I kept my speed steady to avoid attracting attention, especially when I drove by Sandy's modest home. But I needn't have bothered. The place was devoid of lights or any other signs of life. It was either empty or everyone inside was asleep.

I parked down the block across the street at the curb, under a forty-foot maple, killed the engine, and cranked down the windows. If I went up to the door and knocked, no telling what I'd be walking into. From this spot, though, I could safely surveil the Diaz property, including porch and yard.

It was 12:02, according to my dash clock. As stillness filled the air, I leaned back into the upholstery and settled in. Sandy Diaz had chosen the place and time. I wondered where the hell she was. After a while, I opened Whitlow's files. My eye fell upon an article written by a well-known member of *The Sporting Press:*

CODE OF SILENCE

Fraud has always been a problem for thoroughbred horse racing because, unlike other sports, racing's survival depends on gambling. Many people can fix a race, including owners, trainers, vets, and jockeys. A favorite method is doping horses on race day. The cheaters rationalize this practice as helping the horse. Everyone in the sport knows what's going on but won't talk about it openly.

Whitlow had typed, "It's not considered cheating if you don't get caught."

Still no names. I imagined him prowling the backside in search of informants, noting them in his small spiral notebook with a cheap ballpoint pen. I read on. At 12:07, I put the phone down and listened. Nothing but the muted sounds of distant traffic. I rubbed my eyes and yawned.

Bam! bam! bam!

Something stung my forehead like a wasp bite. A whining ricochet told me otherwise and I dropped below window level as another one zinged off the hood. Somebody was shooting at me. Stunned, I walked my fingers up to my hairline. Blood was coursing over my forehead and into my eyes. I grabbed my .45 from the glove box but immediately ran into a problem—I couldn't shoot right-handed without sticking my head out the window. Since that would make me too easy a target, I shifted the gun to my left hand and fired at the continuing muzzle flashes. I squeezed off four rounds, spacing them a couple seconds apart, aiming low to avoid collateral damage.

In response, a spray of gunshots peppered my car from the right, spider-webbing the windshield and telling me the shooter was moving. Hoping to get lucky, I raised my head and shot twice at where I thought he'd be.

The return fire told me he was not there.

The extra ammo in the trunk was no good to me now. I was down to my last two bullets. Firing from this position would make it hard to hit what I was aiming at, especially with blood in my eyes. I sat up straight and switched to a two-hand grip and shot twice through my own windshield. Didn't know if I'd hit him, but bullets stopped whizzing by. Even half-blinded by my blood, I saw someone splashing through a pool of moonlight, gun held out as his or her side—I couldn't be sure which. Seconds after the figure rounded the corner of Sandy's house, I heard a car door slam and an engine start up.

No sooner had I keyed the ignition and shifted into reverse than I felt a thump that told me I had a punctured front tire and wasn't going anywhere soon. I had lost a lot of blood already and would soon pass out unless I acted quickly. Mopping my eyes, I fumbled my seat belt loose and took off my T-shirt. I tied it around my head, then waited for help. Someone must have heard the noise, but they did not come out to see what had happened. Someone called 911, though, because I heard sirens approaching as I slipped into unconsciousness.

FRIDAY

23

"Can you ID the shooter?"

I was snuffling in Brownfield's office at the Edison Center, which despite a ban on tobacco use reeked of cigarette smoke. It had been dark out when I left the hospital, but now as I stared at my reflection in the window, daylight was leaking into the sky and my forehead was half-covered by a massive bandage.

"I'm fine, Leo. Thanks for asking."

Brownfield grunted. He had loosened his collar and tie and rolled up his sleeves as if he expected this interview to last a while.

"The shooter?" he asked again.

"I couldn't see his face. Or hers. Could have been either a man or a woman, but I think it was a guy. Medium height and build. Wore a gray hooded sweatshirt, jeans, and a ball cap with the brim pulled down." It was a description that might have fit almost anyone. "Sorry. I know it's not much. Best I can do."

"Any witnesses?"

"None that I saw."

"Nobody has come forward, either."

"What about the 911 caller?" I asked.

"Used a burner."

"Have you canvassed the neighborhood?"

"Of course. Got nothing. Tell me again about this secret midnight meeting that didn't happen."

We had already been over this several times, but coppers live for inconsistencies. I told it again. How I was waiting outside the house of Sandy Diaz, who was a hotwalker for thoroughbred trainer Keene Kessinger and had information pertinent to the Felipe Rojas murder investigation.

"Why not talk to her at the track?" Brownfield asked.

"Don't think she wanted to be seen talking with me."

"I wouldn't, either."

"Screw you, Brownfield."

"Could she have been the shooter?"

"It's possible, but I don't know why she'd want to shoot me."

"You said you'd cost her husband his job."

"Yeah, but I don't think that was it."

"Well, what was *it?*"

"Something else. Maybe I was getting too close and spooked someone."

Brownfield tilted his head back and wearily pinched the bridge of his nose. "Tell me about this pertinent information she had concerning the Rojas investigation."

"Sandy was having an affair with Rojas."

"What?" He handled the surprise smoothly—if you didn't count leaping to his feet and yelling. "How long have you known this?"

"Only since yesterday."

"And when were you planning to let me in on it?"

The truth—which in this case definitely would not set me free—was not until I had solved the murder, and then only if I had to. But the truth is often a casualty in an investigation, where the ends outweigh the means.

"As soon as I talked to her," I lied.

Brownfield started pacing while giving me a vicious look as if there were invisible bars between us that were keeping him from tearing me apart. "How did you find out?"

"I've suspected it for some time."

"If Rojas was going back to his wife, then the Diaz woman had a motive for killing him," Brownfield said.

"Right, but her jealous husband could have killed him, too. Except for one thing. They were together at the time, so they are each other's alibi."

"Ah, Christ." Brownfield shook his head, fuming. "Do you see any connection with Whitlow's murder?"

"No," I said. Since I wasn't supposed to have the flash drive, I couldn't very well share what I'd learned from it.

Brownfield sat back down. "Okay, but at least we've learned something. Who else knew about your meeting?"

"Only my client and my date."

"Sounds like one of them must've set you up. I'll need some names."

I didn't want to believe it. I hated giving up the information. But I couldn't keep Carlos' identity confidential anymore.

"Sandy could have done it, and she's the only one who knew where and with whom I was meeting. Carlos Rojas and Freya Hall, who I was with earlier in the evening, both knew that I had a midnight meeting, but that's all they knew."

"What if one of them followed you?" Brownfield asked, tugging on his ear lobe like Humphrey Bogart playing Philip Marlowe.

A possibility I had not considered.

"Which one of them wants you dead the most—and why?"

"Neither of them. Why would Carlos hire me if he didn't want his father's murder solved?"

"I'd say that question answers itself," Brownfield smirked.

"Very funny. As for Freya, well, she just wouldn't do it."

"Because she *likes* you?"

"That's right, damn it."

"Then who shot you?"

"Like I said—someone must be afraid I'm getting too close to the truth."

We went over it all again but got nowhere. After impounding the Mustang and confiscating my .45 as evidence, he finally let me go. I called an Uber to take me to the airport, where I rented an anonymous gray subcompact and drove it to Mario's. He lived in a shotgun house in Schnitzelburg, an old German neighborhood three miles southeast of downtown.

"I trust you deleted all the files from your computer?" I said as I exchanged money for the flash drive.

"What am I, an idiot? Why hang on to something guaranteed to bring me trouble?" Mario replied.

"What makes you think it would cause you trouble?"

"My crystal ball."

"How much of it did you read, Mario?"

"Only enough to do my job, and I've already forgotten that."

"Wise answer, young hacker."

I left him and went back to the track.

24

I was looking for Sandy, but she found me first, outside Kessinger's stables.

"We need to talk." She stared at the bandage on my forehead.

"Why didn't you meet me last night?"

"Inside," she nodded toward the barn.

I followed her into the tack room. And repeated the question.

"There was a problem. Juan has not been staying with us. But he showed up shortly before we were supposed to meet. He was a mean drunk. I had to take my daughter away. We went over to a friend's where she could spend the night. By the time I got back, the cops were all over our street. I couldn't deal with them. I left again. It was late before I could go home. That's why I missed you."

As alibis go, it wasn't bad. I could easily verify it. After telling her what had happened outside her house, I said, "You didn't shoot me, did you, Sandy?"

"Shoot you?" she said. "Seriously?"

"Very."

"Why would I do that?"

"To keep me quiet about your affair with Felipe Rojas perhaps."

"Who the hell told you I had an affair?"

"Your friend Daniela Torres. Did you?"

Sandy picked up a curry comb. She'd probably used it a thousand times. Now it was just something to cling to. "Not your business. But I swear on my daughter's life that I didn't shoot you. Whoever did, I want them caught."

"You're saying you don't know who?"

"Yeah, that's what I'm saying."

"Come on, Sandy. You got to have some suspicions. Give me something. A name."

She put the comb down, said nothing.

"Did you tell anyone else you were meeting me?" I asked.

"No. Did you?"

"Could it have been your husband? You said he was there and mean drunk. Think he shot at me?"

"Juan?" she laughed, with an edge. "Why would he want to shoot you?"

"He's jealous. Maybe he jumped to conclusions last night after seeing me outside your house." I could buy it, based on his erratic behavior this afternoon, but I doubted he was a good shot.

"Juan doesn't have a gun."

"It's not hard to get hold of one. But let's talk about Felipe. If you want his killer caught, like you say, then help me by answering my questions."

"I'm trying."

"Do you still deny having had the affair? I'm going to find out, one way or another. You might as well tell me now."

"It just happened." She exhaled deeply and took her head in hand. "It was three years ago. We were both lonely. Juan was drinking too much. We had financial problems. I wanted to leave him, but we had no money. When Felipe saw how miserable I was, he reached out. He was always kind to me, made me feel good instead of like I was nothing."

"But he was planning to bring the rest of their family here. He wouldn't go to all that trouble just to dump his wife, would he? Where did that leave you? Wouldn't that give you a motive to kill him?"

Chin in the air, Sandy Diaz looked down her flat nose at me. "First, I try to shoot you, then I murdered Felipe? Who else have I killed? Kennedy? John Lennon? Let me spell it out for you. I—Did—Not—Kill—Anyone."

I'd heard many lies. This didn't sound like one. "Okay, let's say I believe you. Make me understand."

"I truly loved Felipe. He was the only one. I would never have done anything to harm him. Once his wife was safely out of Guatemala, he was going to divorce her."

"Then why bother to bring her here when it was so expensive?"

"Because Felipe was a man of honor. Things were terrible in Guatemala and she might have been killed. She still might."

"Where did he hope to get the money to do all this?"

Sandy shook her head and sobbed, "I don't know."

"You didn't ask him?"

"Sometimes it is better not to."

She could have been right about that.

She said she had to get back to work. Leaving her in the barn, I headed for my car. Sandy seemed to believe Felipe was going to divorce his wife for her. Ergo, no motive. She also denied trying to kill me. And if she had not killed Felipe, why should she? But somebody had. And they might try again. I kept one eye on my rear-view.

When I arrived at home, I entered cautiously but found no one lurking there. I took out the double-barrel scattergun from the gun safe, broke open the action, and checked the load. I liked the fact that it was descended from the kind used by stagecoach guards in the Old West. I also liked that all you had to do to fire it was to cock the hammers and pull the trigger. I held it ready as I swept the rest of the property for any signs of a prowler. There were none. I came back in and locked all the doors and windows. I put the shotgun away but took my back-up .38 from a low bedside table drawer and kept it handy.

Despite needing sleep, I put on a pot of coffee and showered while it brewed. I re-bandaged my wound and got dressed in jeans, a plum-colored T-shirt, and a charcoal sport coat. I carried my coffee cup into the living room and switched on the TV. After a few local stories aired, a shot of Keene Kessinger appeared on-screen. A crawl across the bottom read, "Breaking News. Police arrest two men in fatal beating. One is Derby favorite's trainer." As I turned up the sound, the trainer's image was replaced by one of Cat Chaser.

"Racing fans and Churchill Downs officials are in shock this morning after Derby Week was marred by murder for the second straight year. But unlike last year's killing, which remains unsolved, this time an arrest was made. In a stunning development, Louisville police charged two men, well-known trainer Keene Kessinger and farrier J.T. Young, with the murder of tip sheet publisher Wyatt Whitlow."

The reporter went on to say that Kessinger and Whitlow had been in a fistfight on the track earlier this week. Crime scene investigators said their fingerprints matched those found on the alleged murder weapon found in Kessinger's stable. After both men entered not guilty pleas, they were released on one hundred thousand dollar bonds.

I switched off the TV.

Surprised that both men had been granted bail, I wondered if their movements had been restricted, such as requiring them to surrender their passports or not leave Kentucky until trial. I was also curious about whether Kessinger, obviously worth millions, had paid for Young's release, as well as his own. If so, this might be interpreted as his way of keeping an alleged accomplice quiet rather than a generous and loyal gesture. The phone rang. It was Harriet Anderson, an old friend, and a top-notch lawyer.

"It's nice to hear your voice," she said.

"Yours, too, Harriet."

Although we had not seen each other in six months, Harriet was never much for small talk. She got right to it, saying that she needed my help. Could I take on a new case? How could I afford not to, when I barely was able to cover last night's emergency room bill? Besides, I owed her.

"Good. Come by my office. I'll tell you all about it."

—

Too Tall John, Harriet's six-foot-seven-inch receptionist, showed me into her office. I was always surprised he was not yet in the NBA. Harriet seemed drawn to tall people and objects—case in point, her office sat on top of the National City Tower. When she saw me, she swept around her desk to examine my bandage.

"What happened to you?"

"Got shot." I told her how it had happened.

She advised me to duck the next time.

I told her she looked great. Not an idle compliment, either. She appeared younger than her years. Not so much a matter of style as attitude. She was a high-powered lawyer and dressed like one—conservative and traditional. It was clear she had not picked her clothing with the intention that they become a conversation point. Today's gray suit was not too short. It had heels and a ruffled blouse that showed no more than standard courtroom cleavage. Not exactly dull, but not flashy, either.

"How's Sarah?" she asked.

I told her my daughter was still in Vegas with her mother. "Haven't seen her for a while. How's Woody?" Harriet's husband—who I had never liked—owned a string of radio stations.

"Woody's fine. Are you seeing anyone?"

Still looking out for me. "As a matter of fact, yes, I am."

"Do I know her?"

"Wouldn't surprise me if you did. Doctor Freya Hall?"

"M.D. or Ph.D.?"

"DVM. She's an equine veterinarian I met through the case I'm working."

"You're already on an investigation. That murdered groom?"

"You're well-informed."

"I'm representing Keene Kessinger and J.T. Young in the Wyatt Whitlow murder."

"Ah," I said.

"I need you for reasons almost too numerous to list. You are an experienced investigator, someone I can trust, and as it happens, you are already involved. You identified the victim's body. I was told by Lieutenant Brownfield that you were already poking around, so I thought might as well keep it among friends."

"Leo's not exactly my friend."

"Mine, either. Want the job?"

I said I was a little worried about having a conflict of interest. We both knew that under Kentucky law, a licensed private investigator could not accept an assignment if it meant that the P.I. would find it "difficult to devote himself with loyalty and singleness of purpose to the best interest of his client or employer."

"Never quote the law to a lawyer," Harriet said.

"I'd like to keep my license."

"Who's the lawyer around here, Jim?"

"You, Harriet. But if I become your agent, I'll have the same ethical obligations as you. Working for you could compromise my work for Carlos Rojas. By hiring me, you might have some ethical exposure yourself."

"Let me worry about that," she said. "I don't see a problem unless my clients are guilty. They say they're not. Based on the evidence so far, they will never be convicted. I believe we're on solid ground."

I didn't feel quite as confident as she did, but she offered to pay my standard rate and retainer. And working for her and a rich trainer like Kessinger might well open some doors previously closed to me.

"I'll have to discuss this with my client before I can give you an answer," I said.

"Fine, but don't dally. Time waits on no man, and neither do I."

She asked me to meet her this afternoon on the backside.

—

I phoned Carlos from my office to update him on the changing situation.

"A private investigator cannot be paid by more than one client for conducting the same investigation," I said, quoting the law, more or less, "unless all the interested parties consent in writing after full disclosure."

"I'm not paying you. What's the problem?"

"I guess there isn't one. But it's wise to be careful when dealing with the law."

"Seems only fair you get something out of this."

"I appreciate that. I'll bring you a contract to sign."

As I hung up, I realized there was another problem. No way could I tell Harriet about the tainted evidence on Whitlow's flash drive—or how I had come by it, namely, by risking both my license and my liberty—without jeopardizing her case. Eventually, I'd have to come up with another explanation for how I knew what was on the flash drive. In the meantime, though, I needed to ditch it along with my phone.

Doing so would be hypocritical as hell, especially after railing at Carlos about withholding possible evidence from me. But after all Whitlow's hard work, it would be a shame if his investigation was thrown out on a technicality. Maybe the flash drive would resurface after this was all over, thanks to an anonymous tip.

25

I drew up the full disclosure forms indicating that I was working for both Carlos Rojas and Harriet Anderson. Then I resumed reading Whitlow's exposé. So far, he had not backed up his suppositions about race fixing with any solid facts or figures. Also, everything on the drive seemed arranged haphazardly. I chose a folder and a file at random. It was written in *The Late Mail* publisher's trademark sarcastic style, but it turned out to have an uncommonly serious purpose. Whitlow was searching for a way to prove that "massive" cheating went on in horse racing. He'd found out about it, he claimed, while "doing a little light reading" in *The Congressional Record.*

According to the *U.S. Senate Hearing on Medication and Performance-Enhancing Drugs in Horse Racing,* conflicting testimony had been given. But the more credible witnesses, in Whitlow's opinion, had testified that horse racing in the U.S. was currently plagued by consistent cheating, mostly by administering drugs illegally.

"And we're not talking about the legal stuff everybody uses

like Lasix or Bute," Whitlow wrote. "We're talking about designer drugs made from stuff like snake venom and—no kidding—South American frog skin. Then there are 'milkshakes,' potent and undetectable drug cocktails made by combining legal medications."

Whitlow said this testimony was contradicted, however, by witnesses representing the Horsemen's Benevolent and Protective Association (HBPA), a trade association of racehorse owners and trainers. According to HBPA, more than 99.8 percent of all trainers did not cheat or dope their horses.

"Anyone who believes *that*," Whitlow wrote, "probably also believes in Santa Claus. And I have a bridge over the Ohio River I'd like to sell them."

Whitlow cited an undercover investigation of one of horse racing's largest and most successful operations, which reported that a trainer and his assistant had administered drugs to horses for non-therapeutic purposes. Also, that a jockey had shocked horses into running faster with an electrical device. The evidence collected by People for the Ethical Treatment of Animals—PETA—included seven hours of video footage showing how often injections and tranquilizers were administered to horses.

In an interview with a major television network, the trainer had denied all accusations. Later, the Kentucky Horse Racing Commission cleared the accused, and no further action was taken.

Nevertheless, an estimated twenty-four racehorses died each week on American racetracks, according to Senate testimony. The calculation came from a comprehensive review of official racing charts, Whitlow said. The Senate report proposed that every horse leaving the track be examined by a regulatory veterinarian. That way, a database of records would exist to help curb the danger.

This proposal was what had given Whitlow an idea of how to prove the amount of cheating that was going on. He would create a database of his own, based on information from *The Daily*

Racing Form and other sources. In it, he'd list racing results for the last three years from a few selected tracks, covering various horses, jockeys, trainers, owners, and veterinarians. Also, times, track conditions, and odds.

Whitlow was only interested in researching three categories: long shots who won, odds-on favorites who lost, and horses injured or killed. The third category was less exact since records of injury and breakdowns were only noted at the track. Since no reporting was required or available at off-track sites, I figured he must have put considerable sweat and effort into that one, possibly through some network of contacts he'd developed for just that purpose. He'd cross-referenced all his data on spreadsheets.

That was the end of the file.

I opened another, where Whitlow's database began. It went on for dozens of pages and must have contained hundreds, perhaps thousands, of raw entries that continued right on up to this week. But that's all they were.

On another file, I found the spreadsheets. This was where it got interesting. Most results fell into the normal expectations range: some long shots came in, some favorites tanked, and only a few horses were injured or died. This group Whitlow dubbed "the HBPA's 99.8 percent." Actually, a much lower percentage, of course.

Fewer fell into the more than expected range with significantly larger numbers. Whitlow called this group the "fancy dancers."

Finally, there was the way more than expected range, where the numbers proved shocking. Whitlow called this group simply the "cheaters." The latter group's results seemed to support Whitlow's thesis about widespread illegality. But the biggest eye-opener for me was a newspaper story:

Jockey Segura hurt after horse collapses

Hallandale Beach, Florida (AP)—Jockey Francisco Segura was injured when the horse he was riding at Gulfstream Park racetrack collapsed and died immediately after winning the "Sunshine Millions Stakes." Racetrack officials say three-year-old Quicksilver, a 35-to-1 long shot, suffered an apparent fatal heart attack following the race Saturday. Segura was thrown off the horse, then lay motionless for several minutes before being fitted with a neck brace and taken by ambulance to a hospital. Segura's agent, Ken Fowler, says the 36-year-old jockey suffered a fractured vertebra in his neck and a "stinger" to the left shoulder and arm. He says Segura will remain in the hospital overnight, but doctors expect a full recovery. Segura suffered no paralysis or other broken bones, Fowler says. "It looks like we dodged a bullet." Post-race tests detected no illegal substances in Quicksilver's blood.

I remembered meeting Segura after Carlos had introduced us. The jockey had been on a long losing streak and was having trouble getting mounts. I looked in the trainer column and found Ned Ericson's name listed.

The vet was Dr. F. Hall.

No, not the same Dr. Hall who told me that everything given to the horses, even legally, was used to make them run faster and win, sometimes even at the risk of their death. Not my Freya Hall. She couldn't be involved—couldn't be responsible for this horse's death.

My phone rang. I picked it up. Freya.

"I was just thinking about you...and last night," she said.

"Me, too." It wasn't a lie.

A throaty laugh. "What are you doing?"

"What private investigators do."

"And what's that, I wonder? Chase blondes?"

"Investigate. And I prefer brunettes."

"I know one who'd like to see you."

"I'll see you later on the backside."

—

By noon, I had finished with the flash drive and made a few

assumptions. I believed Whitlow had put everything he knew
on the flash drive. The last entries were up to date. And it made
little sense to only hide part of what he'd learned in a hollow
cork. I figured that I now knew whatever Whitlow had known.
He didn't have enough evidence to go public, or he would have
done so.

In the case of Quicksilver, the post-race tests had detected no
illegal substances in the horse's blood. That was it, as far as the
stewards were concerned. The Ericson horse's untimely death
was an act of God, an unfortunate accident in a dangerous sport
where many racehorses were dying all the time. The only reason
to suspect wrongdoing in the matter was the big payout. Still, I
couldn't help wondering why Freya had neglected to mention
Quicksilver's death to me. Perhaps she was embarrassed that
one of her horses had died. Or maybe she felt it was irrelevant
to my investigation.

Whitlow's study had rated the Ericson stable in the normal
range, meaning only a few of their horses had ever been injured
or died while racing. That was significant. When Whitlow had
tried to follow up, nobody wanted to believe that a horseman
with Ned Ericson's sterling reputation would risk his horse's life
to cheat. Nevertheless, healthy horses didn't just suddenly die
for no reason. And the temptation to rig a race always lurks in
the shadows. Quicksilver's untimely demise was bothersome. I
had to talk to Freya.

Half an hour later, I ran the gauntlet of snarled traffic on
Central Avenue and parked my rental on somebody's front lawn.
The temperature was hovering in the low fifties and there was a
threat of rain, but that did not dampen attendance. Many came
to the Downs wearing big hats and raincoats or plastic bags. I
wore a rain parka myself. When I arrived, Freya was watching a
groom bathe a sweaty horse. I called to her as the animal shook
off foamy water and steam rose from its back. She turned toward
me and smiled—until she saw my bandaged forehead.

"What's happened to you?" She came over and took my

hand.

"Somebody shot me last night."

"Oh, God. Are you all right?"

"I'll be okay. It's not as bad as it looks."

"You don't look okay. Come with me." She led me into a remote corner of the barn. "Does it hurt?"

"A little. Can't massage that one away, I guess, huh?"

"Maybe a different kind of therapy would work." She kissed me.

"You may be on to something there, Doc."

"Are you sure you're going to be okay?"

"Yeah. Unless they shoot straighter next time."

She grabbed the front of my shirt and bunched it up in her fist. "Don't joke about it."

"Why not? It's funny."

"It isn't. You think there'll be a next time?"

"I wouldn't give up that easily if it were me."

"Tell me what happened."

Leaning against the stall, I described the events after I pulled up outside Sandy Diaz's place.

"Was that who you were meeting? Why? And why there at that hour?"

"She didn't want to be seen talking to me," I said.

"I don't understand."

"I imagine she was afraid of becoming a target herself."

"You don't think she was the one who shot you?"

"Nobody else knew where the meeting was going to be held." Both Carlos and Freya had known about the meeting but not its location.

"What was this meeting about?" she asked, raising her eyebrows in query. Freya's hair had a golden gleam. Behind her was a brightly lit white stall with a bale of green hay in front.

"Sandy Diaz and Felipe Rojas had been romantically involved," I said.

"What? How do you know that?"

If she was acting surprised, it was an award-winning performance.

"You didn't know? Or even suspect?" I asked.

"I had no idea. What did you expect her to tell you?"

"Something that would put me on a path toward solving both murders."

"And did she?" Bright smile.

"Not really."

"What did she say?"

"That Felipe was honorable enough to bring his wife here for her protection. But that he also would leave her for Sandy."

"Honor," Freya scoffed. "What else did she say?"

"She denied killing anyone."

"Did you believe her?"

"That's hard to say."

"You seem uneasy. Is something wrong?"

"I need to discuss something else with you." I brushed a strand of hair away from her forehead. "It's about a horse, one of yours, that died suddenly right after winning a race three years ago."

"Quicksilver."

"Can you tell me what happened?"

"I don't see the connection, but sure. He had a congenital heart defect that never showed up until the race where he died. That's all we know."

"He was a thirty-five-to-one underdog, so there must have been a big payout." I let that hang in the air as a groom wearing a forest green top led a horse into a nearby stall full of golden hay. Taking Freya's elbow, I steered her away from the groom before adding, "The horse collapsing like that immediately after winning must have been a shock. Two shocks."

"It was. What are you implying?"

"I wondered if there was an investigation."

"No, he tested clean. Case closed."

"I admit I'm surprised you didn't bring up Quicksilver when

we were discussing how trainers and owners willingly abuse racehorses for profit."

"I don't believe this," Freya said, with a pinched expression. "I told you I took an oath not to harm the animals in my care. I didn't tell you about Quicksilver because it had nothing to do with anything you're investigating. After what we've been to each other, how could you?"

Eyes glittering, she turned and strode away. I watched her go, with a bitter taste in my mouth. The whitewashed walls appeared green in the odd pale light.

26

I walked down the shed row to Kessinger's barn, where I was supposed to meet Harriet Anderson. A guard let me in. I passed Cat Chaser standing quietly in his stall, ears perked, head rotating to keep from missing anything. A saddle was draped over him, along with a silk reading, "Kentucky Derby." On the wall behind him were three signs commemorating his trainer's Derby winners.

At the end of the double row of box stalls, I found Harriet Anderson in the trainer's office where she had set up a war room. Her briefcase lay open atop an old-fashioned leather blotter.

"Where are your clients?" I asked.

"Doing what trainers and blacksmiths do, I suppose. They'll be along. Here." She shoved a document across to me. "Take a look at this."

It was the forensic pathologist's report on the Whitlow murder. I quickly read through its analysis of the head wounds to Whitlow and Felipe Rojas. In both cases, "the cranial lesions were very typical," the report said. "Geometrical, square-shaped, same size as the tool. On the outer table of the skull, the edges of the wounds were sharp and regular. On the inner table, they were beveled and irregular. The bony penetration in the depressed fracture resulted from a rupture of the outer table of the bone under tension."

"Sounds like the two men have matching wounds," I said.

"I believe that's the pathologist's conclusion. Tends to confirm both victims were killed by the same hand."

"Brownfield agrees. He considers one of my clients the murderer, the other an accessory. But that won't hold up. The second hammer obviously was planted to frame them," I said.

"On the contrary, police claim it's open-and-shut." Harriet ticked off the evidence against them: "One, Kessinger and Whitlow despised each other, as shown by their recent fistfight. Two, Whitlow had damaged Young's professional reputation in an earlier tip sheet article. And three, Whitlow's killer was right-handed and strong enough to crush a human skull with one blow. The fatal blow's angle suggests that the killer was about the same height as my clients, both of whom are right-handed."

A point in Sandy Diaz's favor, since she stood only five-feet-five.

"The shoeing hammer found in this barn belongs to J.T. That explains why his prints are on it. He claims it was stolen recently. An identical hammer disappeared a year ago," Harriet said.

"Where's the first hammer?" I asked.

"I suspect that Brownfield has been holding it back all this time, hoping to trip up the killer."

"Your clients face double murder charges. Is the prosecution trying to plea bargain?" I asked.

"Whoever talks first gets a deal for a reduced sentence."

"Are they going for it?" I asked.

"I've strongly advised them against it."

A groom was holding up a water bucket so that the horse didn't have to bend over to drink as Kessinger and Young arrived unguarded. Good service here for horses and clients alike. I'd met both men before. Harriet made a point of introducing me anyway as their defense team's new private investigator.

"What happened to your head?" Kessinger said.

"I got shot last night while working another case."

"What other case?" He frowned.

"The Felipe Rojas murder."

"Who else are you working for?"

I told him. The cat was already out of the bag anyway.

"Ah, the hotwalker. What have you found out so far?"

"I'm afraid part of that's confidential."

"Confidential? If you won't tell me what you find out, why am I paying you?" He cocked an eyebrow at his attorney. "Harriet?"

"It's an ethical problem caused by the fact that he is representing more than one client in the same legal matter," she said.

"Well, how's that going to work, ma'am?" Young asked.

"Mister Guthrie will report to me on whatever is relevant to our case. Anything else stays with his other client."

"What if there's a conflict of interest? I don't want to be hung out to dry," Kessinger said.

"You won't be," Harriet said, reassuring but insistent. "All of our conversations will be covered by attorney-client privilege. Should a conflict arise, Mister Guthrie will immediately withdraw from the team."

Asked if they understood, her clients glanced at each other, shrugged, and nodded.

"Now we need your signatures to make it official." She provided a pen for them to sign the document.

"A lot is riding on this, Harriet. I hope you know what you're doing," Kessinger said.

"So do I," she said. "Now, gentlemen, Mister Guthrie needs your attention."

"Thanks, Harriet," I said. "I just have a few open-ended questions for you concerning your professional relationships, both with each other and with Wyatt Whitlow."

These men were not used to being accused criminals. They wanted me to believe in their innocence. I needed to not only confirm basic facts but also win their trust. Making an effort to do so, I leaned forward slightly as they talked, taking brief notes, and maintaining eye contact. I nodded when appropriate to let them know they had my full attention. This approach seemed to be working at first as their openness increased with each answer. That might change, of course, when the questions grew tougher. But it was a start.

Most of the information they provided was consistent with what I already knew. A competent farrier, Young had worked for the big-time trainer for years. Both men had disliked Whitlow for the stories he had written about them. Kessinger claimed to have been friends with Whitlow at one time, but as the trainer became more successful, he said the tip sheet publisher had turned on him for spite out of envy and professional jealousy. Young believed Whitlow hated him, too, but simply because he was associated with Kessinger.

"Mister Young, you say you're not surprised to find that your fingerprints are on the murder weapon since it belonged to you. But how would you explain the presence of Mister Kessinger's prints on the hammer, should they be found there?" I asked.

"The explanation is simple. Mister Kessinger is both a perfectionist and a hands-on trainer who likes to be involved in the everyday work with the animals. He was dissatisfied with Cat Chaser's shoes, so he borrowed my hammer to do it more to his liking," Young said, fidgeting.

"What about the other hammer—the one that went missing a year ago?"

"Same thing, probably," Young said.

"You're not sure?" I asked.

Less comfortable wielding words than hot iron, the farrier said, "I told you that Keene is hands-on. He might have done the same thing at another time with another horse. I mean, who remembers something like that?"

"Then you wouldn't be surprised if his prints were found on it, too?"

"Not at all."

The crotchety trainer glowered at Young, then at me. "Whose side are you on, Guthrie?"

"Yours, Mister Kessinger. The police are going to ask you these same questions. Knowing your answers will give me a head start."

"For all the good it will do," Kessinger snorted like one of his thoroughbreds.

"Have any other hammers gone missing?" I inquired.

Young shook his head.

"Where were you at the time of the murders?"

At home alone, both said. No alibis.

"How about Whitlow's accusations that you cheated?" I asked.

"I won't dignify that," Kessinger said, "except to say that Whitlow was a lying sack of shit."

"One more thing. How do you feel about Sandy Diaz?"

"What do you mean, how do I feel about her? She works for me," Kessinger said.

"Is she a good employee?"

"Why else would I have her around?"

"You fired her husband recently."

"So what? You're wasting time. None of my employees had anything to do with this."

"How do you know?"

"I know my employees. Leave Sandy and the rest out of it. Understand?"

Kessinger wanted me to leave his workers out of my investigation. Luke Ericson wanted me to leave out his father. Neither was going to be possible. "As always, I'll go where the facts lead me," I said.

"Anything else, Jim?" Harriet said.

"I need to talk to your Derby jockey. Can you arrange that?" I asked Kessinger.

"Didn't you hear what I just told you?" he fumed.

"Why do you need to talk to Humberto Herrera?" Harriet asked.

"Whitlow implied in his tip sheet that Herrera and Kessinger had cheated using buzzers."

"Another lie. Why should that matter now? Do you think I killed him for saying that?"

"The police might look at it as a possibility. I'm simply trying to learn as much as I can about people like Herrera who are involved in the case."

Kessinger grumbled but agreed to phone the jockeys' dressing room.

"Humberto's there now. He'll talk to you if you get over before his next race."

"I'm on my way."

I took the tunnel to the paddock, where the trainers gave the jockeys their final instructions before each race. It was where the horses were saddled, then paraded around, while above plaques of legends like Sea Biscuit and Whirlaway looked down upon them. As I went up the escalator to the nearby jockey's dressing room, the Derby's long history hit me like stiff a slug of bourbon.

While anyone could visit the paddock, few got by the Clerk of Scales, who was seated at his desk when I went in and showed him my pass. As if to emphasize the point, a handwritten sign was taped over the door: "Absolutely No Press Allowed." The clerk not only served as the dressing room's gatekeeper but also—as his title implied—was responsible for reporting the jockeys' correct weight before and after each race.

There was a lot of loud talk and laughter going on, which gave the place a raucous frat house atmosphere. And it smelled like a locker room, but with hints of leather and lemon-scented furniture polish. The so-called room was really a complex of rooms, each apparently full of short, fit men, some half-dressed in riding pants, others in mud-splattered silks, and still others wet-haired with towels around flat mid-sections.

When I asked for Humberto Herrera, the clerk pointed to a lounge area where a short lean athletic man sat smoking a cigarette. The big gray polka dots on the sleeves of his bright red silks announced that he rode for Kessinger's stables. Despite many years of racing experience, Herrera still looked youthful.

He stood up as I walked over to shake hands.

"I can't have anything either," he said when I declined his offer of food or drink. "Sweating off weight."

"I don't know how you manage," I said, aware that jockeys must weigh in, fully tacked, at no more than one hundred twenty-six pounds.

"Got to, if you want to ride." Herrera's smile revealed a gold canine tooth. "Part of the job, like working for free in the morning for trainers. You help them build a profile of their horse, figure out where to run, over what distance, which track, what race. Then they help you get mounts."

"I scratch your back, you scratch mine," I said, glad to find a talkative jockey.

"Exactly."

The room was noisy with a blaring television, a grinding treadmill, and valets talking loudly in Spanish while gathering around a table full of numbers in the room's center.

"I understand you're on the Derby favorite. What's that like?"

"It's good, man. It comes with a lot of pressure."

"No doubt. Look, I know you have a race coming up, so I'll cut to the chase. What can you tell me about the murder of Wyatt Whitlow?"

"What makes you think I can tell you anything?"

"Riding for Kessinger, you're bound to hear things most people don't. You know he's under suspicion of murder, right? Don't you want to help him?"

"Sure. Mister K's been good to me. He is no killer. Neither is J.T. The cops got it all wrong."

"Can you think of anything that might help clear them?"

As Herrera drummed on the chair's padded arms with the tips of his fingers, the valets continued to talk loudly while assembling saddles, whips, pads. Eventually, Herrera shook his head and blew out some smoke.

"Sorry," he said.

"Do you remember a horse called Quicksilver?" I asked.

Before he could answer, a valet interrupted, bringing him four pairs of clean goggles before drifting away again.

"Why do you need so many goggles?" I asked.

"You strap them on your helmet one pair on top of another. During the race, as one pair gets mud-splattered, you jerk it down to the next one, and then the next one, so you always have a clean lens to see through."

"Ah, detectives must see clearly, too."

He grinned, one old pro to another.

When I asked again if he remembered Quicksilver, Herrera said, "Yeah, I was at Gulfstream when that horse went down at the finish line."

"After the race, did you talk to the jockey who was riding him?"

Herrera nodded. "Francisco Segura. He said the horse ran his heart out."

"How well do you know Segura? Well enough to know if he cheated?"

"Are you kidding?" Herrera's eyes flicked upward.

"I'm asking you if the race was on the up and up, Humberto."

"Okay, jockeys," called the Clerk of Scales. "Seventh race."

"How should I know? I got to go now," Herrera said, saved by the bell. As he scrambled off, I added Segura to my list of people to see.

27

Libby Fontaine phoned as I left the building, asking for my help. Again. Chip Alexander had shown up out of the blue, drunk.

"I'm here at the church. I'm afraid he's going to frighten the children."

"I'm four blocks away. Hang on."

Five minutes later, I rushed into the sanctuary of Victory Kenwood Baptist Church to find Chip Alexander near the altar bellowing and shaking Libby by the shoulders.

"Hey!" I yelled.

Seeing me bounding up the center aisle toward them, Chip turned and shoved Libby aside. I had to sidestep her and when I did, he took a wild swing and clipped me, ripping the scab off my forehead. As coppery-tasting blood flooded into my mouth and my eyes, Chip tried to follow up his first punch with another. I could barely see it coming. Nevertheless, I feinted and, as he missed, struck him a hard body blow that doubled him over and drove him to his knees. Green-faced, he began puking all over the carpet while I dabbed at my forehead with a handkerchief to staunch the bleeding. When he finished emptying his guts, I twisted one arm up behind his back and forced him to his feet.

"Going to behave now?"

He managed to nod.

I asked Libby if she was okay. She said she was just shaken up.

"Want me to call the cops?"

She shook her head and asked what had happened to me.

I told her not to worry. It was a gunshot wound but I was okay. I wouldn't bleed to death. Meanwhile, all the fight had gone out of Chip. I shoved him onto a pew and said, "Stay there."

"Who shot you?" Libby asked.

"Not sure. It's a long story. Sorry about the mess."

"Not your fault." She glared at Chip, who was sitting there mewling. "His fault. I'll get the first aid kit and some cleaning supplies."

When she hurried off, I said, "What are you doing here, Chip?"

"Trying to convince her to go out with me," he said, rapidly blinking his eyes awhile sucking in a breath. "I like her."

I laughed. "Trust me when I say she doesn't like you. In fact, she can't stand you. Listen carefully. Stay away from Libby. If you bother her again, I'll hurt you. Understand?"

He nodded blearily.

"Now get out of here."

"What about my car keys?"

"I'll hang on to them for a while. Phone for an Uber and consider yourself lucky. Now get out of here."

He stumbled out the door. Libby reappeared a moment later carrying a bucket and a first aid kit.

"You look like the Red Cross and the fire brigade all rolled into one," I observed.

"Where's Chip?"

"I sent him home."

"Good. I couldn't find any carpet cleaner, so this will have to do. But first, let's take another look at that forehead of yours." She wiped away the blood with a piece of alcohol-soaked gauze, then applied a sterile bandage.

"Tell the church I'll pay to have it cleaned professionally," I said when she set about the carpet and pews.

"Don't worry about it," she said.

But I insisted.

"It was my own fault. I handled it poorly. Besides, it would be bad for business if word got around that a punk kid like Chip had shed my blood."

"Chip's father will probably sue you." Libby wrung out the sponge.

"He might. But remember that I didn't hit Chip until he hit me. I was a Good Samaritan coming to the aid of a fair damsel in distress. By the way, how come he found you here alone on a Friday afternoon?"

"I'm not really alone," Libby said.

Two of her friends were helping her in the classroom wing, she said. They could not hear the ruckus from way back there.

"How did he get in?" I asked.

"I let him in, I'm embarrassed to say. I thought he was someone else coming to help." She dipped the sponge back into the cleaning solution. "This is Oaks Day. Local public schools are closed. That means many elementary-age children whose parents work at the racetrack have nowhere else to go but here. I got them to let us use the learning center."

Once our makeshift cleanup was completed and my forehead re-bandaged, she wanted me to come and see her students' work. It seemed important to her, so I agreed.

"How are you and Carlos doing?"

"He's busy all the time at the barn. He comes over for his English lessons, then runs right back. We don't go out much because he never has any money. That doesn't bother me, but it bothers him. I really, really like Carlos. But I don't know if it's going to work out for us."

I was not anxious to put on my advice columnist hat, but what are you going to do? "He is under a ton of pressure right now, Libby. Got a lot on his mind. I think Carlos really likes you, too. Why not cut him some slack? I think it will all work out."

"You think so?" She sniffed.

"I do."

Maybe I was in the wrong line of work. Maybe I should trade my magnifying glass for a crystal ball.

In the classroom, a dozen kids were being supervised by two college-age women. The children were gathered around several large round tables supplied with sheets of drawing paper and red plastic mesh baskets full of crayons and colored pencils. Already many had made colorful drawings of animals. One long-braided, dark-eyed kid beamed when Libby praised her drawing.

"Look, Jim." Libby held it up for me.

"Is that a rhinoceros?" I asked.

"No, silly," said the girl.

"Then it must be a hippopotamus."

"*No*, it's a horse," she said.

"Oh. Are you a jockey?"

She rolled her eyes as if to say what a dolt I was. She reminded me of my own kid when she was that age. Feeling a lump in my throat, I wondered what Sarah was doing right now.

"What else do you like to do in school besides draw?" I asked.

"I like show-and-tell." She picked up a fresh crayon.

"You two seem close," I told Libby.

"We've been spending a lot of time together lately," she said. "She's Sandy's kid. I often watch her. Sometimes they both spend the night at my house."

"How come?"

"She and Juan aren't getting along."

"Did they stay with you last night?"

"Funny you should ask. Sandy brought Ana Lucia over just

before midnight. Said Juan had shown up causing trouble."

"How did Sandy get to your house?" Libby lived about ten miles from the Downs.

"She drove their old truck."

"What does it look like?"

"It's an old yellow Chevy pickup."

"Did Sandy stay with you all night? Or did she go back out again?"

"She left for about an hour. Why do you ask?"

"You asked how I got this." I pointed at my wound.

"You don't think that Sandy had something to do with you getting shot, do you?" Libby asked.

"I don't know."

"But why would she shoot you?"

"Time to go," I said, shrugging. "I'll show myself out. Let me know if there's any more trouble."

But trouble had already arrived.

Someone was outside yelling and pounding on the front door of the church. I recognized the voices. Chip had not followed my advice to call for an Uber. Now Herb was giving his son hell.

"Goddamn it, Chip, when are you going to start acting like a man? I can't keep fighting your battles for you forever."

"No, Dad."

I couldn't stomach any more of this. Flinging open the door, I stepped out onto the porch, forcing Alexander to backpedal.

"Why don't you knock it off, Herb? Haven't you bullied your son enough for one day?"

"I thought that was your department, Guthrie. Here you are again, sticking your nose in my business. I hope your health insurance is paid up."

Slipping off his fancy Brioni suit coat, he laid it on a step and moved smoothly toward me in a slight crouch. When he drew close, he screamed and wheeled to kick my legs out from under me. It had worked well for him the first time we met, but now I was ready and blocked his flashing foot. Pinning it with one leg,

I used my other to stomp on his toe. He screamed again, but this time in pain.

He hopped around on one foot for a while until I tripped him and gave him a shove. Then he fell and skidded across the concrete, ripping his knees, elbows, chin. When I let him get up, he tried to head-butt me. I dodged and rammed my fist into his nose three times. Down he went. It felt good to see him lying on his back for once instead of me.

I doubted that Chip saw it that way as he helped Herb into his car.

28

The ninth race was beginning when I returned to the backside. Ned Ericson had a horse in it, a chestnut colt with a black tail and mane named Thief of Time, which seemed ironic as its trainer was dying of cancer. Maybe that's why, despite the cloud of suspicion over the Ericson stable, I found myself rooting for the 5-to-1 shot.

"They're all in line and ready for the start—and they're off."

The crowd roared like MGM lions as the horses broke from the gate. I worked my way quickly through the crowd and squeezed into a guard rail slot in time to feel the thrumming and clacking of hooves as the horses swept past. Sadly, Thief of Time was sitting all alone in the last place as the racehorses reached the first pole.

I had not expected to find Ericson himself here among the hoi polloi when he could have been sharing an owner's box up in the grandstand. But there he was, not far from me, standing with a pair of binoculars on a trainers' observation platform ordinarily used during morning workouts. Of course, the deck was full of spectators now. Maybe Mister Ned preferred to play man of the people. Or perhaps he just didn't feel like walking all the way over there to the other side.

As the race continued up the backstretch, it was Hot Money, Poodle Springs, and Fire Lake leading the way. The rest of the field was bunched up, except for Thief of Time still bringing up the rear. Into the stretch, Poodle Springs had grabbed first place but suddenly Thief of Time began his charge. As the horses headed for home into the final furlong, it was Thief of Time closing fast on the outside.

"Coming to the finish line," said the announcer, "Poodle Springs and Thief of Time are neck-and-neck. And Thief of Time wins it by a nose."

I glanced up at the big board. It said the winner paid $10 on a $2 bet. When I turned to check out Ned Ericson's reaction, the old man was dancing a little jig and hugging everyone around him. Finished celebrating, he grabbed the banister and came down the steps with the steadiness of a much younger man. As he happily shook hands and answered shouted questions on the way toward his barn, I made my move, got there ahead of him, and in all the commotion slipped past the security guard inside.

Time to brace Mister Ned about Quicksilver, but first to congratulate him on Thief of Time's unexpected win.

"Thanks," he said, with a grin spreading over his face until he realized it was me.

"Mind if I have a word?"

His amiability faded, but not the color in his cheeks put there by the thrill of victory. "How'd you get in here?"

"Sorry, Ned," said the deputy upon his return. "I'll put him out."

"No, it's all right. He can stay."

"Whatever you say." The security man looked doubtful. "Congrats on the win."

The trainer turned to me, apparently noticing my wound for the first time. "What the hell happened to you, Guthrie?"

"Somebody shot me."

"Who?"

"I suspect it was someone who wants me to stop investigating the Rojas murder and its connection to a horse of yours named Quicksilver."

"Connection? What connection?"

"Look, we need to talk."

"All right." With a peremptory wave at me, Ericson nodded the way past the stalls where his thoroughbreds swished their tails while feeding. We sat down facing each other on plain wood chairs in his office. It had a comfortable, rustic feel. The room felt warm and humid.

"You asked about the connection between your horse and your groom's murder two years later," I said, getting right to the point. "Three years ago, as you know, Quicksilver collapsed and died on the track just beyond the finish line after winning a race way out of his class. There was a huge payoff since the odds against him winning were 35-to-1. Huge enough for some horsemen to question whether that race was honest."

"That's outrageous," he said, jaw clenched.

"Rumor has it that PEDs were involved. Maybe Rojas found out about it and needed to be silenced."

"Are you accusing me of murder, as well as race fixing?"

"Not accusing you, no."

"Who then?"

"You tell me," I said.

"Where did you get this crap about Quicksilver?"

"Wyatt Whitlow."

"Whitlow. That lying scumbag. Not to speak ill of the dead, but there was nothing to those rumors and nothing for Felipe to find out. My horse ran a good race. Tested clean afterward. You can't ask for more than that. Horses are like people. They die when their time comes. Just like yours and mine. That's all there is to it."

"I'm glad today wasn't Thief of Time's time."

"Now what are you implying?" Ericson stiffened as if to prepare for the next calamity.

"Only that if it happened once, it could happen again."

"It never happened, I told you. You're no horseman, Guthrie, but have you ever watched one die?"

"I have not and I'm glad of it."

"I remember Quicksilver winning that race like it was yesterday," Ericson said, visibly aging as he spoke. "I could see it in his eyes when he gave up. He died with his head on my knee. I wouldn't wish that on any horse or any human being. Quicksilver got no drugs from me, and I'll swear to that on a stack of Bibles."

Ironically a Bible reading came over the stable's loudspeakers. Most of it was drowned out by a fit of coughing and hacking by the old trainer.

Asked if he was okay, Ericson wheezed, "Okay? Who in the hell my age is okay? These old bones never lie. People complain when it rains or is too cold. But there's nothing like a major illness to change how you see life."

"How has it changed yours?" I squirmed a little, realizing I'd never before heard him allude, even obliquely, to his ongoing struggle with terminal cancer.

"Every day I wake up, I feel lucky," he said.

For a fleeting moment, I'd shared the hopelessness that I assumed a fatal illness must engender in the victim. But Ericson's gratitude and optimism in the face of almost certain death made me doubt my assumption. My assumptions. About a lot of things. I found his response so confusing and disarming that it became impossible—temporarily, at least—to push him as hard as my inner detective knew that I should.

And then Luke strolled in.

"You okay, Dad?"

"I am now," Ned said, breathing shallowly through his mouth.

Luke looked at me. "Hey, what happened to your head?"

"Somebody tried to kill me."

"Maybe you shouldn't go around getting everybody all riled up."

"Is that a threat?" Instead of ramming the Luke's words back down his throat, I wrapped up the interview, telling Ned that I hoped he'd feel better soon. I got to my feet and—with Luke dogging me like a border collie herding sheep—started for the barn door. I was ten feet from the exit when he said, "Hey."

"Something else you wanted?" I said, sick of him.

"What did you say to upset my old man?"

"I asked him a few questions, that's all."

"Regarding what?"

"Felipe Rojas' murder."

"Why bother him with that?"

"And the odd death of a horse named Quicksilver."

The statement seemed to alarm him, but he recovered quickly. "What are you talking about?"

"Rojas was the groom who took care of Quicksilver."

"So what? That horse died of natural causes. End of story."

"Not sure I buy that, Luke. You were in charge when the horse died, I believe."

"What does that prove?"

"And Freya Hall was your vet at the time."

"You got something to say, spit it out, Guthrie."

"You must have made a killing on Quicksilver. Or should I say *by* killing Quicksilver? A 35-to-1 shot just drops dead at the finish line? What people must have thought."

"Like I give a shit. You picked out one random day when the favorites all did poorly, and Quicksilver happened to run the race of his life. Who can say why? Maybe we got lucky."

"Plenty lucky, I'd say. How many thousands did you clear?"

"Our horse was underrated. Sure, I cashed some tickets on him. So what? No law against that."

"Unless you cheated."

Luke rolled his eyes as if he couldn't believe my stupidity.

"The horse was tested after the race. No illegal substances were found in his blood or urine. No jockey can throw a race without other jocks' cooperation. There were no such accusations. Ask yourself this. If it's so easy to cheat, why don't we do it more often?"

"Maybe you are. Or maybe you limit it to keep anyone from catching on. As far as cheating goes, not finding evidence of performance-enhancing drugs doesn't mean they weren't used, only that they were undetectable," I said.

"That's a laugh. You come in here with your unsubstantiated bullshit and make charges without having a shred of evidence. I've heard enough."

"Maybe there's more evidence than you realize."

"Then produce it. But you can't, can you? Because you got nothing, you prick. Quicksilver won fair and square, then he died of heart failure. It's sad, but all ancient history now anyway. Nobody cares, Guthrie."

"I think you'll find they do."

"If you repeat one word of this in public, I'll sue you. Now get the fuck out of here!"

—

My phone rang as I walked away. Harriet Anderson called to tell me the good news and the bad. Brownfield had dropped his bombshell at last. The police had the Rojas murder weapon all along. It was a farrier's hammer like the one used to kill Whitlow.

"Let me guess," I said. "The good news is that neither of your clients' fingerprints or DNA is on it. Otherwise, Brownfield would have arrested them long ago."

Harriet said I was right, something I never minded hearing.

"The bad news is that the hammers link the two murders," she said.

"But it's only circumstantial, the only physical evidence they've got. There's no witness to testify having seen the crime committed. It won't stick," I said.

"Be sure and tell the jury that. As you know, most criminal convictions are based on circumstantial evidence, so long as it is adequate to meet established standards of proof."

"Look, we both know that the prosecution's case is weak," I said. "Yes, Kessinger and Whitlow disliked each other enough to have a comical public fistfight. But that is a far cry from lying in wait with a hammer in an alley. Who is dumb enough to leave the murder weapon on his own property where it's sure to be found?"

"Police will point out that perps panic and make dumb mistakes. And they're right, sometimes they do. That's good stuff for my opening statement, but I didn't hire you for that. I need proof. Do you have any for me?"

"I have a theory, but you can't use it."

"Less than nothing, in other words," she sighed. "Let's hear it."

"What if I told you that both murders were connected to fixing a horse race?"

"How? And do you have any proof to support that?"

I summarized my suspicions about Quicksilver.

"But racehorses die all the time, don't they? Dozens of them at Santa Anita alone. Besides, you've already said I can't use your theory. Why bother to tell me at all?"

"So, you'll know I'm doing something meaningful on your dime. I am, but I need more time."

"And I need something quick. Remember, your job is not to prove anything about race fixing. Your job is to help me defend my clients from murder charges."

"I'm doing that."

"Do it faster," she said and hung up.

29

A band of orange and copper clouds hovered on the horizon as I hit River Road heading homeward. Both tonight and tomorrow, everyone in town would be partying, from high-end celebrity galas for charity to basic backyard garden variety bashes thrown for friends and family. I'd been invited to one myself by Clive. But elegance, southern charm, and the best of Louisville weren't for me. I had been in crowds of elegantly dressed drunks all day and was tired of talking to people.

Nevertheless, by the time I got home, my block was bumper-to-bumper with expensive cars and pop music was blaring out from my neighbor's open windows and doors—sure signs that the Derby Eve celebration was already in full swing. There would be food, cocktails, a special bourbon drink perhaps, plus live music later on by Somebody Or Other. Proceeds would benefit a worthy cause.

I entered my house and carefully went room to room, making sure nobody else was there. The air had grown thick and oppressive as if a storm might be coming. I hoped so—anything to reduce the sticky heat was welcome. Before showering, I went around opening all the windows. Afterward, I applied alcohol to my wound, changed into my standard cutoffs and T-shirt, and went to the kitchen to make myself a whiskey sour.

I was sipping it while swinging on the porch when Clive turned up for a drink. He arrived with great panache—in a pastel blazer printed with red roses and pale green stems, tailored shorts, a matching bowtie, and a black Victorian top hat last seen on Masterpiece Theatre. He plunked himself into the cane-backed rocker and helped himself to a double shot of a little known ninety proof, plus lemon juice and simple syrup from the icy cocktail shaker.

"Ah. Smoother than a reverse-mortgage salesman's pitch, but without the hangover," he said. "You look..." I began, but words failed me.

"You're pretty underwhelming yourself. What on earth's happened to your head?"

I explained.

"Jeepers criminy almighty. You are in a damn dangerous business, you know that?"

"Maybe I like living dangerously."

"Better than being bored, I suppose."

Maybe boredom was why Clive had an extravagant waxed mustache and goatee, brassy curls creeping over his ears and hanging down the back of his neck. In the rapidly diminishing twilight, I realized that he looked like a poet, or a clever alley cat, dressed up for the ball. But he kept asking such pertinent questions.

"Who might want you dead?" he asked.

"Someone trying to keep me from solving two murders, I imagine."

"Two, is it now?" Clive raised his glass in a toast. "'Best while you have it use your breath, there is no drinking after death.' Sláinte."

Of course, he wanted to hear all about the investigation—

and already had formed his own theories based on mystery novel conventions.

"How about your client as the murderer? That happens all the time in books," he said.

"Do you seriously think Carlos could have killed his father, especially after being rescued by him from Guatemala?"

"Stranger things have happened."

"But if Carlos had already gotten away with it, why would he rake things up a year later by hiring me?"

In a gesture only he could make elegant, Clive shrugged.

Before this, I hadn't felt much like talking. But Clive was smart and imaginative, and I enjoyed his company. He had often served as a useful sounding board, too. Besides, if I didn't bring him up to speed on the two murders, he'd soon be prying into my love life. As I was thinking how intolerable that would be, an image of Freya appeared before my eyes in half shadow, complete with an endearing smear of mud on her cheek and an amused look in her intermittently hazel eyes...

"Guthrie," Clive said, impatiently summoning me back to reality. "I still want to know who shot you."

"Me, too. Any other ideas on the subject?"

"Nope. That's all I got," he said.

"Okay, thanks."

"Are you not coming to the party?"

"That's right, I am not coming."

"Well, in that case, here's to happy crime-solving."

We drank to it.

As Clive was about to take his leave, I said, "Hang on a minute. I have a hypothetical question for you."

"Oh, my favorite kind. Let's hear it."

"It's about betting on the ponies, a subject I believe you know something about," I said.

"Well, I don't want to brag, but I have been known to pick a winner every now and then."

"Good. Suppose you had an inside tip that a real longshot

was about to come in. Suppose you felt so certain of winning that just before the race you bet a really huge sum, say a hundred grand, on the horse."

"All right. Sounds exciting so far."

"Here's the question: wouldn't making a bet like that screw up the odds and defeat the purpose of betting?"

Clive frowned and squinted the way people do when they want to look like they're thinking hard. "Not if you bet online, or at various simulcast outlets, and correctly spaced or hid exotics. That would not dramatically affect the odds."

"I see. What if you were the horse's trainer or jockey? That would look fishy, right? Maybe get you in trouble with the law?"

"In that case, you would offload the wagers, use a civilian to place your bets. That way, you wouldn't get caught. Why do you ask? Is somebody going to do that? If so, I want the name of the horse so I can bet on him."

"Take it easy, Clive. I told you it was just a hypothetical question."

"Does it have something to do with your case?"

"I'm not sure."

"All right. See you later."

After he left, I went up to my painting studio. I'd been neglecting my craft for days now. I didn't want to lose my touch. Once I got started it felt good to slash away at a fresh canvas. After a while, I sat back and looked at what I'd done. I decided that my first go at the painting was too cluttered, too busy with trees, a boat, grass, the Indiana shore. I studied the brush strokes and wondered whether I'd painted what my eyes had *seen*, or if my brain had gotten in the way. That happened sometimes when I thought too much instead of allowing the painting to flow from my eyes to the brush to the canvas.

When nothing clicked, I took out a large brush and dipped it into the water, and rubbed it on a rag. Choosing an acrylic color lighter than the tree, I painted over it. I stepped back and looked at the result. Lightening the tree had made it stand out less. Still,

I felt the painting too cluttered. It was supposed to be about the yellow sailboat tethered to the shore. The poet Emerson said, "People only see what they are prepared to see."

It had been my experience that the hardest thing to see was often right in front of me.

I dipped my brush into the same color as the grass and used it to paint out the details in the grass. I stepped back and thought that the image was getting better. Not so many things to look at now. I dipped the dirty brush into another color. I wanted all these colors to blend. I brushed out Indiana, leaving only an abstract background.

Idly, I recalled once reading an article that said the brain doesn't passively record what our eyes see like a camera, but actively interprets the input. If the brain doesn't expect to see an object, it will blot it from consciousness. In one experiment I'd read about, nearly everyone on a basketball team successfully counted the number of passes during a drill made by the white shirts. But while they were counting, only half the players had noticed that a gorilla walked right in front of them for fully ten seconds.

What wasn't I seeing?

I had not changed the boat itself, but by removing distractions I had made it stand out. Was there a corollary here for solving the Rojas murder? Maybe I should rely more on my gut instinct instead of trying to think it through. Maybe this painting had shown me the way.

Of course, being contrary by nature and a slave to reason, I did no such thing. I was not about to abandon logic, especially when being shot had focused my mind so wonderfully. But as I stared at the yellow sailboat in my painting, I realized that this insight could still be beneficial. I had been wounded last night and I didn't know why, but I doubted it was a random event. Someone was angry, or frightened, enough to try to kill me. I couldn't think of any old enemy—not in prison—who might be nursing a big enough grudge to do it. No, it had to be linked to my current investigation. There were several possibilities for the culprit, but I liked Herb Alexander. He was full of rage. Who knows what else he might be capable of? His ownership of Speckled Band was also suggestive.

Speaking of which, I was convinced by Whitlow's exposé that massive cheating was still going on in thoroughbred horse racing as it had been from time immemorial. Hardly shocking to the cynical-minded, but what had changed was the cheaters' modus operandi. In old movies, jockeys were always being bribed or threatened in order to fix a race. Today, illegal drugs seemed more likely. That was why winners were tested, and violators disqualified. But what if some substances were undetectable? It was widely assumed that attempts to develop PEDs were ongoing. Despite the racing industry's checkered past, the betting public wanted to believe that horse racing was on the up and up. If they ever stopped believing it, then pari-mutuel wagering was in deep shit—along with the track's built-in seventeen percent take.

Everyone in the industry had a vested interest in fostering that continuing faith. That's why my favorite veterinarian had marched off in furious denial when I'd confronted her with the possibility of cheating. Everyone else with whom I'd brought up the possibility had also reacted with angry denial, from Humberto Herrera to both Ericsons. Maybe that helped explain why horrendous events such as Quicksilver's sudden death had not registered more forcefully with the public.

I stared at the yellow sailboat in my painting until my eyes drooped.

—

I was startled awake, still in front of my canvas, by a knock on my front door. I didn't know the time, but it felt like hours had passed since I nodded off. I picked up my gun, opened the door, and found myself face-to-face with Freya, who was silhouetted by the party lights from two doors down.

"Can I come in?"

"No," I said.

"I wanted to see you." She palmed my chest and slid her hand up to lightly touch my wounded forehead. "I'd never hurt you."

"You already have."

But I let her in.

She went straight to the bedroom, dim and shadowy as if lit by candle-light, and with her back to me let her thin dress slip off her shoulders and down her hips to the floor. She crawled onto the mattress on her hands and knees and lay back, watching me now, all milk and honey like the Promised Land.

"I shouldn't let you ever touch me again," she said.

But she bunched my T-shirt in her fist and pulled it over my head. Then I yanked down my cutoffs and climbed in beside her. With our bodies melding and her face inches from mine, I touched her hair, felt her warm bourbon-scented breath against my cheek. She kissed me on the mouth, then spread her thighs and sat on top of, pulling me inside until our breathing grew ragged and rhythmic together, and we were both completely out of control.

—

Later, resting against the headboard, I gazed down at Freya's fair form and realized how utterly silent the rest of the house seemed. She stirred, raising an eyebrow.

"Let's do that again," I said.

Afterward, Freya slid from the bed and stood before me, hiding both nothing and everything.

"Why don't you just let it go?" she said.

"Let what go?"

"The investigation. I can tell that it's on your mind. You know you'll never prove anything now. It's not your fault. Too much time has gone by. It's hopeless and I don't want you to get hurt."

"How would I get hurt?"

"You already have. Look at you. Come with me to Mexico. I know a quiet little town in Baja. You'll love it. We can leave right after the Derby."

"You're up to your neck in this, aren't you?"

After giving me what might have seemed like a long last look at the goods, she slipped her dress back on.

"What if I am? If you felt the same way I do, it wouldn't matter. Let it go. Please."

"You know I can't do that."

"That's a shame," she said and walked out the door.

I watched her go, registering her exquisiteness once more. What a fool I was letting her get away.

I couldn't sleep after that. Maybe I'd become a permanent insomniac now. I filled the long hours till dawn swaying back and forth between helplessness and resignation.

Early in the morning, I phoned Harriet Anderson to tell her what seemed to be going on and what needed to be done. Predictably, she requested proof. I still had none. But when I asked her for a better idea, she admitted having none.

"I won't be a party to anything illegal," she warned.

Me, either. I hoped.

SATURDAY

30

It was already 11:45 when I stepped through the backside gate cleverly disguised to fit in with my dark sunglasses, cargo shorts, untucked T-shirt, and Louisville Bats baseball cap. The third race winners were lined up happily at the windows to cash their tickets. The sun was shining. The grandstands teemed with the colorful and the tipsy. Judging by appearances, all seemed well. But with the clock ticking, I couldn't shake the conviction that something terrible was going to happen, and soon.

As I made my way through the huge crowd, the contrast between Millionaire's Row and the infield leaped out at me. On one side were box seats, a lavish indoor dining room, and private viewing platforms. Occupied by celebrities from all over the world—and protected by the FBI, CIA, and Secret Service. On the other side, eighty thousand rowdies were standing or sitting on the grass, tarps, camp chairs, and blankets. Security there was provided by the National Guard along with state and local cops, including Brownfield.

Moving cautiously to avoid the ubiquitous patches of mud

and vomit, I found him with a rolled-up newspaper jammed into his suit coat pocket and his bulldog jaws clamped around an unlit cigar. He was standing between the medical tent and the drunk tank, which was in a big LMPD trailer, scanning the multitudes for trouble spots through binoculars strapped around his bull neck.

"How's life out here in the mosh pit?" I asked.

"About what you'd expect," he answered, without lowering the binocs. "Overdoses, medical emergencies, pickpockets, grifters, aggressive drunks, and nosey private eyes."

"I'll try not to take that personally."

Brownfield sniffed at that but otherwise made no reply.

Moonlighting on crowd control was making him testy. That was unfortunate, but I still had no choice. "I need your help, Leo."

"What else is new?"

"I think something terrible is about to happen," I said.

"Like what? Poison gas attack? Plane crash into the grandstands?"

"Nothing like that. Don't laugh, but I think someone's going to fix the Kentucky Derby."

Brownfield laughed.

"I'm serious, damn it. We've only got maybe six hours to prevent it."

The police lieutenant stared at me intently. "You don't seem that shitfaced, Guthrie, but are you?"

"Don't talk shit, Leo. This is serious."

"Sure, it is. All right, come with me."

We went inside the medical tent and found a relatively quieter space to talk without being overheard.

"Okay, I'll bite. How are they going to do it?" Brownfield asked.

"With PEDS. Performance-Enhancing Drugs."

"I know what they are. Wouldn't the winner test positive?"

"Not if the drugs are *undetectable*."

"The Holy Grail of cheating. Except undetectable PEDs don't exist," Brownfield said, chewing his cigar.

"I think they do."

"What makes you think so?"

"They've done it before," I said.

"Who has?"

"Luke Ericson and Freya Hall."

"Go on."

Taking a breath, I said I believed that two years ago they had darkened the form of a promising colt named Quicksilver. First, they'd given the horse PEDs to relieve his chronic pain, which allowed him to run faster. Then they'd stopped the pain medication Quicksilver needed, which dramatically slowed him down. When his losing streak was long enough to boost the odds against him sky high, the PEDs were resumed. As a result, the horse ran dramatically better in his next race and they cleaned up.

"Betting like that would've screwed up the odds," Brownfield said.

"Not necessarily." I shared Clive's explanation of how that might be avoided with careful betting.

"How did you find out about this scheme?"

This was where matters got sticky. "Whitlow told me right before he was killed." It was not exactly a lie.

"Why didn't you tell me?"

"I'm telling you now."

"You've been withholding evidence. What else did he tell you? And how did he know?"

"Because the horse in question died immediately after winning the race."

"Racehorses die all the time. It's a huge controversy. Don't you watch the news?" Brownfield said.

"Not like this, they don't. I'm telling you they must have gotten the formula wrong and it wound up killing the horse."

"And you're saying no illegal substances showed up in the

post-race testing?"

"None."

"Where did this happen?" he asked.

"At Aqueduct in Florida."

"Tell me how Whitlow knew about it?"

I kept it simple, saying only that the tipster had been looking into cheating in racing.

"Hold on a minute. You don't care about racing. What does all this have to do with your investigation?" Brownfield said.

I told him that Whitlow's words, plus an odd chain of events, had convinced me that both murders—Rojas and Whitlow—were linked to Quicksilver's death. That Felipe Rojas must have seen Luke and Freya cheating. I said I didn't know what he'd gotten hold of, or how he'd done it, but he must have obtained some physical evidence. That's the only way he could have made a charge stick.

When I went on to hypothesize that Rojas must have blackmailed Luke and Freya to bring the Guatemalan's son to America, Brownfield wanted to know why they would've paid Rojas when they could've just killed him.

"It's a big leap from fixing a race to murder," I said. "At that point, I don't believe they'd ever killed anybody. Besides, Rojas must have had an accomplice, who he claimed that if anything were to happen to him, would turn over the proof to the authorities."

"But they killed him anyway. What changed?"

"I don't know. Maybe Rojas got impatient, put too much pressure on them and they acted impetuously."

"Who was this partner? And why wouldn't they have just killed him or her, too?" Brownfield asked.

"It must have been Sandy Diaz. Rojas was secretly having an affair with her, which meant that no one would have known his partner's identity."

"But once they killed Rojas, if I'm following this correctly, why didn't the Diaz woman make good on the threat to turn them in?"

"I think she was afraid," I said.

"And the blackmail ended?"

"Unless Whitlow, having found out about it, took over."

"Are you're suggesting they shut him up, too?" Brownfield said.

"Yes, and after having committed two murders to stop the blackmail, suddenly they find it has resumed. This time, it's Sandy Diaz who's behind it but they don't know that."

"I thought you said she was too afraid."

"That might be my fault." I quickly explained how I'd inadvertently caused Sandy's husband to lose his job, thereby increasing their desperation.

"Then she could still be blackmailing them," Brownfield said.

"Yeah, making them even more desperate and dangerous."

"Weren't you supposedly meeting her when you got shot?"

"Yeah, but I don't think she did it," I said.

"If no one else knew where this meeting was taking place, who else could it have been?"

"I don't know. But I think I was shot because I'd gotten too close to the truth. The most pressing problem facing us now, though, is the likelihood that Luke and Freya are going to try to make one big score."

"By fixing the Derby. Do you know how that sounds?"

"It's up to us to stop them," I said.

Noting the rolled-up newspaper in his pocket, I asked him to check Speckled Band's odds. When he did, the morning line was sixty-nine to one. "It says here that in his last race, Speckled Band finished eighth, twenty-one lengths back," Brownfield said.

"You could win a lot of money at those odds—if you knew the outcome in advance."

"Okay, I admit it's a nice payout. How am I supposed to prevent it from happening? Arrest Ericson and Hall? Stop the race?"

"If that's what it takes. Or you could warn them off. A threat from you would carry some serious weight," I said.

"And when their horse tests clean, what then? Hand over my badge and gun?"

"You're going to do nothing?"

He nodded. "So are you if you're smart. Or would if you were."

I kept trying but couldn't budge him.

Threading my way out of the infield, I phoned Ray Hines and asked for a meeting. The Downs' security chief seemed reluctant at first, claiming he was too busy. But when I told him what it was about—preserving the integrity of the Derby—he became cooperative. He was waiting for me in his office when I arrived.

"I hope you haven't said anything about this to anyone else," Hines said.

"Only Homicide Lieutenant Brownfield of LMPD." I summarized Brownfield's response. "I hope you intend to do something about it."

"Look, we've heard the rumors about widespread cheating going on in the sport. Sure, we have. But the science is way out in front of us, and there's no national czar to enforce compliance with the rules we have. As a result, only so much we can do on suspicion alone. Like the police, we require hard evidence."

"You could test Speckled Band before and after the race," I said.

"And we will—based on your allegation."

"And you could keep an eye on Speckled Band from this moment forward, maybe catch them in the act of administering the PED."

"We've already got 'round-the-clock security in every stall. But if they are as smart as you say, there's little likelihood of catching them no matter how many of us are watching."

"Yeah," I said, "but think of the scandal if I'm right and they pull it off. With so many horses dying and the public's other concerns, racing already is in deep trouble. Imagine the uproar when it comes out that the Downs was warned about this scam and did nothing about it."

Hines went pale. "Is that a threat?"

"No, but this is going to come out, sooner or later. Best get out in front of it."

"We already are. Rest assured that every precaution has been taken," he said.

"Save the speech for after the race. That's when you'll need it."

"Obviously, I expect you to say nothing about this to anyone, Guthrie."

"Obviously. But I don't work for you. It doesn't matter. What good would it do now? It's like standing helplessly on the beach watching the tsunami roll in."

"Let's hope you're wrong," he said.

Hoping didn't sound like enough.

Leaving Hines to his other duties, I went to the Ericson barn, where I slipped in without being challenged. While waiting for Carlos, I noticed an unfamiliar groom in a back stall tacking up a horse I did not recognize. He used a curry comb, checked its eyes and nose, and hoof-picked caked dirt and rocks out of the hooves. Finally, he polo-wrapped the colt's lower legs with a strip of Velcro cloth and led him out of the barn for the walk over to the paddock.

The walk to the paddock

Suddenly I realized that Speckled Band's stall wasn't the only place where the colt might be doped. What about on his way over to the paddock? That scenario might seem unlikely with so many cameras focused along the route. But every step of the way from the barn to the tunnel and beyond needed a thorough inspection before the race. Perhaps it would only take a momentary distraction to slip the horse a "mickey"—or rather, a PED—perhaps laced in a sugar cube.

Carlos came in as the horse left. Naturally, he was

impatient for a progress report, which was not an unreasonable request. Fearing he might overreact if I shared my suspicions prematurely, though, I put him off till day's end with a promise to tell him everything then. He still seemed eager to help despite this and agreed to stick as close to Speckled Band as he could until post time.

"Be alert for anything unusual. I mean anything," I said.

I asked him to secretly surveil Luke Ericson, as well.

"You want me to watch my boss? What's he done?"

"I'm not ready to say. But it might prove helpful. Will you do it?"

"I'll try."

"Good man." I clapped him on the shoulder as we parted company.

31

Everybody at the racetrack believed in pure luck or they wouldn't be there. There was no other explanation for why so many bets were based on a horse's name, color, or number. Even professional handicappers were not immune. They knew that despite all the study in the world, a race's outcome could turn on the tiniest fraction of an inch. That's why when the starting gate opened, many preferred trusting to fortune rather than skill. Even investigators. Since luck was not for sale, I settled for the next best thing—a beer. There was a long line at the counter. Francisco Segura was standing at the very end, dressed in civvies and moving stiffly as if in pain.

"Hey, Francisco, remember me?" I asked.

His eyes narrowed as recognition slowly dawned.

"You're the private eye."

"Correct. Are you not riding today, of all days?"

"Does it look like it?" he said bitterly.

"How come?"

"Why do you think?" he said.

"I don't know."

"Because I been blackballed, that's why."

"Blackballed?"

"Kicked out of the club. One bad ride—that's all it takes."

He stopped talking.

He looked as spooked as a rainbow trout diving back into his hidey-hole. The only way to lure him out again was by slowly floating the bait past him on the rushing stream.

"Hey, Francisco, how about we forget this line and get one of those juleps instead?" I nodded at a nearby julep vendor who was shouting, "Who's ready? No waiting. Who needs me?"

He nodded and I bought us a couple of traditional bourbon cocktails. Segura inhaled his drink while I was still savoring the first icy burn and tongue-numbing properties of mine. I offered him another, he accepted. Hoping he'd be more forthcoming now, I said, "Tell me more about being blackballed."

"It's cut-throat. A rich man's club. Piss one of 'em off and see what you get."

"Who did you piss off, Francisco?"

"The Goddamn owner and the trainer. Dirty bastards."

Bitterness in his voice, sparks of rage in his eyes

"What happened? Are we talking about Quicksilver?"

Segura's head snapped up.

"Why should I tell you anything?"

"Because I'll pay you."

"How much?"

We haggled, starting at $100 and settling on $300.

"Show me the damn money," he said.

I showed him. "Information first."

"What do you want to know?"

"Every detail."

"Nothing much to say. Quicksilver was a long shot. Ran his goddamn heart out though. We won, but then he fell down dead. That's it. Pay me."

Segura reached for the cash, but I pulled my hand back.

"Not so fast. Tell me something I don't already know."

Clenching his jaw, he said, "They said it was my fault the horse dropped dead, but it wasn't. He wasn't himself that day. I tried to warn the trainer that something was wrong. The horse was jumpy before the race, harder to saddle, harder to ride. But he wouldn't listen. Who did I think I was, he says? Who made me trainer? He was threatening to take me off the horse. Told me to keep my trap shut and do what I was told if I ever wanted to ride for him again. So, that's what I did."

Segura held out his hand again. This time, I gave him one Benjamin Franklin.

"Now tell me more about what was going on right before the race."

"Like what?"

"Who was in the stall with Quicksilver?"

"The groom, the vet, and the trainer. Then the old man called the vet and the trainer over for a talk."

"Not the groom?"

"No, he stayed where he was."

"Doing what?"

"Taking care of the horse. What do you think?"

I handed him another hundred-dollar bill.

"Did the groom stick around for long?"

"No, a minute later I saw him take off."

"Did he carry anything off with him?"

"As a matter of fact, he did. A feed bucket."

"Was there anything in it?"

"Yeah—feed."

Segura grabbed the third C-note and took off himself.

—

An hour later, I was breaking into Daniela Torres' one-story duplex.

Segura had unwittingly given me the idea to do so, and though it was an even longer shot than Quicksilver, it was still the best hope of cracking the case and possibly preventing a catastrophic Derby outcome. It didn't take a genius to figure out that Daniela would be at work. Or that her place would be empty, seeing as how she was single.

Due to gridlock, I'd walked the eight blocks from the Downs to her quiet narrow street lined with modest houses and parked vehicles. There was hardly any foot traffic at present, I noted. The front doors and windows were closed. Dense foundation plantings offered only minimal concealment. On the other hand, I found no "Beware of Dog" or security signs in the yard. No plastic-wrapped phone books left on the front walk. No notes on the doors for an afternoon package delivery. No indication that anyone might return home soon. Very encouraging.

Daniela lived on the right side of the shabby white frame house. I knew because her name was written on a wall-mounted mailbox in letters too fancy for the place. I rang her neighbor's doorbell. No answer. I searched for an Internet-enabled webcam, one that could record my activities in real-time and bring the cops. No webcam.

As I continued pondering how to gain entry, I was also thinking about the hypothesis I was operating on—namely, that Felipe Rojas had removed the needle and syringe, or another delivery system used to dope Quicksilver. He'd hidden it in the feed bucket and carried it away from the horse's stall. Doubtless, it contained DNA and/or fingerprints that could prove what had been done to the horse. Since it was never turned over to the authorities, though, it followed that Rojas meant to use it for blackmailing purposes.

If that assumption was correct, he'd have needed a safe hiding place. But finding one at the Downs seemed highly improbable. Almost every inch of its 150 acres was in use or under observation 24/7 during the racing season. On the front side, fans and employees were everywhere. On the backside, workers were everywhere. A child could have successfully searched a tiny barn apartment like Felipe's.

A much better hiding place would be somewhere off-track. If the night has a thousand eyes, the Downs had tens of thousands. Of all the possible locations I could think of, Sandy Diaz's home seemed the obvious choice. Rojas had no other friends living away from the Downs and he wouldn't have done something like burying it in the park, where access would be a problem, and anyone might stumble over it. No, Sandy's home made the most sense—except that her husband and daughter lived there, too. Even better was Daniela's domicile, which I recalled had served as Felipe and Sandy's love nest.

I banged my fist on the neighbor's screen and waited, all the while asking myself what did Rojas hope to get from blackmailing Luke and Freya? Probably money and assistance to bring his entire family to the U.S. But only his son had ever made it. Something must have changed to keep the others back in Guatemala. And that same something was probably what had gotten Felipe murdered. I did not know what had changed, but right now the most important objective was to get my gloved hands on that evidence. Unfortunately, I had no gloves with me. No lockpicks or crowbar, either. I'd have to make do, as I'd done many times before.

Getting no response to my knocking, I concluded that no one was at home. The preferred way in would be to open Daniela's front door. But it was solid wood and had a deadbolt that I'd never be able to jimmy. Needing a better option, I circled the house while also observing the rest of the block. No prying neighbors surfaced, and only one dog-walker. I appraised the usefulness of a full-grown shrub that stood slightly higher than a side window as my best place to break in.

There was a small patio in back, where I worked a moss-covered red brick out of its basket-weave pattern and hurled through the window I'd selected, making a loud crash. I froze, waiting to see if anyone had noticed, but when nothing happened, I scraped away the shattered glass and climbed through and began the search.

As I did, I kept coming back to why Rojas' killers had also waited—an entire year—to bump him off when they could have done so immediately. Had they been paying him all that time? That made no sense. Unless maybe he'd told them that he had an anonymous accomplice, who I was pretty sure had been Sandy Diaz. He just didn't have anyone else. He'd say that the accomplice would turn the bad guys in if anything happened to him. That would keep Rojas and Sandy both safe. Until it didn't.

I searched for thirty minutes. When I did not find what I was looking for, I gave up.

—

I was running out of options. I had considered, and rejected, the possibility that Rojas might have hidden the evidence in a bank safe deposit box. The trouble with that approach was access. Should anything go wrong with his account, he might be unable to retrieve his most prized possession.

If I was right, another alternative would have been for him to stash the evidence at the off-track home of a friend. The trouble with that option was that he had no friends or at least none I'd identified.

Again, if I was right, that narrowed it down pretty much to Sandy Diaz's place. The downside was that her jealous husband and their daughter lived there, too. When in a tight spot, take what you can find. I figured that's how Felipe Rojas had looked at it, too. Sandy's house was six blocks west of Daniela's. By the time I walked there, fortune had another surprise in store for me—the unanticipated and nearly simultaneous arrival of Sandy herself on a bicycle.

Fortunately, I saw her coming before she saw me. I just had time to duck behind the building before she rode up to the front, laid down her bike, and rushed inside. Her hair was pulled up and she was wearing her work clothes, as one might expect on a workday. But what the hell was she doing here? I assumed she must have had a damn good reason for going AWOL from the track, on today of all days, since it might well cost her job and sole source of income.

Wait a minute. Could this mean that she'd come for the same reason as I had, i.e., to retrieve the evidence? If so, what a bonus! Maybe I should place a few bets myself despite my aversion to gambling since this really could be shaping up as my lucky day. But five minutes later I felt a sinking sensation in my chest when she left the place apparently empty-handed.

Damn, there went that theory. But if not that, what was she here for? There was no guarantee that I'd find out by following her, and no certainty I could keep up with her on foot without being spotted, either, but what other recourse did I have? I tried to keep up, trotting after her through the steamy motionless air, my running shoes pounding the streets like exceedingly weighty metronomes. It was grueling. Wet patches had bloomed under my armpits and I was gasping. Every so often, I'd bob down behind a parked vehicle, tree, or fence to hide in case she looked back. So far, she hadn't. Not that it would matter much longer because she was pulling away.

As she turned a corner and I lost sight of her, I experienced a pang of despair because my last chance to solve the case and save the race was slipping away. Solve the case, save the race.

Catchy. I was probably giddy from oxygen deprivation. But in my darkest hour, destiny lent a hand in the form of a rusty old one-speed Schwinn bicycle that an elementary-age kid came riding down the street. Instantly I changed directions and intercepted him. Seizing the bike by its gummy handlebars, I grabbed the boy and lowered him gently onto a grass strip separating blacktop from the sidewalk.

"What are you doing?" the young rider yelled as I mounted the purloined Schwinn. "You're stealing my bike."

"I'm not stealing it. I'm commandeering it to make a citizen's arrest."

"You can't do that, you asshole!" he screamed.

"Yes, I can under the power of eminent domain."

"Bullshit!" He was jumping up and down. "You're stealing it."

"Sorry, kid. You'll get it back," I yelled over my shoulder as, now mounted, I again took up the pursuit of Sandy Diaz. A block later, I could still hear the bike's rightful owner cursing after me with amazing fluency for someone so young. The urchin was right, of course. What I had said was bogus. The power of eminent domain had nothing to do with seizing his bike. As I vaguely recalled, it meant taking private property for public use, such as confiscating land to build a dam. I was not an agent of the government and stealing someone's bike to make a citizen's arrest was plain stupid. Nevertheless, I needed the bike.

Unfortunately, I had apparently snatched the city's worst bicycle. It jumped gears when I pedaled, rubbed its pads when I braked, and shimmied and shook so bad I feared it would judder itself apart. The tires were under-inflated, misaligned, and had spokes missing. Nevertheless, I was only a block behind Sandy when she turned north on Southern Parkway. To reach Victory Kenwood Baptist Church, she swept across four lanes of honking traffic and nearly paid for it with her life. But she made it and, abandoning her bike, dashed up the wide concrete steps to the entrance. I watched from behind a parked car across the street.

I assumed she'd come to pick up her daughter since the BLC was running daycare here for the Derby. As the minutes passed, I grew anxious wondering what she was doing in there. I was poised to go in after her when she came back out by herself but with a pink backpack strapped around her shoulders. What was inside that backpack? Could it be the evidence I was seeking? She picked up her bike and climbed aboard, but paused to make a brief, apparently intense phone call before speeding away.

According to my watch, it was nearly five o'clock when she pocketed the phone and aimed her bike south on the parkway back toward Iroquois Park. A mere few minutes remained before the start of the Derby.

32

Sandy skidded to a halt outside Freya Hall's house, threw down her bike, and rushed to the front door. I watched from behind a Rose of Sharon bush halfway down the block as she pounded on the door until Freya let her in. Then I was up and running across the intervening lawns and flattening myself against an exterior wall. I toed a shaky strip of brick edging to peer inside and found that the living room was unoccupied.

Next, I slipped around back. All the windows in the cottage were dark, the back door locked, and the kitchen curtains drawn. Seemed the only way to find out what was going on inside was to knock on the front door, which I did after pulling out my cell phone and tapping record, then shoving it into my back pocket. Freya appeared in the door of a hallway wearing a white T and khaki shorts, her dark hair falling around her shoulders. She looked ready for the infield. Or anything.

"Jim, darling! What are you doing here?" For a moment it seemed possible she was about to stretch up and enfold me in an embrace. But the moment passed.

"Where is Sandy Diaz? I saw her come in."

When Freya pressed her lips tightly together, I brushed past her and followed the hallway to an open door that led to the basement.

"Sandy, it's Guthrie. Are you all right?" I called.

No answer from the basement. Hearing the click of footsteps behind me, I turned only to find Freya pointing a semi-automatic pistol at my chest.

"No need for guns," I said, wishing I had not left mine in the rental car glove box. "We're all friends, right?"

"Show me your hands," Freya said.

"What have you done with Sandy and her child?" I raised my arms slowly.

"Nothing much. Turn around."

She jammed the muzzle into my back and frisked me one-handed. Perhaps I could have taken the .22 away from her then and there, but it might have gone off and there might be civilians in the house. She found my phone and stopped it from recording.

"Making a documentary?" Tight little smile.

"You should end this now before something else goes horribly wrong. You're only guilty of race fixing and accomplice to murder so far. You can still cop a plea."

"Shut up." She flicked her gun toward the basement. "Go."

At the bottom of the steps, an old-style television set rested on a wall-bracketed shelf. The TV was on and tuned to the races at low volume. Freya herded me past it into an area fitted out like a chemistry laboratory with a microscope, test tubes, and a Bunsen burner. After placing my phone on the upright workbench beside a pink backpack, she picked up a roll of duct tape and nudged me with it toward a hardwood door in a dividing wall.

"Unlock it."

The key was in the old mortise keyhole. I turned it counterclockwise until it threw the bolt. The door opened, revealing exposed ceiling joists, pipes, and ductwork. A washer and dryer marked it as a laundry room that also housed the furnace and hot water heater, plus storage—including Sandy and her child, who were huddled at the far end near the only light fixture.

"Tie him up good and tight." Freya tossed the gray tape over to Sandy.

"Is that really necessary? Let's talk it over, work something out," I said.

"Tie him up first. Then we'll talk," Freya said.

I held out my wrists, keeping my elbows as close together as possible while Sandy bound me. Freya told her to wind it tight, then made sure she had. When I complained that my circulation was cut off, she said, "Stop being such a big baby and sit down against the wall."

Not so easy trussed up, but I managed. I leaned back and felt the pegs of a perforated hardboard dig into my back. At least there were no tools stored on it.

"Now tie up Ana Lucia."

"Don't make me do that," Sandy begged.

"Do it—or I'll tape your mouths shut, too."

Soon, all three of us were tied up on the floor.

"Stay put." Freya left for a moment, returning with the backpack, which she unzipped with a flourish, and pulled out a large clear plastic baggie containing a hypodermic needle and syringe. "Voila!" She opened the baggie and sniffed, presumably seeking any remaining traces of her undetectable PED on the paraphernalia. I studied her face for a clue, but she was undetectable as well. Zipping up the bag wordlessly, she started texting on her phone as she went out the door. She shut it behind her, leaving us in semi-darkness.

"I'm scared," said the child, resting her head on her mother's lap.

Sandy tried to soothe her, saying, "Don't worry, angel. It will be all right."

But with time running out, the kid was right—the situation seemed grim. I had to try something, so I tugged at the duct tape confining my arms. It didn't give much but then it wasn't supposed to.

"We've got to get out of here," Sandy said.

"You traded that baggie for your child's life, didn't you," I said in a low voice. "Well, I don't mean to alarm you unduly, but I wouldn't count on Freya holding up her end of the bargain."

"But she promised!" Sandy yawped.

"Keep your voice down. Do you think she'll let us go after kidnaping your daughter? Especially since we know who and what killed Quicksilver?"

I sensed, rather than saw, her holding her head in her hands, and then looking up at me with a sheen of moisture in her eyes. "What can we do?"

"I think I can get us out of here, but I need the truth and I need it now," I said.

"How?"

"Don't worry about that. Just tell me about what happened today."

Freya had phoned her, Sandy said, and threatened she would never see Ana Lucia again unless she brought the bag in an hour. Sandy had phoned Libby at the childcare center to confirm that Ana Lucia had been spirited away under some pretext. After that, Sandy had gone to her apartment to get the evidence she'd hidden there—in an oatmeal box. She'd kept it safely stored there for months, knowing that neither her husband nor her daughter cared for oatmeal.

"When I looked and saw that it wasn't there today, I nearly fainted," Sandy said.

It was possible that her daughter, a naturally curious child, could have stumbled across the needle and syringe and, since she loved everything about horses and taking care of them, recognized what it was used for. In that case, what would she do with it? In a sudden flash of insight, Sandy had realized that Ana

Lucia might have taken the needle and syringe to the church learning center for her favorite activity, "show-and-tell." Hoping it was still there, she had rushed to the church—unaware that I was in quiet pursuit—where a frenzied search had turned up her daughter's backpack stashed in a basement locker.

"I was holding my breath while I opened it up. You can't imagine what a relief it was to find the stuff in it. I immediately called Freya back and she told me to bring it here. Which reminds me—how did you know to come here?"

"I follow you on a borrowed bicycle. Now tell me about the blackmail," I said.

Sandy admitted demanding $50,000 to keep quiet about the PED used to dope Quicksilver. "I was careful, even used a burner phone and disguised my voice, but Freya recognized it somehow and went after Ana Lucia."

I asked when the blackmail scheme began.

By the time of his murder, she told me, Felipe Rojas had been extorting money from Freya and Luke Ericson for over a year.

"Since we know they were eventually willing to commit murder, why did they agree to pay instead of just killing him at the start?" I asked.

"Felipe had threatened that his unnamed accomplice— meaning me—would turn them in if he was ever harmed."

"Why didn't you follow through and turn them in? Or continue blackmailing them immediately?"

"At first, I was too afraid. But when Juan lost his job recently because of you, I was desperate. I could have asked for so much more, you know, but I am not a greedy person. All I wanted was enough to get away from here and start a better life—"

The dividing door creaked open, casting a cube of light upon us.

"Should my ears be burning?" Freya stood there in silhouette.

"Think what you're doing. You have to know this can't work," I said.

"I tried to warn you, but you wouldn't listen. Now it's too late."

"Too late for what?" Sandy cried. "What's going to happen to us? Please, don't hurt my baby."

"I'm not going to hurt anyone—unless you make me."

"Then how about putting the gun away?" I asked.

"I think I'll keep it handy, thanks," she said, still holding it at her side.

"You'll never get away with this," I said.

"You don't think so? Well, think again, Mister Private Eye. Sandy's not going to tell anyone, are you, Sandy?"

"No, no."

"Are you really just doing this for the money?" I said, hoping to steer us away from threats.

"And you think you're going to help yourself by analyzing me psychologically?" Freya looked at me with what seemed like genuine disappointment. "If we're going to talk intimately, we need more privacy."

She left the room with the gun and came back without it. Then showing surprising strength, she half-dragged me up off the floor and shoved me out of the laundry room and onto a sagging sofa in the lab, where I noticed the gun resting on the table beside her microscope.

"Sorry to leave you in the dark, Sandy," Freya said, as she shut the utility room door.

From my new perch, I could see the TV screen. The walkover was in progress at the Downs as owners and trainers led their Derby horses from barn to paddock. The on-screen time display read 5:45, only forty-five minutes before the big race.

"Why shouldn't money be reason enough for me to do this? It's enough for most people," Freya said.

"I thought it might be something else."

"Such as?"

"I don't know. You seem so angry now. I didn't see that in you at first."

Sadly, I recalled how oddly appealing she had looked with that little smear of mud on her cheek. Now I noticed the lines etched on either side of her full-lipped mouth, though of course, her eyes were still large and quite beautiful.

"Aren't you mad yourself? Don't you dare tell me you're not," she said.

She was right. I admitted as much.

"Where does your rage come from?" she said.

"I'm not sure."

"Yes, you are. Don't you remember how your no-good, gambling-addicted wife dumped you? Took you for everything you had?"

"Okay," I said. "We're both angry. But that doesn't explain how you got involved in this mess."

She seemed lost in thought for a moment. "Started when I met Luke in college."

"You were a couple?"

"For a while."

Hardly surprising, considering the way she knew how to make a man feel good just being around her.

"He had everything, I had nothing. I could see us together one day when he would replace his father. Luke would be a big-time trainer. I would be a top-notch equine veterinarian." She slumped, arms limp at her side as if the memory remained unbearably raw even after all these years.

I was surprised to find that even under these dire circumstances I couldn't help being drawn to her.

"Why?" I asked. "How could he dump you?"

She smiled for a moment as if grimly amused, then straightened her posture and lifted her chin. "I'm still asking myself that same question. But he should have known better. Getting rid of me is never that easy."

Chilling words. But the dark laughter that followed was worse—like nothing I'd heard from her before.

"Yet here you are with him again," I said.

"Not exactly." She leaned back against the tale and picked up the .22. "After the breakup, I went on to finish my DVM degree, then got a job with an established equine practice. I was still very idealistic at the time. But the work soon forced me to make ethical compromises at the expense of the horses under my care."

Hearing her talk about ethics while holding a gun in her hand was surreal, but she didn't seem to notice.

"I thought about quitting daily. But then I would never have been able to achieve my goal of getting into the racing world at the highest level. Finally, I decided that if I couldn't beat them, I'd join them." She had a dreamy look in her eyes just from thinking about it

"How'd you manage that?" I asked.

"By creating an undetectable performance-enhancing drug, the Holy Grail of horse racing."

"Quite an achievement," I noted.

"To be sure, but I had a knack for equine research. I was passionate about it and willing to put in the time and effort it took. I spent years experimenting in secret, getting closer little by little until at last, I had it."

"That's amazing," I said, to keep her talking.

"You're trying to flatter me, but it truly was. The only remaining question was how to turn it to my own best advantage. I could have sold it, of course, no shortage of buyers out there. Just look at what was already going on. But I wanted more than money out of this. I wanted to be in the racing business and to win the biggest races. For that, I needed a stable. That's when I heard the news that Ned Ericson was deathly ill with cancer."

In her excitement, Freya had started waving the pistol around. I asked her to be careful.

"Why? Afraid that I'll shoot you? I won't—not by accident anyway," she said, seeming even more delighted. "I remembered Luke telling me how obsessed his father had always been with winning the Derby. I mean, Ned was one of the best trainers in the country who had never won a single Triple Crown race. Just imagine how he must have felt when his illness forced him to turn over day-to-day training operations to his son.

"I knew Luke was just as obsessed as his father and would stop at nothing to win the Derby. I got in touch and made him a business proposal. Hire me as your official veterinarian, I said, and I'll give you the Holy Grail. He was skeptical at first, of course, assuming I was trying to rekindle our failed romance or some such. But he couldn't resist such a golden opportunity for long—and sure enough, he didn't."

"Did his father know anything about this?"

"Saint Ned? Don't make me laugh."

"What I want to know is how could you do this and still make that speech about the oath you'd sworn to protect animals and prevent their suffering?"

"Oh, grow up for God's sake. You bend the rules just like me. I told you I do it for the money. I also do it to make horses run faster. That's all."

"Two bodies in the morgue—that's a lot of bending," I said.

"Science requires making some sacrifices."

"Human ones?"

"I haven't hurt anybody." Her red lips parted over white teeth and she smiled as if bitterly amused by the question.

"How about horses? How about Quicksilver?"

"That wasn't supposed to happen. I gave him the wrong dosage. He was not himself, being all moody and skittish like he didn't want to run. His groom noticed and told Luke about it. He said to let it go and keep his mouth shut. But he went to Ned while we were dosing the horse, and the old man interrupted us. We barely had time to hide the needle and syringe under the hay. When we went back, it was gone.

"Right after that, Rojas started using it to blackmail us. His claim to have an accomplice seemed to leave us no choice when he demanded money and legal help to get visas for his whole family. But since there were only a limited number of visas available, it would've meant bribing immigration. We'd won some serious money on Quicksilver, but Luke had gambling debts to pay. We just couldn't swing it all at once. So, we agreed to bring Rojas's son here right away and give him a job. The others would have to wait until we won more money."

"What was the next target?" I asked.

"That fat three-million-dollar Derby purse."

"But then why did Felipe have to die?"

"We figured to only get one chance at the Derby and didn't want to screw it up. But the situation in Guatemala went downhill and Rojas got impatient. When he wouldn't listen to reason, Luke decided we had to...well, you know."

"Kill him, you mean? But what about his accomplice?"

"Luke decided to call his bluff—except it wasn't a bluff—and without asking me. Bad move until the blackmail started up again, and this time we didn't know who was behind it—until you led us to him."

"Whitlow?" I lowered my gaze, regretting that I had inadvertently endangered his life. "Is Luke the one who shot me?"

"How could he when nobody knew where you'd be?" she said.

"You knew when, and you could have followed me to Sandy's place, too, and phoned *your* accomplice the location. Is that how it went down?"

Instead of answering, she said, "My God, you look tense," and laid the automatic down on the workbench, which immediately made me feel better. But my shoulder muscles were cramped. After all I'd been through lately, I felt knotted up all over. She sat down beside me on the padded sofa arm and dug her clever fingers into my flesh. I relaxed in spite of everything.

On TV between races, a man dressed in a white straw hat and a light green suit with a bamboo print stood at the rail. Beside him was a bare-shouldered woman wearing a crimson fascinator. She waved a lit cigarette around until a colt passed by, then leaned over and tried to kiss him. She was way too far away for that to happen, but Freya seemed inspired and planted one on my lips.

"Kinky," I said. "First time I've ever been kissed while tied up."

"You really haven't lived much, have you?" She brushed a strand of hair away from her forehead. "I feel it's very romantic to trust someone enough that you're willing to literally put your life in her hands."

"*Willing?*"

"I do wish you trusted me more." She moved in closer and put her arm around my back and pulled me in.

"Is this what is meant by 'keeping your enemies close,' I wonder?'" I said as she pressed her chest against mine.

"Maybe it started that way. I didn't count on falling in love with you."

"This is love?"

"I did ask you to come away with me, remember?" she said.

"Probably too late now."

"Is it?" she asked, pushing me away.

"What happens to Sandy and her daughter?"

"They'll be fine. Once I collect my winnings, everyone goes free."

"Just like that?"

"You've got nothing on me, so why not?"

She was right—unless Sandy agreed to testify that Freya had abducted her and Ana Lucia. Then there was also the physical evidence of horse-doping currently residing on the workbench right in front of me.

"Are you sure Luke will go along with that?" I inquired.

"Doesn't matter. I don't even like Luke. He never listens to me, yet always expects me to accomplish the impossible."

"Selling you short?"

"Now who's massaging whom?"

But I was still drawn to her, God help me.

"That's what I like about you, Jim. Your mind. Of course, I like the rest of you, too." To demonstrate, she kissed me again and held the kiss while tracing her fingertips down between us. Now I knew why they say fear is an aphrodisiac. She pulled off her shirt and posed for me, unashamed, velvet skin pale as rose petals.

Then her phone rang. Looking frustrated, she picked it up.

On TV horses were in the paddock being saddled. Thirty minutes left before the start of the Derby. Any hope of preventing it from being fixed was fading fast. Freya turned her back on me, obviously confident that I represented no threat, and therefore did not see me straining against the duct tape wrapped around my wrists.

"Don't worry. Sandy's too scared to open her mouth," Freya said into her phone.

I strained against the duct tape, which felt as unbreakable as ever. Like most people, I had used it myself to do amazing things, suspend colossal amounts of weight. It did not seem possible that it could just be pulled apart with brute force.

"That wasn't part of the deal. I don't think I can do that," Freya said.

A moment later, she hung up. Still facing away, she said, "I wish you hadn't followed Sandy here."

I didn't like hearing those words, or the finality in her voice.

33

Now was my chance before she turned around. But quickly getting to my feet from a sitting position, without using my hands, would be a challenge—Freya obviously thought so, as she was paying no attention to me at all. It could be done, though, in about a second and a half *if* you knew how. A physics professor could better explain the Newtonian mechanics involved, but what I did was simple. Basically, by rocking back and forth once, I created enough momentum to pull my body forward and then pushed myself upward in one smooth movement.

Now I was on my feet. With the battle half won, all that remained was to create a lateral stress powerful enough to break the seemingly unbreakable duct tape. The trick here was to raise my hands over my head as far as I could and then swing them down as hard as I could, like a man ringing a bell with a sledgehammer at the state fair. I had seen it done by an ex-CIA agent on YouTube. It had worked for him and now it worked for me, too, ripping the duct tape apart and freeing my hands.

Before Freya could react, I scooped up her gun, turned the

safety off, and pointed it at her head.

When she saw this, she seemed dumbfounded. "How—?"

"No time to explain," I said.

I took her phone away and listened. Hearing only a dial tone, I pocketed it along with my own phone and Ana Lucia's backpack. I grabbed Freya's T-shirt and tossed it to her to slip over her head. Pulling her arms behind her, I tied her up with my belt—no duct tape for her! Then I escorted her upstairs. I lowered her into a sofa and pulled up a hassock for myself.

"I need you to talk," I said and once again hit record on my phone.

"Can't you let me go? I was willing to do the same for you."

"No chance."

"Come on, let's work something out."

"What did you have in mind?" I asked.

"I'll tell you what I know, but you can't record it. Otherwise, I'll lose all my leverage."

A taped confession would be ideal, but any information at all could possibly help prevent the looming calamity at the Downs. I stopped recording. "Talk."

"That last phone call? It was an order to get rid of you. All of you."

"You're giving me the cold robbies," I said. "Who gave the order?"

"Who do you imagine?"

"Were you going to do it?"

"I told you before that I'm no killer—though I may be a fool for love."

"Love or no love, now that you're no longer a threat, Sandy will testify against you. With her testimony and mine, you'll be found guilty of child kidnapping and likely get twenty years to life."

Hearing this, she went white around the lips. "Is that what you want?"

I wasn't sure. And that bothered me.

"It's what the law will want. What I want doesn't come into it. I'm not the Commonwealth Attorney. I can't promise you anything. But it's possible that your sentence could be greatly reduced if you gave up Luke and any other accessories. It's the only way to get Luke for double homicide, so the prosecutor might go for the deal. Start by telling me how Luke killed Rojas without being caught, even though all that security was around."

"After the races were over that day," Freya sat quietly, "Luke hid in the Ericson barn until after dark. He slipped over to a vacant barn that was on Rojas' way home after the poker game and waited. When he came by, Luke ambushed him by sneaking up from behind hitting him with a stolen farrier's hammer. He dragged the body and hid it inside the empty barn. Then he went back to his barn and stayed out of sight there until dawn when he blended in with arriving workers. A decent plan, considering he came up with it all by himself."

"And you had nothing to do with it?"

"I was his alibi. We were supposed to have been at an off-track party together."

"What happened after that?" I asked.

"We were afraid Felipe's alleged accomplice might give us up. We sweated it out for months. When no one ever came forward, we figured we were in the clear. If we won the Derby and betted right, we'd be able to retire."

She stopped speaking and stared straight ahead of her.

"But?"

"But then the blackmailing started again. This time, it was Whitlow. He'd been sniffing around, hinting that he knew what we were up to. When he tried to cut himself in for a share, we agreed that something had to be done."

"Exit Whitlow. Did Luke 'act impulsively' again?" I asked.

She nodded.

"And he used an identical stolen hammer to confuse investigators?"

"Right."

Now that I knew virtually everything, time to do something about it. That meant Freya and Sandy would have to be arrested while I rushed back to catch Luke in the act of trying to cheat his way to winning the Derby.

"You still haven't told me how Herb Alexander fits into all this. I know he's dirty. I won't help you try to make a deal unless he gets bagged in the bargain."

"Is that all?" she snapped, swinging around to stare at me. "Are you sure that will be enough to satisfy you?"

"It'll be enough."

"All right then. Ned was training Herb Alexander's horse—well, Luke was—and Speckled Band was on course to qualify for the Derby. But Herb was impatient and dissatisfied. He demanded faster times, more purses, and he wanted them now. The guy is a blowhard and a jerk, but a dangerous jerk, as I believe you discovered."

"Go on."

"He's also a coke head."

"Thanks for throwing that in. Does Luke like blow, too?"

"Oh yeah."

"And what about you? You like coke?"

"Only Diet," she quipped and fell silent briefly. "Several months ago, Luke and Herb got drunk at a party. Herb likes to throw his weight around and tell everybody what a bigshot he is, but he was not himself that night, according to Luke. Despite the dope, Herb broke down, confiding that his business was in trouble. He was desperate to turn it around before he went broke. He begged Luke to find some way to "improve the horse's chances to generate income."

We locked gazes. There was disappointment or despair in her eyes, or something even more implacable.

"Luke said there might be a way. He knew that we couldn't do what we wanted without the owner's cooperation. So, he started educating Herb about PEDs, hinting that they might be the solution to his cash problems. Herb bought into it completely.

He even proposed selling doses of the PED to other trainers through his pharmaceutical delivery company."

"How would that work, I wonder."

"Maybe by misbranding it as an equine dietary supplement. Or some such."

"Clever."

"And lucrative."

I felt I had gotten all I could out of Freya. "One last question. Do you really believe that your horse, even juiced, can outrun Cat Chaser today?"

"You haven't seen the real Speckled Band yet," Freya said.

Locking her up in a closet was not easy for me, especially with her warm breath on my cheek or while hearing her unspoken plea. For what? Forgiveness? Release?

But I did it.

In the basement, Sandy and her daughter seemed bewildered to see me at first but then relieved. When I made no move to free them, though, they exchanged troubled looks.

"Aren't you going to untie us?" Sandy said.

"Not just yet," I said, feeling like a heel for leaving the child's hands bound.

"What do you mean? You're can't just leave us like this. My daughter's been traumatized, and so have I. You have to let us go."

"Soon. But first, we need to talk."

"No, untie us first."

"Can't do that."

"Talk about what then?" She sounded fearful and exhausted.

"Sandy, you realize that you're in deep trouble, don't you?"

"What are you talking about? Freya Hall is the one who's in trouble here. I haven't done anything wrong."

"Not counting blackmail and extortion."

Her face lost its color.

"Mama, I'm scared," Ana Lucia said.

"It's all right, angel," Sandy said.

I searched for the words that would convince her to cooperate. "Your testimony could nail Freya for child kidnapping, Sandy. But hers might convict you of extortion. That way, they'd get you both."

She chewed her lower lip, unsure how to respond. Finally, she said, "And if I agree to testify?"

"I can't promise anything. That's up to the prosecutor. But if you turn state's evidence, and your testimony helps convict Luke Ericson, they might let you walk on the extortion charges."

She stared at the floor. "Okay, I'll do it."

"Good. It's the smart move."

"Can't you take this tape off us now?"

"Sorry."

I went into the lab and shut the door behind me, leaving the light on in the laundry room. As I started to phone Brownfield, who I assumed was still manning his post in the infield, the crowd on TV began the traditional sing-along with "My Old Kentucky Home." I waited for it to end. Only one person in a thousand would know any of Stephen Foster's lyrics beyond "weep no more my lady." But everyone knew the hell out of those five words and happily faked the rest. Then they cheered.

"They're going to try to fix the Derby, Leo. They're using a performance-enhancing drug on Speckled Band." It was now 6:16.

"How do you know this?" Brownfield asked.

I gave him a thirty-second summary of events, concluding with, "You've got to do something."

"Like what?"

"Stop the race."

"It's too late."

"Can you arrest Luke Ericson and Herb Alexander?"

"On what evidence—your say so? You know I can't."

"Well, at least send a patrol car here to pick up Freya, Sandy, and Ana Lucia."

"That I can do."

"Good. Make sure you keep those two women apart. You let them get together, they might change their stories."

"Roger that. What are you going to do?"

"Try to set a new land-speed record on the worst bicycle possible."

34

Only fifteen minutes remained before post time. Like most everybody else in Louisville who watched the Derby on TV every year, I knew what would happen almost by heart. While I pedaled furiously back to the Downs, a bugler in a red hunting jacket would be playing the "Call to the Post." Then red-helmeted riders would herd the twenty horses toward the starting gate, which spanned the entire track. Workers in yellow vests would man the gate's X-shaped cages reminiscent of bridge struts and girders and topped by a broad green Churchill Downs banner.

When all the horses were loaded into their respective slots and pawing the dirt, the bell would ring and the track announcer would shout, "They're off."

I heard him saying it when I reached the suddenly deserted concourse under the grandstands as spectators flocked outward to watch the race live in the open air. That being the case, there was nothing else I could do but watch the race along with everyone else. Since the view was better on TV, I stayed where I was, hoping that the world's signature race would be on the up and up, but dreading that it might fall prey to greed and chicanery.

With everything up for grabs, and deafened by the massive crowd's cheers, I watched Cat Chaser, the 6-to-5 favorite, get off to a great start. His jockey, Humberto Herrera, wearing Keene Kessinger's red silks with polka-dotted sleeves, stood in the stirrups, bent at the waist, perfectly balanced over the mane. And Cat Chaser, looking every inch the blueblood super horse, broke clear and moved outside to lead the field in the early going.

In striking contrast, with mud flying up in his face and on his jockey's goggles, Speckled Band had already fallen far behind—not just trailing the leader but the whole field. Normally I wouldn't give a hoot who won, but I found myself feeling oddly conflicted. On the one hand, I hoped honesty and fair play would triumph. But on the other, doped or not, Speckled Band was my client's horse and I always rooted for the underdog. Absurd maybe.

Still, my heart pounded right along with the thundering hooves as Cat Chaser maintained his steady lead and Speckled Band remained bottled up in traffic through the first turn. At the frantic urging of his jockey, Bud Devlin, in yellow and blue diamond silks, the 69-to-1 longshot valiantly attempted to advance. But with other horses bunched up on the inside, it was tough going.

"They're in the back stretch," the track announcer said. "Cat Chaser is pulling away from Raven, Ivory Grin, and Hot Money. Speckled Band remains trapped next to the rail." Keene Kessinger was probably already counting his winnings, but Freya and the two Ericsons must be feeling quite grim about their chances now.

Seconds later everything changed dramatically as Devlin crawled up the mane of his galloping horse and perched there like a bird on a wire and started toward a gap. But then the jockey made a split-second decision to go right instead of left, and all at once Speckled Band was on the outside sitting all alone. With the crowd in a frenzy, the announcer said, "Cat Chaser's still in the lead, but look out for Speckled Band. He has begun his charge, coming wide. Look at him go."

Seeming to explode in a fireball of energy, Speckled Band passed up the field. One by one, they fell back until only the favorite remained ahead. As they came for home, Speckled Band finally pulled even.

"They're neck-and-neck coming to the line. And at the wire, it's Speckled Band by half a length. The longshot has beaten the favorite to win the Kentucky Derby!"

Speckled Band's electrifying come-from-behind effort kept delirious racing fans screaming like they would never stop. It also produced a huge payout. On TV, Devlin waved to the masses while answering questions posed live by a mounted reporter. "He did it, not me," Devlin said, of his horse. "I didn't use the whip. All I did was hold on. Speckled Band—what a ride!"

Cameras lingered on Ned Ericson in his box seat, where he smiled jubilantly while hugging Luke and slapping Herb Alexander on the back. For me, it was a truly bittersweet moment. Despite the race's undeniably exciting outcome, the fun was over. Now hard questions remained, starting with whether I had failed. The bad guys seemed to have won. With so much money at their disposal, could they buy their way out of trouble? The plea bargains I'd cobbled together to implicate Luke and Herb were likely doomed by this cash flood.

Slowly I began blustering my way through the rapturous throng to reach the rail directly across from the winner's circle. A euphoric Ned Ericson and his party were already at the epicenter of the celebration, waiting for Devlin to arrive and toss the garland of roses over Speckled Band.

That moment, however, was when the epic tableau all fell apart. In a scene eerily reminiscent of Quicksilver's tragic death, Speckled Band abruptly let out a horrific noise and jinked, throwing off his rider. In front of thousands of shocked spectators, Devlin went down and was knocked unconscious when his head struck the ground, the force of the blow splitting his helmet.

In the sudden silence that followed as we held our collective breath, Speckled Band went jelly-legged and dropped. For a seeming eternity, probably less than twenty seconds, the colt groaned and struggled to rise. He rolled not quite from side to side, his great chest heaving, but couldn't make it. Speckled Band stretched out his head and laid down motionless as Ned Ericson rushed onto the track to cradle his neck and comfort him. But long before a veterinarian could euthanize the colt with an injection of pentobarbital, Speckled Band had already drawn his last breath.

Closeups on the big screen showed Mister Ned's horrified expression as race officials dragged a tarpaulin in to cover the fallen horse and hide the fatal breakdown. When Luke Ericson joined his father, Ned grabbed him by the lapels of his blazer and was heard screaming, "Son, what have you done?"

Horror and mass confusion reigned as replays of the race appeared on the screen. In the chaos, both Luke and Herb Alexander slipped into the crowd and disappeared. Not knowing where they went, I was betting on the backside. It was in a quiet uproar, like a movie with the sound turned down, as dazed workers scurred about wearing stunned expressions. Somehow my inner GPS guided me to a group of strangers who were clustered around Carlos Rojas lying beaten and bloodied on the ground outside the Ericson stables.

"What the hell happened?" I asked.

"Luke hit Carlos when he tried to stop him," said Libby, cradling the young hotwalker in her pale arms.

"Jesus, Carlos," I said as my client's eyes fluttered open. "You were only supposed to watch him, not try to take him down."

"He killed our horse. I think he might have killed my father, too. Don't let him get away," the kid rasped.

"I won't."

When I asked which way he'd gone, Carlos pointed toward Gate Five.

"Take care of him, Libby," I said, and rushed off through the mob. I raced after him for five minutes along the clogged sidewalks of Fourth Street and was about to give up when I spotted him in a green taxi stuck in bumper-to-bumper traffic. I charged through the crowd of Jaywalkers surrounding it, catching up just in time before it began to move. I slipped out Freya's gun and yanked the door open.

"Get out." A metallic stink rolled over me. Sweat was running down Luke's panic-stricken face. With my left hand I reached in and grabbed a handful of his sticky shirt front, which proved a mistake.

Because just as I dragged him out, someone in the crowd bumped into me. Luke seized the opportunity to slash up at my wrist with his forearm and knock the gun out of my hand. As it went skidding across the asphalt, he drove his other fist into my gut, catching me flat-footed and knocking the breath out of me. I hung onto him like a boxer in a clinch as he tried to follow up with a left, right combination.

Hanging on with my left hand, I slammed the heel of my right into his nose, smashing it and staggering him. I took a breath, then grabbed the neck and the back of his shirt and drove him headfirst into a parked car. He slid down the dented door slowly until he was lying in a heap with his legs splayed out in front of him. Amid the honking horns and curious stares, I picked up the gun and waited for the police.

Within twenty minutes after the race, he was under arrest, the dead horse had been vanned off the track, and the winner of today's Derby remained in doubt due to a steward's inquiry. While some members of the huge crowd were leaving, most remained through the turbulence undulating like a school of traumatized fish. On the big screen, perhaps as a reminder of simpler times, was a shot of the life-sized bronze statue of

Barbaro, the tragic 2006 Derby winner, which stood in front of
the Downs museum.

—

In the days that followed, a necropsy was performed, and more
was known as the stewards' report came out. PETA called for
an investigation and the release of Speckled Band's veterinary
records, plus a list of his recent medications. Brownfield
dispatched the needle and syringe used on Quicksilver to the
state crime lab for DNA testing.

A tag team of LMPD detectives who made no secret of
their resentment toward me for working a high-profile open
case—and worse, solving it, tried to trip me up but failed. In
his office at the Edison Center, Brownfield produced a thumb
drive he had received from an anonymous source containing
Wyatt Whitlow's investigative data. Brownfield asked if I knew
anything about that. I said no, but he probably didn't believe
me.

Luke Ericson was arrested for murder and Herb Alexander
for felonious doping of racehorses. Harriet Anderson mailed me
a bonus check for getting her clients off. My client, the hotwalker,
thanked me for apprehending his father's killer. He and Libby
Fontaine were getting married, he said. And a certain south-
end street urchin received a brand-new ten-speed Schwinn and
an apology from a certain sheepish private detective. The kid
cursed him anyway.

Acknowledgments

For bringing *Hotwalker* to life, I am deeply grateful to Susan Brooks, my highly esteemed editor and publisher at Literary Wanderlust, and her entire publishing team. My heartfelt thanks to Sena Jeter Naslund and Chris Helvey for their generous endorsements of *Hotwalker*. I thank Michele Ruby, Bob Sachs, and Gayle Hanratty for invaluable critiques and support. I am also deeply grateful to my first reader, Cora Rouse Neumayer, and to all my other wonderful readers including Mark Klein, Ed Wong, Peter Fields, Kathy Loomis, Charlie Merkel, Marianna Schakel-Metcalf, Dave Caudill, and John McCarthy.

About the Author

Rick Neumayer's debut novel, *Journeyman*, was published in September 2020. *Hotwalker* is his second novel. Rick has also published short fiction in many literary magazines, and three of his full-length Broadway-style musical collaborations have been produced. A career teacher, he has had a wide variety of experiences, including working as a newspaper reporter, book reviewer, literary magazine editor, and singer in rock bands. He is a Louisville native and resident with degrees from Spalding University (MFA), University of Louisville (MA), and Western Kentucky University (BA).